## Praise for *Today Tonight Forever*

"*Today Tonight Forever* brims with wit and charisma and blooms with every kind of love: love won and love lost, love changed and love reborn. This is a page-turner with heart."

**—Alison Wisdom, author of *We Can Only Save Ourselves* and *The Burning Season***

"Dazzling! *Today Tonight Forever* unfolds at a seaside wedding where memories, secrets, the reverberations of mistakes, and the hope for renewal collide. Readers will love these flawed, tender characters."

**—Deb Rogers, author of *Florida Woman***

"*Today Tonight Forever* beautifully encapsulates all the ways people come together and break apart. This book is moving, sweet, funny, and I fell in love with its characters over and over again."

**—Ilana Masad, author of *All My Mother's Lovers***

## Praise for *The Golden Season*

"*The Golden Season* will sweep you up, make you laugh and cry, and leave you wiser… Madeline Kay Sneed is a blazing talent."

**—Mako Yoshikawa, author of *One Hundred and One Ways* and *Once Removed***

"[A] gorgeous, thoughtful debut novel…vivid, layered and ultimately satisfying."

**—*Shelf Awareness***

"A *Friday Night Lights* for a new generation, a heartfelt story of finding yourself, coming out, and coming home… Tender and bighearted."

**—Sarah McCraw Crow, author of *The Wrong Kind of Woman***

"Breathtaking… I wish I could read it for the first time all over again."

**—Julia Glass, author of *Vigil Harbor* and the National Book Award–winning *Three Junes***

## Also by Madeline Kay Sneed

*The Golden Season*

# TODAY TONIGHT FOREVER

*A Novel*

# MADELINE KAY SNEED

GRAYDON
HOUSE

GRAYDON
HOUSE®

Recycling programs
for this product may
not exist in your area.

ISBN-13: 978-1-525-81959-9

Today Tonight Forever

Graydon House
22 Adelaide St. West, 41st Floor
Toronto, Ontario M5H 4E3, Canada
www.GraydonHouseBooks.com
www.BookClubbish.com

Printed in U.S.A.

For Miranda,
My world's most wonderful surprise.

*At least—it solaces—*
*to know—*
*That there exists—a Gold—*
*Altho' I prove it, just*
*in time—*
*Its' distance—to behold!*
*Its' far—far—Treasure—to*
*surmise—*
*And estimate—the Pearl—*
*That slipped—my simple fingers—*
*thro'*
*While yet—a Girl—*
*at School!*

    *Dear Sue—*
       *You see I remember—*
           *Emily.*


*When the Best is gone—I know that other things are not of*
*consequence—*
*The heart wants what it wants—or else it does not care.*
                                —Emily Dickinson

# ATHENA

The best day of someone's life is always the worst day of somebody else's. This is especially true at a wedding—even more so when you're separated.

Since her college graduation, Athena had been a bridesmaid in seventeen weddings. Twenty, if you count being in the house party, which Athena never did since it was the same as making it onto the junior varsity team, a consolation prize, an afterthought. Not bad, but not good enough for the big time.

For most of her twenties, she'd done the whole hog, Katherine Heigl, *27 Dresses*. An overpriced and cheaply made gown for every wedding she'd been in, except for the one right after she came out, where the bride insisted Athena wear a tux so that the bride could showcase her acceptance and allyship to the one lesbian she'd ever known.

Now, at thirty-three—her Jesus year, as her mother so constantly reminds her—Athena drives down a Floridian highway full of billboards advertising Heaven and Hell to be a bridesmaid in her eighteenth wedding. Her longtime family friend, Daisy, is getting married in Watercolor, Florida, a sprawling beachside resort with large, spaced-out, two-story vacation homes, each painted in a distinct pastel color, like, as the name suggests, a watercolor palette. The wedding party had made their mantra for the weekend: Best Wedding Ever in the History of Weddings.

Athena knew that, for her, this could never be true. The best wedding Athena had been in was her own. To Sydnee. The great light of her life.

It was nothing like the other weddings, with their churches and their pomp and circumstance. It was small and full of lights that twinkled from tree branches and wrapped around columns on the back porch of Athena's parents' house. They didn't need a priest, they had their best friend, Deacon, to marry them, and he recited Dickinson instead of First Corinthians, and they danced on the grass in bare feet until the neighbors complained about the noise. There was no prayer, but they still felt blessed.

It was the happiest day of Athena's life.

Now, after six years, they are divorcing. The papers are due in the mail next week. They have been separated for eight months, and soon it will be official.

Divorce does not suit Athena. She's been too busy burying herself in work to do anything about it. It's as if she believes that sorting through the fragments of Emily Dickinson's envelope poems in her tiny, dimly lit cubicle at the University of Houston can help heal her heartbreak without her ever having to face it straight on.

There's always a snag, though, some little reminder of Sydnee, who never particularly liked literature. She did, however, love Athena and how much she loved Dickinson, so she had a few favorite poems of her own: *Split the Lark— and you'll find the Music*—was a much-loved line between the two of them.

"I like the way it sounds," Sydnee explained. "It's weird. Twisted."

"Unnecessary bloodshed, uncanny music," Athena said after they first moved into their house in Montrose when they settled down in Houston, a few months before their marriage. Athena was organizing her books and flipping through the pages of the poet's collection. "I don't think I'll ever get tired of her."

"And me?" Sydnee rested her head in her hand, her hair swaying to one side, a curtain of darkness.

"Maybe after seven lifetimes, I'll start to get bored," Athena said, and Sydnee smiled, and they came together like Athena thought they would continue to do for the rest of their lives.

When she comes across the line, or anything similar (*I split the dew—But took the morn*), her heart cleaves, an open wound. She tries to hide from it, but it always finds her eventually. Not even her most sacred pleasures are safe from the pain of separation.

As Athena drives, she imagines her mother would tell her to snap out of the past and keep her eyes peeled on the present. *It's your Jesus year, Thene*, she could almost hear her mother saying through a jaw tensed with superstition. Her mother is obsessed with the concept and terrified of it, too. Thirty-three was Jesus's age when he was crucified, betrayed by his friends, strung up for all the world to see. It feels like a warning to her. Nothing good can come from thirty-three. *And your Jesus year?* her mother would say. *It's trying to kill you.*

Athena grips the steering wheel tight, closing her eyes for a moment, exhaling, before jolting back into awareness as she swerves slightly into the other lane.

*Not today, Jesus year.*

A gulp of coffee. A turned-up stereo. Athena slaps her cheek and drives on. In the rearview mirror, the horizon blares bright and blue with the high noon sun doing its best to heat up the unseasonably chilly November day. If the cold stays at bay, it's going to be a beautiful weekend for a wedding.

After half an hour of nothing but pine trees and billboards, Athena finally exits the highway, passes the Publix, and finds herself in the strange, beautiful, pristine, idyllic world of Watercolor, Florida.

Athena and her brother used to join Daisy's family on their weeklong trips to the resort during the summers in high school. It hasn't changed much since then. It's expanded, but otherwise remains timeless. People cruise down the paved roads in their three-row golf carts or beach cruiser bikes with baskets on the front, going from their homes, to the Publix down the road and to the beach club across the high-way. The sidewalks are manicured and lined with pine trees and magnolias, the needles and leaves of which are finely collected on the sides of the paved walkways, never a twig out of place, giving the residents and guests a taste of nature without all the messiness it brings.

Back then, Athena loved the sun-soaked days at the beach, salt water settling into her hair, making it coarse and curly and wild. They spent summer nights riding up and down the streets on their bikes, going on ice cream and soda runs until their stomachs got sick. Life was simple then. Athena had been happiest here, after days spent diving into the crashing waves, riding their force toward the shore, her belly scrap-ing the shallow sand once the wave died out and deposited her back where she belonged.

It's November now. Too cold for waves, and she's too old to ride them, anyway. Her back might tweak or her knee might shift in the tide at the wrong enough angle, leaving her sore for weeks. The world had seemed so open when she was young. She realized now the scope was much smaller.

Caution cursed her every step because she had known consequences and understood they could come when you least expected it.

Athena's father used to say that age gave you double vision. You see the world both as it is and as it was before. *It's like your friend says*, he'd say, always referring to Emily Dickinson in this way, *"the past is such a curious creature!"*

She wonders what her father would think now. About Daisy's wedding, about her own divorce. He's been dead three years, and still, every day, she wonders what he'd say. Three years of questions. Three years without answers.

Athena blinks away the thought as she turns off the 30A highway into the massive, sprawling beach resort, circling past the bustling beach club before finally finding the towering town house where Daisy and the other bridesmaids will spend the night after the rehearsal dinner and then spend tomorrow getting ready for the wedding. It's blindingly white, exactly like the row of townhomes it stands beside, with two decks that overlook the white sand beach and emerald coast of the Gulf of Mexico. Behind it, the midafternoon waves swell and crash onto the coast, the sun starting to sparkle in the water. All nature, no artifice.

Once she cuts the engine, Athena slowly gets out of the car, relishing her last moments of silence before the chaos of the wedding begins. The air is thick with humidity. She savors the smell of salt air and pine needles, happy to have the sun on her cheeks. She's spent so many hours inside her office and classroom these past eight months. She hadn't realized how much she missed the world—the natural, reviving tonic of fresh air and warmth.

"There she is," a voice calls from the front door. "The divorcée."

Deacon steps out from the house, an enormous grin

stretched across his face. Tall, lean, and shirtless as always, he leans against the doorframe, two cups of coffee in his hands, his board shorts sagging slightly. He sets the coffees down and tugs up his shorts before walking over to Athena, his arms outstretched. His blond hair sticks up straight at the back, like he's just woken up from a nap, and he traces the now faint and faded scars underneath his pecs, a habit he's kept up for over a decade since he got them. Athena embraces her best friend, burying her face in his chest, the tufts of blond chest hair tickling her cheek.

"So," Deacon says, pulling her away from him so that he can look at her. "How *is* the divorcée?"

"I told you that's not funny yet." Athena smiles despite herself.

"I guess I'll keep doing it until it is," Deacon says as he takes her arm in his. "Come on. I'll show you to your designated chambers."

They walk through the house, steering clear of the rest of the bridesmaids for the time being, and make their way to Athena's room, which has one tiny twin bed.

"Doesn't seem like Daisy has *any* faith that you'll be hooking up at this wedding," Deacon says, gesturing to the bed.

"What else is new." Athena sets her bag down at the foot of the bed before taking the hot cup of coffee from Deacon. It's strong, with a hint of vanilla and cinnamon. "What are the other dudes doing?"

"Getting ready for the rehearsal dinner." Deacon checks his watch. "Still got a few hours, but Chad wants to experiment with gel in his hair. Doesn't want to take a chance in case it's terrible—which it will be—and he has to start over."

"At least he's thinking ahead," Athena says. She pulls out her suit for the dinner and tugs at her messy bun. "Wish I could just gel this mess. My hair is driving me bonkers."

"Shave it off," Deacon says, digging through Athena's bag. He removes a pair of her white sneakers and tries them on. "Can I borrow these tonight?"

"I can't shave it, I have an egg-shaped head, we've discussed this," Athena says. "And no, I'm wearing them."

"More like a bowling pin."

"Any cone-shaped object will do." Athena points at the bridesmaid dress she will wear tomorrow. The lavender silk will hug every curve and constrict her breathing so badly she worries it will induce a semi–panic attack. "Wish Daisy would have let us choose our dresses."

"She's an influencer, Athena," Deacon says, running the fabric of the dress through his hands. "The only thing that matters are the pictures, tagging her designer sponsor and making sure that everyone seems the same, and by same, I of course mean not quite as good as Daisy."

"So I'm getting punished because she has half a million followers she needs to impress?"

"Dude, you're going to look good, a real heartbreaker." Deacon walks around in Athena's sneakers, checking them in the mirror. "I'll catcall you when you walk down the aisle if that makes you feel better."

"Exactly what I need at all times, a mobile fan club, thank you very much for understanding." Athena points at the sneakers and gestures toward her suit, trying to get him to take them off. "What about you? You getting ready with us tomorrow?"

"Bride's orders." Deacon nods as he takes off the shoes and puts them under Athena's suit. "She wants me by her side every step of the way. Until the *actual* wedding. A guy standing with the bridesmaids would ruin the aesthetic. At this wedding, gender is very much a binary."

"Why push boundaries when you could just reinforce them, right?" Athena says.

"Well, she'll have plenty of pictures to post for all the trans awareness, appreciation, whatever-the-fuck hashtag weeks they come up with."

"Gotta feed the followers."

"Name of the game." Deacon rubs his forearm slowly, tracing the tips of his fingers over his bluebonnet tattoo. "Talked to Sydnee recently? We'll see her tomorrow. At the wedding."

A jolt rushes through Athena. It happens every time she hears her name. When they first started dating, she'd get a similar flood of electricity. It is still a marvel: the dread, excitement, giddy joy contained in one name. The thought of her face is instinctual. The dark hair, curly when left untouched, hanging just above her shoulders. Her easy smile, her eyes, green unless in sunlight, when they transformed into an almost translucent blue. Her hands were always in motion, when she talked and when she was silent, where they'd move from the back of her neck to the front of it, fiddling with the crucifix necklace she wore every day, a reminder of her family and the Catholicism of her youth. She called it a bad habit, but Athena had always known that the comfort of home could take many forms.

"We've talked a bit," Athena says, trying to play it cool. "You know lesbians and their exes. Always staying best friends."

"Don't bullshit a bullshitter." Deacon opens his mouth to say more, but hesitates, tugging on the thin wisps of hair at the end of his chin instead. "I gotta shave or Daisy will kill me."

"What is it?" A flush of panic heats through her. She'd dreaded this possibility so much it almost felt prescient, like she could sense Sydnee's shifting heart, moving on from her to someone else without having seen her since she asked for the divorce. "She's dating. *Her.* Isn't she?"

"I thought you weren't on social media anymore."

"I *knew* it," Athena says, kicking herself for talking through lawyers instead of staying in the loop. There is no dignity in silence. Knowing is always better than being blindsided. "I *knew* it was more than just sex."

"I don't think it'll last…" Deacon trails off. He bites his lower lip. "It's hard."

"Staying faithful shouldn't be hard."

"I mean for me." He clears his throat, his voice dropping in the hollow sort of way that means he's telling the truth. "Y'all are both my friends…"

"Let's just not talk about it," Athena says quickly, going back to her suitcase and unpacking her pajamas. She gets up and puts them in the mahogany chest in the corner, her back to Deacon.

Athena is not willing to listen to other people talk about how *her* divorce has affected *them.* It is her pain, her isolation. She doesn't *want* to be miserable, but she's settled into her misery in such a way that it's now become a part of her. Every step she takes is steeped in the stuff. No one can top her in terms of agony. Her father is dead. Her wife left her. There is nothing else that matters.

Deacon clears his throat. She senses his frustration, but does nothing to ease it. It's not his fault that her marriage ended. Outside of her mom and brother, Deacon is the only person she's willingly let into her life during this period of upheaval. He's shown up for her. During their weekly meet-ups at their favorite pub, he chomps on fries as she regales him with all the reasons she should have seen the divorce coming. He never complains. He rarely talks about himself. He sits, and he listens, and Athena does nothing to change that.

She does wonder, sometimes, when she's alone and she can't sleep, why he doesn't stop her, why he always sits and takes it, all her anger, and all her frustration, and all of her grief. It's a purgatory with an open exit that he never seems to take.

"Put down the coffee," Deacon says before Athena can reflect further. "And get your tennis shoes."

"What?" She puts her suitcase under the bed and clutches her coffee closer, not ready to leave so shortly after her arrival.

"We're going for a run."

"The rehearsal dinner's in a few hours."

"Just a quick one." He fishes through Athena's bag to find her running shoes and throws them at her. "Come on. Lace up. We need it."

They run on the beach. The sand is pure white and cool in the winter sun. It's like snow. In the midafternoon, the beach is crowded with people. But when Deacon and Athena run, there is no one else in the world.

Deacon is faster, but they never try to match pace on their runs. Athena watches him kick up sand as he speeds up, his body built for this, unencumbered as it had been in years before, when he felt small and alone and afraid. Athena smiles as Deacon takes off in an all-out sprint, testing his limits, always precise with his intervals. The sun shines on his bare back, and, next to him, the ocean glistens, like a patch of stars bobbing in the crashing waves. It is beautiful. He is beautiful. Athena's heart swells with a rush of love, that curious purity of affection that can only come from friendship that has endured many years and withstood as many changes.

Any exercise takes Athena out of her head and puts her back into her body, but nothing grounds her like running. It's been that way for her whole life. Playing outside when she was a kid with her brother, Leo, and the other boys on the block. Bare feet in grass, on concrete, dribbling soccer balls, basketballs, running receiving routes in front yard football fields, diving, tackling, feeling fast and free.

When she was in high school, high-strung and closeted, much of her existence felt like a dream. She was so dissociated from herself that she spent most of her time invested in the lives of other people, either through fiction or her family and friends. But when she went out onto the soccer pitch, took her position, and the game began, she was catapulted into her body. Her calves burned, her lungs heaved, her shoulders bruised (she did not play delicately). It was such a freedom and such a privilege, to move and strain and fight. To put her body on the line. The soreness centered her. She could not, in those moments during and after a game, help but recognize the body she so often ignored in her daily life, its instincts and desires and natural attractions. When she played, she got the faintest glimpse of the glory that would come from finally being in tune with her mind and her body at the same time.

As sand kicks into her shoes and the wind blows strong behind her, Athena feels her pulse quicken, her breathing become more labored. She embraces the ache in her legs. She is out of shape. Too many hours spent at her desk, not enough on the move.

Seagulls caw as they soar in the sky, then dive down into the water in search of fish, a feeding frenzy. She inhales the heavy brine of sea air mixed with the sharp sweetness of her sunscreen. The beach, the ocean, the smells she loves. She squats down and splashes water onto her face. When it rushes over her and the salt water stings her eyes, Athena finally feels at home. *Find the sea, Athena, you're built from the sea,* her father would always tell her when they sat around his globe, his finger tracing a cragged island near the Aegean Sea. *Your blood is built from salt water and sea, your bones made from islands down here*, he'd say, pointing to Greece. Then, moving the globe slightly to the right, he'd trace to the coast of Western Ireland. *And from up here. So if you ever feel lost, just find the water, and you'll be home again.* Athena remembers her father's voice, an echo that rings clear in her mind. She lets the thick ocean air fill her burning lungs as she pants, her legs on fire.

Athena checks her watch. She's gone a mile. That's enough. She slows to a walk, putting her hands on her head, catching her breath. She takes off her shoes and sits, letting the sand squish between her toes. After a while, Deacon turns around and joins her. The ocean inches up toward their feet, the cool water a relief after the run. Deacon digs into the ground next to him and finds a sand dollar.

"Good luck," he says, grinning, putting it in his pocket.

"You trying to get lucky at the wedding?" Athena shoves his shoulder.

"I'm giving monogamy a try, if you can believe it."

"With the bartender?"

"I'm not sure it suits me, though."

"With the tattoos?"

"She has one on the back of her neck that says, 'live, laugh, love,'" Deacon says, wrinkling his nose. "Except the *o* in *love* sort of *droops*. So, it looks like *lave*."

"Deacon, I *lave* you." She throws her arms around his shoulders. "But I don't think things with the bartender are going to work out."

"Such a cynic." Deacon pushes her off him. He plows his hands into the sand, collecting it in his fists and spilling it out onto Athena's outstretched leg. "No, but. There's something about her. Tattoo aside. Haven't felt this way before. Like, ever."

"She coming to the wedding?"

"My parents wanted me to invite her," he says, trying hard not to smile. He's never been good at nonchalance. "They're hoping I'll finally settle down. But Daisy says it's too soon to have her here. What if we break up and she's in the pictures and then Daisy can't post them? A tragedy, you see. Can't risk it."

"Can't Daisy crop her out or something?"

"That would ruin the authenticity of the image, which is her brand, Athena, how could you forget?"

"I would mock, but she knows what she's doing."

"Five hundred thousand followers and counting."

"So," Athena says. "When it's you and—what's her name?"

"Mel."

"When it's you and Mel, are your parents gonna throw you a wedding like this?"

"Yes." Deacon shakes his head in exasperation. "Which is why, no matter who the person is, we're gonna elope. You can come. Bear witness."

"Sounds like a plan."

"Your mom's coming this weekend, right?"

"Tonight. Your mom would kill her if she missed the rehearsal dinner. They have to see everything and take notes for their—what do they call it?"

"'Ladies luncheon,'" Deacon says. He sits up so he can use air quotes. "Weekly wine, oysters and gossip. The perfect combination."

Deacon fixes his gaze out toward the ocean, his eyes squinting against the reflected light on the water. A seagull dive-bombs down into the waves and shoots back up with a fish in its beak. A wave crashes on the shore and water rushes up to their legs, cool and crisp. The natural rhythm of the coast envelopes them. They sit in comfortable silence for a few moments, drinking it all in.

"How's she holding up?" Deacon asks, still focused on the ocean in front of him. "Your mom, I mean. She started dating or anything?"

"No." Athena's chest seizes, her breath hard to find. It *had* been three years. But the thought of her mother moving on makes her nauseous. She hates herself for that. Selfish, she knows. She steadies her voice. "I mean, I don't know. We don't talk about that stuff. All I know is she's doing just fine. Nothing knocks that woman down, you know that."

"She was built from iron, it's true."

"Still working on all her recipes. An unstoppable force."

"And you?" Deacon asks, a little uncertain. He speaks slower than usual. "We don't really talk about your dad much and—"

"Why is Sydnee coming to the wedding?" Athena filters sand through her fingers as she watches a large wave forming and then cascading down in the distance. She'd been waiting to ask the question. It's plagued her since Daisy told her Sydnee would be at the wedding more than two months ago. It was awkward, Daisy explained. She and Sydnee had spent so much time talking about the wedding. And Daniel loved Sydnee (everyone loved Sydnee). Athena could have pressed Daisy. Could have even insisted that Sydnee's invite get revoked. Daisy was Athena's friend, after all. They were practically sisters. But Athena, committed to the illusion that her heart had not been cracked and crushed by the love of her life, wanted to seem nonplussed by it. *I don't care, she can go wherever she wants, she's a free woman, and so am I.* It was a stupid thing to say, even if it was true.

"What do you mean?" Deacon knits his eyebrows together in confusion, her quick change of subject giving him whiplash.

"Sydnee," Athena says, meeting his eyes directly, as if in accusation. "Why is she coming?"

"She's not bringing *her*," Deacon says quickly. "She's not a dick."

"No, she's not," Athena agrees. "So, why is she coming?"

"Daisy's her friend, too." He leans back on one hand as he siphons more sand onto her leg with the other. "And mine. My parents love her."

"Everyone loves her," Athena quips.

"People love you, too," Deacon says, half-heartedly.

Athena doesn't take offense. She knows that if their friends had to pick, they would choose Sydnee. It isn't just that she's more fun—she is. But Sydnee is *vibrant*. The whole world elevates when she's around. When people tell stories, Sydnee is enraptured. When they tell jokes, she has the best laugh in the room. She makes even the dullest person seem to shine. Where Athena is rooted in routines and plans and certainty, Sydnee thrives in spontaneity and improvisation and joy. Every moment is fully lived, and she forces the people around her to do the same. It's grounding and life affirming, being in the presence of someone so effervescent. Athena knows that she can never compete with all that lightness.

"I just think it's weird, is all." Athena tries, and fails, to sound casual. "Since I'm going to be here. *In* the wedding."

"Athena," Deacon says, standing up, brushing the sand off his shorts, an edge of irritation in his voice. "Don't you get it?"

"Obviously not." She stands up, too.

"You have to know." He cocks his head to the side.

"Clearly I don't." She grits her teeth. "So just explain it to me."

"She's coming," Deacon says, turning around to walk back to the house, his voice muffled by the wind, "so that she can see *you*."

# DEACON

When a sibling gets married, their wedding takes up your entire life. The world is a motion blur. The only clear point of focus? The bride.

The year leading up to the wedding had whizzed by. There were bridal showers, engagement parties, and the bachelor and bachelorette parties. Deacon had been blessed (cursed?) with being invited to both, after which he swore off booze until the wedding, the groomsmen and bridesmaids taking no prisoners when it came to anyone's livers.

Between Daisy's wedding events and teaching his American literature class at Houston's performing arts high school, Deacon didn't think he'd have time to have much of a life. Saturdays spent celebrating Daisy, Sundays spent buried underneath rushed essays by students who always put his class last, behind their ballet and their orchestra and their musical theater rehearsals. But, somewhere, through the fog of lace and veils and velvet, Deacon had managed to find more than a life. He had fallen in love. With Mel.

Daisy's fiancé, Daniel, had introduced them. After he met Deacon for the first time, Daniel kept repeating, "You *remind* me of someone, I just can't put my finger on it." That someone was Mel, the bartender with the live, laugh, love neck tattoo who worked at Daniel's favorite dive bar. When he finally connected the dots, he introduced them, and the rest was history. Well, four months of history. It had been enough.

But not quite enough to get Mel invited to the wedding. When he asked if Mel could come, Daisy looked at Deacon up and down, her blue eyes narrowed as if searching for the joke. When she realized he was serious, she sighed, exasperated, as if it had taken all her energy to keep herself from exploding.

"That's not possible," Daisy said, her mouth in the stubborn straight line she got when she was digging her heels in. "Six months? Sure. But four? Be real, Deacon. Think about the pictures. If y'all break up, we'll see her everywhere."

He knew there was no sense arguing, even with his parents' consent. The bride got to call the shots. It was a once in a lifetime power that Daisy wielded well. Deacon retreated to the role of supportive sibling and said no more on the subject of Mel's attendance. It was Daisy's day, and she'd always have final say.

It seemed impossible that, after their lives had hurtled toward the event for over a year, the weekend had finally arrived. Earlier in the day, Daniel and Daisy had a small, private ceremony with their immediate families, two of Daniel's best friends, who would serve as witnesses, and the rabbi so that they could sign the ketubah, an ornately designed marriage contract that bound them together in Jewish law. Technically, they were supposed to sign it half an hour before the ceremony, but Daisy absolutely refused to be seen by Daniel in her wedding dress before the ceremony. It was one of the few traditions she wanted to preserve, and Daniel's family's rabbi was more than willing to accommodate the desire.

Once Athena arrived and got settled in, they headed to the brief wedding run-through on the beach. Now Deacon and Athena drive together down the 30A highway to the rehearsal dinner venue, which is tucked away in the quaint shopping center where *The Truman Show* was filmed. They walk through it, and Deacon checks himself out in a shop window, brushing sand off of his pants. He wears a velvet tux and black Chucks. He looks good. He feels good. It's all going to be *good*.

He repeats the mantra in his mind, trying to breathe away the slight spike of anxiety that always comes from entering a room of strangers and, worse, people from his past.

It was his parents' friends he was most worried about. There were a handful of good ones—who'd visited him after his top surgery, who consulted Google with their questions instead of peppering him with them, who'd loved him just the same through every transition in his life. They were family, and they were safe.

Friends of his parents to avoid: the LeBlancs, the Marches, the Catalinas. His mother would fuss if she knew he kept their names so closely knit together in his mind's "Do Not Disturb" section, but it is a necessity of, if not survival, than comfort. They're nice enough. They look him up and down, squinting, as if trying to see the kid he once was etched in his face. The thoughts running through their mind... Deacon does not like to think of them. He'd heard enough of that line of thinking for all his life. There is no more room for their strained smiles and raised eyebrows and whispered comments of cruelty, guided by the rigid rule of religion that they called love.

Perhaps that devotion to a higher law is a form of love. Who is Deacon to declare such things? But it's stiff with starch, inflexible until the end, with no room for expansion or transformation. No, Deacon wanted no part of that, and he will not indulge their pleasantries and small talk so they can feel better about themselves at the end of the day. Acknowledge from afar and avoid at all costs: that is the game plan. Deacon always has a game plan. Analyze the situation, mitigate risks, trust your instincts.

"You ready for this?" Athena asks, brushing a stray strand of hair off his forehead. She clasps his hand in hers and gives it a squeeze.

"Let's do it." Deacon repeats the pressure in her hand, then drops it before leading the way up the stairs to the rooftop deck where the rehearsal dinner will take place.

He and Athena are the first to arrive. Deacon gasps when he walks in. The restaurant bar is normally unremarkable, with splintered wood columns matching the old wooden deck, a perfect place for people in board shorts and flip-flops to sit and drink while the rest of their families spend hours in the small township's shopping center. There's a beautiful view of the ocean, which had always seemed to be enough decoration for the place.

Now, however, it's been overtaken by white lights and lace. Sheer curtains hang between the pillars and billow in the wind, a dreamy entrance into a heavenly world. Deacon pulls apart the fabric and enters. There's an elegance to the excess. In vases on the tables, peonies burst open, white and blush, surrounded by red roses and the dark, thick branches of a magnolia tree. Jasmine vines wrap around every one of the salt soaked wooden columns, the white flowers in full bloom, their perfume wafting through the air, mingling with the sea. There's one long table in the middle, lined with twenty or so chairs, an elegant white table runner serving as a natural canvas for the bright blue and yellow goblets, the green plates, and the sparkling silverware. Twinkle lights are draped from the rafters, falling down in a curtain of light. When night finally comes, they will be boxed in by the artificial sparkle swirling in the wind.

Scattered around the long table, where the wedding party and families will sit, twelve tables are arranged on the patio, surrounded by so many column heaters that Deacon can hardly feel the cold. A waiter approaches with a tray of wine. Deacon grabs a goblet of red, sniffs it, appreciating the overwhelming aroma of dark plum and tobacco, and takes a sip, savoring the flavors: dark cherry, sage and earth. Every detail is high-class.

"The good stuff?" Athena asks, watching Deacon drink.

"The best stuff." Deacon swirls his goblet and admires the legs running down the sides.

"There's my son!"

Deacon's father walks over from the bar, holding a glass of scotch, beaming, the smile lighting up his pockmarked face as he spots Deacon. His white hair blows askew in the wind and Deacon fixes it for him before giving him a hug, the medals on his father's army blues cold on Deacon's cheeks.

Deacon's dad sees Athena and gives her an awkward side hug, mumbling his hellos. Athena's greeting is stiff and formal. She never did know how to interact around Deacon's dad.

"Good to see you, Scott," Athena says, before excusing herself to join the other bridesmaids who had just arrived.

"She still scared of me?" Scott asks as Athena walks across the deck.

"It's the uniform," Deacon says, adjusting the medals on the left side of his coat. "Intimidating as hell, Pop."

"Could be." Scott sips his scotch, then smiles into his glass. "Think it's more about the time I caught her and Daisy with a bottle of peppermint schnapps their senior year in high school. I threatened to tell her father if I ever caught her breaking into our liquor cabinet again. She's probably still scared I'll tell him."

"You gonna start a séance just to rat out Athena to Jason?"

"Wish I'd told him," Scott says. He tilts up his head to the sky, as if he might find Jason up there, waiting to hear the story. "Good man. He'd have loved this." He lifts his glass to Deacon's, and they clink them together, a toast to the past, and the people who must perpetually live there. "Can't believe Daisy's getting married."

"Can't believe we get to see it this time."

"Don't mention that, Deacon, not today." Scott clutches his glass tighter, always furious when any mention of Daisy's first wedding is brought up. "We're seeing the one that lasts. That's what matters."

"Cheers to that." They clink glasses once more. "Where's Mom?"

"Something with the flowers got fucked up," he says. His tone is gruff but affectionate. "She's putting out fires, as per usual."

"And you had to make sure the Lagavulin wasn't poisoned."

"Most important job there is!" Scott lets out his booming bark of a laugh. He claps Deacon on the back, nearly buckling his knees, then pulls him into another hug. "You know we're going to do all of this for you, too. When you get married."

"Maybe just do half of it," Deacon says, glancing around at the growing crowd of people.

"Thatta boy, my wallet will thank you for it." He drains his glass then taps the top of it. "Gonna get a top off and mingle. You try that Cab yet? It's supposed to be the best."

"Lives up to the hype."

"Save the rest of us a glass, then."

Deacon salutes, and his dad walks away.

As he follows Athena's path across the deck, Deacon hangs his head down, not wanting to make eye contact with anyone by accident, knowing all of Daisy and his mother's friends would take that as an invitation to come chat. There's nothing he'd rather do less. Small talk grates on him. He can't avoid it forever. What else is a wedding for, but time for mindless, mutual politeness without an inch of depth? He had his talking points ready. Yes, he loved teaching. Yes, it was hard. Yes, his students never put away their phones, ever. Yes, they still read. Yes, they still write. Yes, they do actually have interesting things to say outside the internet. There were always bad faith assumptions about his students (Teenagers today are worse than they've ever been!), and his school (An arts school? Do they know how to do math?), and his own competency as a teacher (But you didn't get your degree in education, did you?). Luckily, questions of transitions and identity required more nerve than was allotted for small talk. Though it might be more engaging, if no less comfortable, to talk about something with conviction.

Finally, he finds Athena near a group of influencers huddled together by the bar. They all have a drink in hand as they stare down at one phone. They debate loudly, deciding which pictures to AirDrop and which to delete forever, an agreement they'd all come to at one of their meetups to ensure that no one posted a bad photo of any of them. From what he gathered from Daisy, Deacon knows there are no legal ramifications if a kill shot gets posted. But, the organized ostracization that would follow is more than enough to keep everyone honest.

Of the influencers, Deacon only knows the three other bridesmaids—Katie, Reghan and Clare—and, not wanting to be roped into any of the photo selections, hangs back, waiting to catch Athena's eye.

The bridesmaids are alright. Not Deacon's cup of tea, but they've been good to Daisy. Reghan runs a plant-focused Instagram and exudes all the crunchiness of Colorado, while Katie's focuses on yoga and mindfulness and the ongoing effort to make Houston more bike friendly, and Clare's has no real brand except wealthy and white, with a vague hint of Christian morality mixed with modern sensibility. One Sunday could be a post about a pastor's sermon and her women's Bible study, while another could be a booze-filled drag brunch in Montrose, where Clare stuck twenties into the queens' bras, letting them slap her ass in gratitude. She is a mixed metaphor, but her kind of money allows for an opaque sense of identity.

Before Deacon can get Athena's attention, Katie breaks away from the photo selection committee and comes up behind her. She taps her on the shoulder, introducing herself. Deacon notices Athena give her a once-over. It's smooth. He forgot how cool Athena could look when she wanted to. But then, as if on cue, her mother, Mollie, shouts at her from across the deck, and Athena starts fumbling her words, the facade of effortlessness over even before it could begin.

"I've got to go say hi to, uh, my mom, um, and brother, but…" Athena says, her voice awkward and stilted, as if words have suddenly become illusive.

"We'll have lots of time tomorrow," Katie says, giving Athena's shoulder a squeeze before walking off to the table to find her seat. Athena's face is strangely transfixed as she watches Katie go. Deacon tries hard to stifle a laugh. He does not succeed. Athena doesn't notice.

"Athena!" Mollie shouts, impatient for her daughter's attention. Still dazed, Athena walks toward her mother, leaving Deacon alone.

It's like she's been waiting for a moment to swoop in. He sees her shawl before he sees anything else. Bright yellow with pink polka dots, cashmere had never looked less elegant. Her black bob is the same as it has been for the past thirty years. Shorter in the back, longer curtains that frame her face. Her thin lips curve up in a smile that does not meet her pale blue eyes, adorned with heavy eyeliner on the bottom lid.

"Hello, darlin'," Mrs. March says. She never uses his name. "How are you?"

"Fine, thanks, and yourself?" Deacon answers mechanically. Polite, but not warm. He will not give her an inch.

"I'm fantastic, of course! It's Daisy's wedding weekend!"

Deacon stays silent. He smiles. But he does not respond. Mrs. March taps her hand on the top of the purse. Deacon imagines she has a Bible tucked away in there, ready to whip it out at the last moment, perhaps to read him a passage, or hand over the whole book itself, as if the archaic text in his hands would change everything he knew to be true about himself.

"So, things are going…well?" The question is layered with incredulity, as if Mrs. March could not envision a world in which this could be true.

"Hey, Mrs. M.," Leo, Athena's brother, rushes over. He grabs Deacon's shoulder. "Got a really important question for the brother of the bride. Mind if I steal him?"

"Oh, well, I was—"

"Thanks," Leo says. He flashes her his signature grin, a little coy, a touch devilish. She giggles. Deacon can picture, underneath the thick coat of foundation, that she's flushed slightly. Leo always had that effect. Charming, handsome, polite. Southern women in particular had a difficult time preventing themselves from fawning over him.

"The charm never fails," Deacon slaps Leo on the back once they walk over to Mollie and Athena, who huddle together in whispered conversation. "Thanks for saving me."

"I didn't fly across the country to see our moms' tasteless friends passive-aggressively bully you, bro."

"Bro? You really are LA, huh?"

"We're not family? Come on, man."

Deacon nods, knowing it's true, even if not official. There was a time when Deacon thought it could be. That they might be brothers-in-law. Leo had loved Daisy since they were kids. Daisy didn't give him much thought, with him being three years younger, until after college, after the end of her first marriage, when she started hanging out with all of them again in Houston. The two of them were inseparable. Deacon assumed they went on a few dates, but neither would confirm. They tried to be covert, secretive, but the way Leo looked at Daisy made it clear: he'd never stopped loving her. It'd seemed like they were going to make a real go of it, but then Jason died, and everything crumbled. Leo went off to Los Angeles to chase his dreams—or run away from their family's nightmare, Deacon was never sure which. The budding love between the two died in their throats. A few months after Leo left, Daisy met Daniel. The rest is history.

"Besides," Leo adds, "we all send out a distress signal when one of the Marches approaches, you know that."

"Good to see Los Angeles hasn't changed you too much."

"I'm 60 percent more vapid and vain, don't worry." As if to emphasize the point, Leo rubs his hand up and down his bicep, which has grown considerably in the past year.

"Beefing up for a Marvel movie?"

"Gotta be ready at a moment's notice." Leo flexes his arms and gives a Captain America–worthy grin, cheesy and overdone, showcasing his bleached white teeth.

When Mollie gets flagged down by Daisy across the way, Athena joins Deacon and Leo, but Deacon only gets a brief moment with the siblings together before he spots his mother on the far side of the deck, nearest to the beach, making her way into the hunched circle with Daisy and Mollie. Knowing it's his responsibility to help put out any potential fires, he leaves his friends to assess the damage.

"We wanted lilies of the valley, you know, the same flowers I had," his mother explains, smacking the back of her hand into her palm. Her dress is aquamarine with sequins running up and down the skirt, which sparkle in the lights as she emphatically turns from Daisy to Mollie. Her hair, blond like her children, maintains all the elegance of the '80s, high volume, short cut, plenty of hair spray. She does not notice Deacon approaching.

"*We* wanted them," Deacon asks. "Or *you* wanted them, Ma?"

"Deacon, you don't know what you're talking about." His mother dismisses him with the wave of a hand before she stage-whispers to Mollie, "He tries to help as best he can, but he just doesn't have that vision, that ass—what's the word, Daisy? That you and your friends are always using?"

"Aesthetic." Daisy looks at Deacon and crosses her eyes, their old signal for when they needed saving from their mother's more overbearing moments.

"Daisy," Deacon addresses his sister, pretending Mollie and his mother do not exist. "What do you think of your flowers?"

"Well, Deacon." Daisy boxes out both of the women. Their mother scoffs. Mollie says, "Not this again!" Daisy does not stop. "It seems to me my flowers are most perfect, but our overlord, Mother, has other plans in mind."

"Will she succeed? Find out on next week's episode of *The Takeover.*"

"Starring Diane, with a special guest appearance by Mollie!"

"We get it," Mollie says. "We got it fifteen years ago."

"No one asked you two for a rerun," Diane says, scowling, biting the inside of her cheek to stop herself from laughing.

"Reboot, Mom, and they are *in* right now, let me tell you."

Daisy uses her influencer voice (a high-pitched monotone), but crosses her eyes once more as she says it.

"Aren't you supposed to be elegant, or effortless, or classy, or whatever your brand is?"

"She'll appear for the cameras," Daisy says. She transforms her face in an instant into her signature Instagram pose, her eyes vacant, her mouth slightly open. "Y'all just get the behind-the-scenes look."

"If you're not careful," Diane says. "I'm going to write a tell-all book about how weird you actually are. Blow that whole cool girl cover."

"Luckily for me," Daisy says, snatching a champagne glass from a waiter and taking a healthy sip of it. "Nobody reads anymore."

"Shake it off, Ma, the lilies of the valley will live to tell another day," Deacon says. "But that day will not be tomorrow. We good here?"

"Yeah, yeah," Diane says, squeezing his shoulders and kissing both Daisy and Deacon, and Mollie for good measure, on the cheek. She must have already hit the wine, Deacon thinks. He and Daisy share a look. She's thinking the same thing. They hold in their laughter as they go to find their spots at the main table.

As Deacon heads toward his seat, a crowd of suit jackets and pastel pants engulfs him, shoving a fresh drink in his hand as they clap him on the back. The traditional groomsmen's greeting. They are violent in their affection, which can only come out if they've had enough booze to justify the vulnerability, the intimacy. Punching shoulders, crushing hugs. Even their most tender moments are hardened. They toss Deacon around, squeezing his shoulders and slapping his back, hard. Chad, whose gelled hair experiment has held up well, catches Deacon up on the eighteen holes they played that day. Mike invites him to play pickleball with them tomorrow. Nick asks if he knows if any of the bridesmaids are single.

Daniel meticulously maintains his friendships. It's a community he's cultivated since camp, with the men he knew as boys, inviting more into the fold as he grew older, from the linebackers he played with in high school, to the fraternity brothers he pledged with in college. He delights in all of them. He has no siblings of his own, so he met his brothers along the way. There was no greater pleasure for Daniel than his friends becoming friends with each other.

Their friendships are not complex, but, on the whole, they are kind. To each other. To Deacon. He was skeptical of them at first. Good-looking jocks who had spent the majority of their lives as well-liked, popular and generally accepted by every room they walked into. Deacon imagined their birthday parties and Bar Mitzvahs were coveted invitations by everyone they grew up around. Guys like that were not typically kind to guys like Deacon. But Daniel's groomsmen had gone above and beyond all of Deacon's expectations. He had actually started to like hanging out with them.

After they release him from their gruff greeting, Deacon sits down next to Athena at the table. Leo sits to Athena's right, staring down the table at Daisy, at Daniel. Deacon wants to catch Athena's eye, to draw her attention to her brother's obvious longing, and to get her to get Leo to fix his face. But she's trapped in a conversation across the table with Clare, one of the other bridesmaids, who pitches her the subscription-based skin care company she's been sponsored by. Before he can save her from Clare's rundown, Deacon's phone rings.

It's Mel. Deacon debates whether or not he should answer. They'd fought right before he left. It was a bad one.

"I need to take this," Deacon says, leaning in toward Athena.

"Oh, no, Deacon, hang up to hang out, remember!" Athena wants him to stay, but he has to go.

"Be back in a bit."

Deacon can just make out Athena giving him the finger as he walks away. He raises up his own middle finger over his head in return. A few older guests gasp as they catch it. He pays them no attention.

"What's up?" he says, answering the phone. He finds a quiet corner by the balcony railing. He stares out at the ocean, the white foam distinct in the otherwise dark night.

"What a greeting," Mel says. "Real nice."

"Hello, my darling, my love, how art thou?"

"I think the phrase we were looking for was, *I'm sorry.*"

"I forgive you." Deacon knows he's being a dick.

"You're being a dick."

"The fight was stupid."

"That's not an apology."

"Look," Deacon says, running his hands through his hair. "I'm sorry we left like that. Let's not fight anymore."

"This is bigger than us, and you know it."

"This isn't your business," Deacon says, his cheeks flushing with anger, blazing warm in the cold wind. "This is my decision. I'm not changing my mind."

"You've kept this from her for over eight months!"

"So?" Deacon calms himself and stops his voice from rising. "She can wait a little longer."

"That's almost a year."

"I can do math, Mel, thank you."

Mel sighs. Deep. Heavy. Deacon can almost imagine the exhalation making its way through the phone all the way from Houston. As if it has, the hairs on the back of his neck stand up and goose bumps run down his arm.

"At some point, Deacon," Mel says, knowing how much he loves hearing her say his name. "You have to tell the truth."

"But what if it—"

"You can't control anything except what you say, how you say it and when. So." Mel pauses. She takes a loud sip of her tea. "Don't be mean about it or anything. But…"

"I get it," Deacon says. He traces his bluebonnet tattoo, his heart softening, the stubbornness melting away to reveal to himself something terrifying: she is right, and he is wrong.

"So," Mel says. "You'll tell her?"

"Yeah." Deacon observes the bridal party table, where Athena listens intently to something Reghan is explaining. Her hand supports her head under her chin. Deacon imagines the dark brows contracting together, trying to follow whatever it is Reghan is saying, but not quite grasping it. Despite this, she maintains her polite, strained smile, never unkind but always overworked. There is a delicacy he can sense in Athena. It formed when her father died, and it spread farther after everything with Sydnee. He doesn't want to cause her any more cracks. He wants to hold her close to him, protect her from the truth, protect her from the pain.

"Deacon?" Mel's sharp tone demands an answer.

"I'll tell her," Deacon says, resigning himself to it.

"You promise?" Mel asks.

"I promise." Deacon closes his eyes, making the promise to her, to himself. "Athena deserves to know."

# LEO

Since he landed at the Panama City airport, up until the very moment he arrives at the rehearsal dinner, Leo's mother has not stopped warning him.

She warns him of Daisy's father's fury. She warns him of what everyone will think. She warns him that Daisy doesn't love him. She warns him that Daniel will never let him see it through.

She's worried—as is Athena, and, most likely, Deacon—that Leo has traveled across the country to attend Daisy's wedding with the intention of stopping it from happening. After hugging Leo and helping him with his bags, the first thing Mollie said to him was, *Don't get any ideas, mister, this weekend isn't about you.*

Perhaps if they lived in a sitcom, or if Leo were a different man, this fear would be justified. But he's just here to be a guest. No agenda, just a good-looking suit and a hope that they'll play "Proud Mary" at the reception. He's perfectly content to show up at the wedding with his mother, to sit back and watch the woman he always thought he'd eventually marry, give her hand over to another man.

"Don't try and think about it too hard," Mollie says at the foot of the stairs that lead up to the patio where the rehearsal dinner is taking place. She straightens his tie and pushes his hair out of his face. Leo shakes his head, getting his hair back to the way he likes it.

"Think about what?"

"That you love her."

"I don't love her."

"And don't try to corner Daniel and size him up or intimidate him or whatever. He's a very nice boy."

"I'm not a mob boss, Mom."

"Are you wearing your father's watch?" Mollie stops on the stairs as she glances over at Leo's wrist. Several guests behind them bump into their backs. Mollie profusely apologizes and ushers Leo on, as if he was the one who caused the traffic jam. Mollie pulls him aside at the top of the stairs, bringing his left arm up so she can inspect. It is, indeed, his father's watch. Technically his grandfather's. The first purchase he made for himself after arriving in the country. But seeing as Jason's father had cut off his son as soon as he married a girl who wasn't Greek—instead marrying Mollie, the strawberry blonde Irish Catholic—Leo had never met the man. He associated the watch much more with Jason. Gold face, gold links. It's a little large for Leo, who has to shake it back up his wrist every so often. He keeps forgetting to get it resized. Still, it feels good to glance down and see a piece of his father there. Patiently waiting to tell him the time.

"It fits," Leo says. He tugs his arm away from his mother, and shakes the watch back up his wrist, self-conscious.

"He'd love this," Mollie says, kissing Leo's hand. "It's wonderful on you."

"Thanks."

"But just because you look good, doesn't mean you should go off and make a scene, you hear me?"

"Mom, I'm not going to—"

"Oh, there's Athena, let's say hi."

Instead of waving, or walking up to her herself, Mollie yells out for Athena to come over, gesturing wildly with her arms in order to get Athena's attention. Leo shrinks back a little bit, trying not to be noticed.

"You shrieked, Mother?" Athena asks as she finally comes over. Mollie crosses her arms in fake exasperation, her thin, straight, strawberry blond hair tied up in a perky, high ponytail that sways back and forth as she shakes her head, her pale, symmetrical face lighting up into an inviting smile. Leo mimics their mother's body language as Athena comes over, making his sister laugh.

Leo assesses if any physical changes have come out of his sister's emotional upheaval. Athena's cryptic song lyric tweets before she deleted all social media led him to believe her to be in a dark, abysmal place. Other than a general gauntness around her eyes, she seems the same, ever consistent in the storm.

"I have to go talk with Diane, she's so nervous about tomorrow, something about Daisy's bouquet," Mollie whispers before Leo can say anything. She holds Athena close, but her voice still carries. "But keep an eye out for Leo. I don't want him drinking too much and making a toast about lost love and regret."

"That would kill the mood," Athena agrees, as if Leo is not standing right there next to them, hearing every word. "I'll make sure he's got water in the mix."

Leo grits his teeth, about to stick up for himself and his own impulse control, but, before he can, he notices the hawklike visage of Mrs. March swooping down upon Deacon, cornering him into conversation. Leo grabs Deacon and brings him back toward Mollie and Athena.

"Mrs. March was hunting Deacon," Leo explains to Athena

as Mollie walks off toward Daisy. "You know how she likes to swoop on y'all."

"She came up to me earlier," Athena says. "Asked where my friend was. I said, *You mean my wife?* And she gave me this look. You know the one." Athena raises her eyebrows and purses her lips and tilts her head back so that her nose sticks up at them. "Then, I had to tell her that we got divorced. Walked away before she could start dancing on the grave of our marriage. She sucks."

"So hard," Deacon says. He sees Daisy, Mollie and his mother all huddled together in a corner. "I should go see what's up."

"You know, I don't need to be babysat," Leo says once Deacon walks away. He rubs the back of his neck. His life's most two important women always tried to tell him what to do.

"Of course you do, you're my baby brother." Athena pinches his cheeks until he slaps her hand away, smiling despite himself. This is their language. Leo was worried it got lost in all the grief. It's a relief to see it returned.

Leo is three years younger than Athena, and, in many ways, her complete opposite. Where Athena inherited all of her father—dark, curly hair, thick, ever-overgrown eyebrows, dark brown eyes, broad shoulders and wide everything else, palms and feet and hips and thighs—Leo is all Mollie. His strawberry blond hair is stalk-straight and glossy. He'd had the perfect Justin Bieber swoop in the early 2010s, and, now, with the resurgence of the '90s, parts it in the middle and lets it drape across his forehead like a young Leonardo DiCaprio. He has his mother's freckles and his father's olive-toned skin, with dark green eyes no one else in the family had. He is beautiful.

*An Adonis*, their father proudly claimed.

*An ab-less Adonis,* Athena clarified, always wanting to curb her brother's ego from the endless enthusiasm of their father.

Though she could not say this anymore. Out in LA, he'd started working out every chance he got. His life was simple: wake up at six, work out, audition, waiter at an upscale vegan restaurant until midnight, go to sleep, repeat. It was a miracle he was able to get away. He hated leaving the city in case a callback or audition popped up. But he needed to be here for this. To see the end of his chance with Daisy. To watch the consequences of his choices come to fruition, and officially close the door that he'd always left open between the two of them.

"Weird being here," Leo says, looking around. "For her, I mean. With him."

Athena takes his arm in hers and leads him to their table. "No pining, remember?"

"But I've gotten so good at it." Leo swoops his hand through his hair in an air of artificial exasperation.

"Save it for the auditions, movie star."

"You know, women like a sensitive man these days." Leo pulls out Athena's chair for her before sitting down in his. "I'm breaking up a long upheld toxic cycle of masculinity that requires repressed emotions. My yearning is for the good of society, really, if you think about it."

"You've been doing too much of that Tok talk."

"So, listen, Thene," he says, lowering his voice, avoiding her eyes and staring down at his bright white tennis shoes. He'd been bracing himself for this. He figured he might as well get it out of the way as soon as possible. "You talk to Sydnee recently?"

"Why does everyone keep asking me that?" She reaches for a roll in the bread basket in front of her.

"She's coming tomorrow, you know."

"So I've heard," Athena says, buttering the bread, then picking up the silver plate embossed with her name in gold lettering. "Nameplates. Cute. Think we can take these home?"

"I haven't talked to her or anything."

"Gold and silver. Classic combination. A little stuffy, though."

"Mom was talking to Daisy, you know." Leo glances down the table at Daisy. She seems to glow from the twinkle lights surrounding her.

"Please no grand romantic gestures," Athena says. "You had your shot, you blew it, you chose LA over—"

"Sydnee's bringing Alex," Leo says quickly before Athena can continue. He hates being reminded of his choices.

"She's…" Athena starts but can't quite finish. Her cheeks, already red with flush from the wine, grow a dark shade of magenta.

"Coming. To the wedding. With…"

"With," Athena begins. She clenches her jaw as she says it. "The woman she fucked while we were married."

Leo watches her. He can almost see the steam coming out of her ears. When Athena gets mad, her whole body boils. When they were kids, and someone changed the rules in the middle of a pickup football game, she'd stand right in front of the boy (it was always a boy, who was always several inches taller than her), ball up her fists and tell him he wasn't playing fair. The boy would start to tease her, but Athena would stand her ground, staring up at him, her face growing red, the veins in her neck popping out, as she told him—quietly, she never yelled—to stick with the rules. Injustice set Athena off like no other. All teasing would die in the boy's throat when he heard that quiet, but deadly serious, tone in her voice. It was a grown-up's fury bottled up in a little kid's mind. Nothing was more volatile. And everyone knew it. They played by the rules and stuck with them.

Leo isn't sure what Athena will do now. You can't stare down someone and make them fall in love with you again, or, even more simply, respect you enough not to rub salt in the gaping wound they left behind.

Sydnee might think of it as empowering. Taking back the space that she could once walk through so effortlessly. She'd probably done a great job convincing herself it was the right thing to do. He remembered how she'd get after a few drinks. The bar became her courtroom. Her speech was abrasive and persuasive. She could talk her way into anything and convince the rest of the group that she was right. Even if she knew it was wrong. It was a remarkable gift. It was a lot like acting. Building a world for yourself to sink into. Crafting a character's internal life, their beliefs. Jason had pointed that out to Leo during Thanksgiving one year.

*You can learn a lot from Sydnee, you know,* he said after Sydnee had launched into one of her speeches. *The commitment, the guts. She never yields. Ever. With your characters—never yield, Leonidus.*

*Never yield.* It was good advice. He'd thought about getting it tattooed on his bicep. He wished Sydnee would let up, though. Give Athena a break. But maybe Sydnee didn't think about what she was doing at all. Athena hadn't talked to her in so long Sydnee might have forgotten her fury, her hurt, her love.

"Shitty of her," Leo says. There's no reason to dance around the truth.

"It's fine." Athena shoots a look down the table at one of the bridesmaids. Leo recognizes her face but doesn't know her name. "No, it's good. It's...an opportunity."

"That's the spirit."

"I'm just going to…"

Athena gets the attention of the bridesmaid. She starts leaning forward, running her hands down her braid, rubbing the back of her neck as she talks. Leo downs his wine in one gulp. He can't stand it when Athena flirts. It's grotesque, unnatural. She'd been with Sydnee so long he forgot how horrible she is at it. And now he has to sit here and witness it firsthand.

He gets the unmistakable urge of a little brother to poke holes in her stories, to rip off the mask she's put on to make herself seem smoother, cooler, better. Her voice goes down an octave and her eyes never stop wandering, as if this gives the impression that she's evasive, cool, unfazed by anything anyone has ever said. When, in reality, Leo knows she will go back to her room that night, ruminate on every reaction, and think about it for the next two weeks, letting the anxiety of the unknown render her incapable of making any moves. She talks a big game, but she's never been able to back it up.

He holds his tongue and drinks his wine and makes mental notes of every little moment he'd like to mock her for later. For now, he lets her have her fun. It's been a while since she's lit up like this. It's healthy, he's sure of it, for her to move on.

He doesn't have to stomach Athena's flirting for long. He feels a slight tug on his jacket sleeve and turns around.

It's Daisy. In the twinkle lights, she seems to glow. Her blond hair is down and curled, and she has a headband made out of jasmine vine that holds her hair out of her face. Her eyes are wide and kind and full of light. On her cheek, there's the slightest smudge of black makeup. Leo resists the urge to reach out and wipe it off.

"Is Los Angeles everything you ever hoped for?" Daisy asks. She gives him a playful shove. "Was it worth abandoning all of us in Texas?"

Leo smiles, but he does not answer. Los Angeles is not what

he imagined. He craved the ocean and open spaces, early mornings spent surfing in the Pacific and hiking hill trails. He wanted to escape the concrete streets of Houston that encased him in their claustrophobic, oppressive, unyielding grip of mediocrity and burst forth into Hollywood, that glittering oasis of promise and possibility and potential.

But, as it happens, in California, beauty demands an expanded budget. The closer something is to what Leo craves, the more unattainable it becomes. Leo can barely afford his three-hundred-square-foot studio apartment with views of concrete highways and strip malls. With the notable exceptions of the perfect weather, the distant, hazy hills and the palm trees that line the roads, he could have been in Houston. Still stuck, surrounded by cement and traffic jammed streets.

He thought it was going to be easier. Aided by the effusive praise of his father, Leo had always been convinced that he had something special. Whatever the world dubbed the "It" factor, Leo believed he oozed the stuff.

In LA, though, everyone is magnetic, and everyone seems the same. It's lonely. He has a few friends from school in town, but they all live on the West Side, in Santa Monica. Leo lives on the East Side because one of his favorite musicians sang about it in a wistful falsetto, and he wanted to live inside her songs. It takes more time to get across Los Angeles than it does to get to College Station from Houston, and he is usually too exhausted from waiting tables and putting together self-tapes at the end of the week to do anything other than plop into his bed, put on his TV, and eat the same roasted chicken and vegetables he meal prepped for the entire week.

How could he tell Daisy the truth? That this life isn't what he wanted? That he's less happy than he's ever been? The truth held nothing for him here.

"It's even better," Leo says. "Best decision I ever made."

"Well, I'm glad." Daisy tilts her head to the side, her eyes narrowed, as if trying to figure out whether or not she believes him. She did always know him well enough to catch his bullshit. He expects her to call him out on it. Prepares for one of their old sparring matches. Instead, she smiles and says, "Congratulations, Leo."

"That's what I'm supposed to say to you."

"No time like the present."

"Daisy," he says, putting on his best Mr. Darcy impersonation, the one she always asked to hear. "I must offer my most sincere and utter—"

"It was great seeing you, but I've got to go." She nods over to her mom. "Have fun. Drink a lot. It's an open bar!"

He watches Daisy go. She talks with her mom, then sits back down next to Daniel, kissing him on the cheek as she does. Leo clenches his fist, then reaches for the bottle of wine on the table. He pours himself too much. He drinks. He leans back in his chair.

If he could get one part. Land something to make himself stick. In the minds of an audience, of the executives. Then it would all be worth it. Giving up his shot at love, leaving his family in their moments of grief. He knew that love would come again, with someone else, and he knew the well of grief his family felt would never get more shallow with time. Maybe he didn't want success for any reason deeper than he wanted to do what he loved and be recognized as good enough to do it for a living. He wanted all of this to be worth it. The rejection and the sacrifice.

Though, if he's honest with himself, he never thought of leaving Daisy as a true sacrifice. She had always been there. For years, he'd waited for her to notice him as someone more than Athena's little brother. It never kept him from dating other people, but Leo always believed that, when Daisy ever came around, he'd drop everything for her.

It took longer than expected. His crush started at fifteen, when Daisy was eighteen and too checked out to notice anything new about their high school, let alone the fact that he'd grown a foot and started shaving and landed the lead in the school musical his freshman year. She went off to the Baptist college and got swept away in the church, spending her holiday breaks on mission trips and breaking away from Athena, who resented the distance so much she would not stand to hear any of the questions Leo wanted to ask her about Daisy.

When he and Deacon were eighteen, they followed Athena to the University of Texas. Leo studied theater, and everything else fell away. He took on a new personality, wearing all black, bleaching his hair, parting it in the middle. He read Chekhov and smoked cigarettes and enrolled in film classes and became enamored with the concept of anarchy. He did not understand it, but he liked the chaos it evoked. An agent of anarchy, that was his acting philosophy. He starred in students' short films, he landed an Austin agent, he let Daisy fade away to the back of his mind.

He graduated. Los Angeles was always there, beckoning, begging, but he was not ready, and he was not funded. Indulgent as his parents were, they could not provide him a stipend to move across the country with no plan and no savings. They supported his dream, but they needed him to support himself first. He moved back home, got a job waiting tables at the sister restaurant of the high-end one he'd worked at in Austin, and kept auditioning when he could, making the drive out to Austin when he didn't have shifts. He found a cheap, one-bedroom apartment. He saved all that he could, though most of his money went to gas for his road trips and rent for his apartment, and he wondered if he'd made a mistake in delaying, in not going straight to Los Angeles after graduation. This choice did not bring the anarchy he had envisioned. It was a hard year, that first one after college. Misery snaked into his bones, filling them with lead, making it hard to move, tanking his motivation. He kept his head above water, but every day he struggled, he sank a little more.

That was the year Daisy moved back to Houston. She was twenty-five that fall. She'd spent three years building up a church plant in Waco, and she got promoted to the same church's campus in Houston. Leo ran into her a few times at a coffee shop in town. They exchanged pleasantries. "Morning devotional time," she said, lifting up her Bible. "Hangover cure," he said, lifting up his coffee cup. She was still beautiful, but distant, like her whole personality was being held back by some force Leo could not see. He remembered her involvement with the church and assumed the force was God. She lacked her signature sarcasm, her fiery wit. There was no more banter. Leo left each interaction wondering why she'd ever had such a hold on him in the first place.

The next three years were a blur of mundanity. Work, auditions, home. Leo dated a few people he'd met on the apps, but he never fell into anything serious. Athena and Sydnee moved back to Houston, so he spent most of his free time with them. They helped him prepare for auditions and made him dinner and bought him drinks whenever they went out, encouraging him to save his money, to not give up his dream of Los Angeles. Deacon hung around with them, too. He saw his parents every week. It was a bright spot, the miniscule community he'd cultivated, in an otherwise unremarkable life.

Then, Daisy came back to them.

It was sudden and strange. One day she was ignoring them, and then, the next, she was at her parents' house, begging her dad to help her move her stuff out of the apartment she shared with a man from the church, who she had eloped with two years prior. The man, they realized later, had been their youth pastor back in high school.

Slowly, after her return, Leo started meeting up with Daisy. They went to coffee shops on his days off. Flat white for him, vanilla latte for her. She started off quiet, clutching on to her mug with both hands, holding it close to her chest as she looked out the window at the packed parking lot in the Heights, shaking her head. No makeup, hair pulled back in a clip. Her lips chapped, her eyes red, dark circles underneath them. She had trouble sleeping in those first few months, finally free to stay up and think about all that had transpired. He hated those people who hurt Daisy, because they were cruel, but also because he loved her.

A few months after they had consistently started meeting up, Daisy sat down and showed Leo her phone. It was an Instagram account with five thousand followers. The Faithful Foodie.

"So," Daisy said, apprehensive, not meeting his eyes. "I've started this thing, and I think you might hate it."

She wanted to become an influencer. "With a purpose!" she clarified. Leo hated the culture around it, people transforming themselves into commercials, sponsoring posts and getting free stuff just because they were good-looking and good at editing. But Daisy had done her homework. She'd met with a dozen new restaurants in Houston, promising to give their food the buzz it deserved by posting about it on her page. That was the main premise, new restaurants in Houston. But on Sundays, she wrote about her experience in the church, the disorientation she felt after leaving it, and kept her followers updated on lessons she'd learned and was still learning.

It wasn't a bad idea. It gave Daisy something to do, something to work toward. Leo went with her to meetings with restaurants when he could. He stood by her side. He supported her when she needed it.

After a meeting with the marketing person at a local Viet-Cajun restaurant, she took his hand and said, "I think I should take you out on a date."

He'd waited so long for it, once it finally became a possibility, it felt like fate. She finally saw him as a man, worthy of her attention, like he always knew she would, if she'd just give him a chance.

They told no one. Deacon suspected it, Leo knew, but he never pressed them about it. They were all too tangled together. Athena had just started talking to Daisy again. If they were going to date, they needed to make sure it worked.

And it did.

Leo was swept away by Daisy, only sacrificing seeing her to pick up extra shifts or drive to Austin auditions. They went on Bayou walks and took in the pocket of lush green beauty in the otherwise concrete encased city of Houston. He made dinner for her at his apartment. They spent nights together, taking it slow, waiting six months to do anything more than make out and cuddle. Leo was happy to wait. That had always been his story with Daisy: waiting for the right time to come.

Los Angeles became a hazy dream. Daisy pulled his focus. His life was quiet and happily held in her hands. Nothing else mattered to him. He even thought about giving up acting, going into real estate, and tying himself down to Houston, to her.

And then Jason died. His death shocked them all. Where grief sent Athena sinking, it energized Leo, his dreams, his ambition. Los Angeles had been patient, but, he knew, it would not be kind if he waited any longer. He was twenty-seven, breathing down thirty's neck. Hollywood was a young man's game. He had to act fast, or else he might lose his nerve for good.

His time in Houston had given him so much. He'd gotten to spend the final years of his father's life in the same city as him. That was a gift and a sign to leave.

There was Daisy, of course, but he had waited years for her. He had stood by her side when she needed support. He had been there for her. It made sense, to Leo, that this time around, once he left, she would wait for him, too.

Leo studies Daisy at the other end of the table. She's staring at Daniel in a way that she never looked at Leo. Not with those blazing eyes, with that sureness, an absentminded hand resting on his thigh, as if the emotional connection must be solidified with some form of physical touch.

Leo always thought his moving to LA was the reason they never got together officially. He starts to worry his move was irrelevant. He needs to know if he mattered. If he meant as much to her as she does to him. He clutches his wineglass, and he starts to plan.

# DAISY

The rehearsal dinner flies by at an alarming speed. Kind speeches from Daniel's family, compliments from every person Daisy's ever met, good wine and good food consumed with great gusto and pleasure. By the end of it, Daisy's voice is hoarse from talking with family members and friends. She never realized it would be so exhausting, to become the concentrated center of attention.

As the guests file out, Daisy pulls Deacon aside in a corner away from it all.

"I just need a minute." Daisy lets her face fall, her cheeks numb from smiling. "To be neutral."

"You're doing great out there," Deacon says, rubbing her back. "Effervescent, if I do say so myself."

"It's all nice." Daisy slaps her cheeks, trying to get the feeling back in them. "Just requires so much smiling."

"Makes sense." Deacon glances over Daisy's shoulder. "FYI," Deacon says. "You've got some chemistry brewing in the bridal party."

"What?" Daisy turns toward her bridesmaids. "Bad or good?"

"Chemistry is always good, dude." Deacon shakes his head. "But, Athena. And Katie. Should have seen Leo's face. You know he hates it when Athena flirts."

"Goddammit." Daisy watches Katie closely as she edges closer to Athena, trying to get her attention. She's harbored a crush on Athena for years, begging Daisy to introduce the two of them. Athena, though, in her current emotional state, is too fragile to be trusted with any emotionally potent situation. "I'll talk to her."

"They're just having fun."

"But what does that fun become when it's combined with Sydnee's arrival? You know how Athena gets."

"A taut string ready to snap," Deacon says, nodding. "But nothing we can do about it now. They're adults."

"I'll talk to Athena."

"Good luck," Deacon says. "You know she'll deny it until they're U-Hauling it all the way to Montrose."

"Here, you go grab the car, I'll tell her to meet you downstairs." Daisy shoves him toward the stairs. "Quick so she doesn't see you."

Deacon does as he's told, in part, Daisy knows, because he's committed to doing whatever she asks of him this weekend. Younger siblings never quite lose that inability to disobey their older one's instructions.

Athena is wandering around the patio, her black suit tailored and sleek, unadorned but classic, her usually messy bun is tamed in a long braid that sways side to side every time she moves.

"So," Daisy says as she walks behind Athena. "Hear you've been having fun."

Athena's braid flips over her shoulder as she faces Daisy. Her face lights up when she sees her, the dark brows raised, the smile quick to come, creating dimples on either side of her cheeks as she throws her arms around Daisy, pulling her into a hug.

"Finally," Athena says. "I get the honor of talking to the bride."

There was a time, after Daisy broke away from the church, that she feared Athena would never look at her that way again, her vibrant brown eyes wide with recognition and love. They could become cold so quickly, Daisy knew well. It left you exposed and stripped of all that once made you feel beloved. Had Daisy lost Athena in the mess she'd made of her twenties, she never would have healed completely.

She probably would have lost her, too, if it weren't for Sydnee. Athena was reluctant to welcome Daisy so easily back into the fold. Daisy had, it was true, let their friendship go by the wayside, instead prioritizing a church that excluded people like Athena and Deacon.

Daisy blew off Athena when she was in Houston, she responded to her texts days later, she made little effort to let Athena in since she was not a part of her world. Daisy's cheeks burn at the thought. The memory of that time, so much of it, filled her with a shame she could not quite disperse no matter how long she spent exorcising those years from her mind.

In Athena's place, Sydnee accepted the invitations to hang out with Daisy and Deacon. It was odd that Daisy met Sydnee alone before she saw her with Athena, but you can never script the moments that will bond you with someone else forever. The only person who listened to Daisy more than Sydnee in those first few months of freedom was Leo. Sydnee let Daisy vent, and, more importantly, she worked on Athena, encouraging her to give Daisy a chance. When she finally did, Daisy knew it was because of Sydnee. She is forever grateful to her for preserving the friendship that very well would have been otherwise lost.

They grew closer as the years went on. Athena and Daisy had been friends for longer, but Daisy spent more time with

Sydnee in the past five years. Before everyone found out about the affair, Sydnee and Daisy had spent six straight months using all their free weekends to plan the wedding. Sydnee's strong opinions and decisiveness were welcome assets when Daisy couldn't make up her mind. Sydnee picked the peonies and the playlist and encouraged her to honor Daniel and his family's wishes for them to have a Jewish ceremony because it was such an integral part of their lives and history, and it cost Daisy nothing to honor that part of her new family. Sydnee talked her through the spike of anxiety that came from entwining herself too closely with religion once more. She'd been so attentive and so kind, holding it down whenever Daisy spun out about one choice or the other. It was hard to believe that during that time she was being a great help to Daisy, she was already setting the stage to break Athena's heart.

It's a contradiction. Daisy misses Sydnee, her friendship, the impulsive spontaneity that always made life more fun, but her anger at Sydnee for what she did still simmers inside of her. Daisy reflected her torn feelings with her invitation to Sydnee. No rehearsal dinner, but she's welcome at the wedding. All the most intimate moments of the day would be shared with Athena. Daisy loved them both, but time favored her. They had been friends for nearly two decades. That meant something. That meant everything.

Daisy holds Athena closer, squeezing her hard around the waist, crushing her.

"You're being a python," Athena wheezes, pushing Daisy away from her and coughing after she's released.

"I'm the bride, you can't complain about getting crushed this weekend."

"So, you were saying. You heard I was having fun?" Athena

asks. She glances behind her, looking for someone. Probably Deacon. "Aren't I supposed to have fun?"

"Fun with one of my friends," Daisy says.

"Well." Athena narrows her eyes, then shrugs, not denying it. "Seen Deacon?"

"He's grabbing the car," Daisy says. "Said to meet him downstairs."

"I better go, then."

"Not so fast." Daisy puts her arm around Athena's shoulder and holds her close, protective. "You need to be careful."

"With the stairs?" Athena asks, pulling away. "I'm not wearing heels. You know my ankles can't handle that."

"With Katie," Daisy explains, pressing ahead. "She's had a crush on you for a while."

"You're full of shit." Athena blushes and tries to hide her smile. She does not succeed. Daisy frowns. Athena hasn't looked like that in years. Embarrassed, but pleased.

"So you were, then?" Daisy asks. "Flirting with Katie?"

"That's ridiculous." Athena can't quite meet her eyes. "What makes you think that?"

"Hear Leo had that nauseous face."

"He's so dramatic."

"He is an actor," Daisy says, glancing over at Leo, who's waiting for Mollie to finish talking with her mother. He's more handsome than he's ever been, and less happy than she's ever seen him. There was a time when the emotional state of Leo could take up her whole week. She'd work to help regulate his mood, stand by him when his anxiety spiked or his despair made him lethargic and listless. Now, though, the sadness she feels for him is distant, not pressing, not hers.

"Mr. Hollywood. That's what he keeps telling us." Athena smiles, her face full of affection. She's always loved her brother. Daisy's heart clenches as Leo notices her, giving a small wave before leaving with Mollie. Athena checks her watch and says, "It's late. I want to get back to the house. Hoping to slip into bed unnoticed by Reghan or Clare."

"And Katie?"

"Daisy," Athena says gently. "I can take care of myself, I promise."

"It's just, I don't want you to get—"

"I know, I know." Athena crosses her arms. "No drama, nothing to take attention away from you."

"That's not it!" Daisy always gets defensive at the presumption that she needs the attention or demands that everything be perfect. She just wants her day clear of distractions. There's so much she can't control, but Athena diving headfirst into something she's not prepared for... "I just want you to have fun tomorrow. Not put pressure on yourself. Or get wrapped up in something you can't handle. Or..."

"That would all be easier if Alex wasn't coming."

"I'm sorry about that, I—"

"It's fine."

They stand in silence, staring at each other. The twinkle lights hanging from the columns sway in the wind. The staff shuts off the heaters. A chill rushes into the air. It's not fine, and they both know it. A mistake Daisy knows she'll never hear the end of.

Their decades-long friendship affords them the same rights as sisters: anger can flood out and course between them, pulsating energy, before it dims and dies out. Athena sighs.

"You're beautiful, by the way." Athena steps toward her with her arms wide. They hug. When they break apart, she says, "You're going to be a stunning bride."

"And you'll look great by my side," Daisy says, softening, letting go of her anger and interrogation. If Athena wants to put herself out there, to try to move on—even if Daisy doesn't think she is ready for it—there is nothing she could do. You can't control the people you love. If you could, she would have taken Sydnee by the shoulders last year and told her to pause. To think. To wait. To communicate. But she couldn't. Sydnee had her own autonomy, and their friend group in the process disintegrated. Everybody lost something in their divorce. Athena, Daisy reminded herself, most of all. "Any Dickinson to send me off? I could use a line right about now. The poetry kind, not cocaine."

Athena laughs, the sharp sound loud and unrestricted. It's a gift to Daisy, the reverberation of her friend's delight.

"Of course," she says. Athena liked to leave big moments punctuated by the words of the poet. She thinks for a moment, her dark brows raised in concentration, as if she is rifling through the lexicon of one-hundred-year-old words in her mind.

*"It's all I have to bring today—This, and my heart beside—This, and my heart, and all the fields—And all the meadows wide—Be sure you count—should I forget, Some one the sum could tell—This, and my heart, and all the Bees, Which in the Clover dwell."*

"I don't know what that means." Daisy embraces her friend again and also the strange fever of her mind. "But I love the way it sounds."

"The beauty of poetry." Athena squeezes Daisy, then heads down the stairs to meet Deacon, who will take her back to the town house.

"There's the bride," a voice says behind her. Daisy smiles before she whirls around. She knows that it's Daniel. He grabs her hips and pulls her into him, hugging her around the waist. "Feel different than the first time?"

"Everything about this is different than the first," Daisy says, twisting her diamond engagement ring up toward her knuckle. She keeps her first marriage buried within her. If she doesn't think of it, then it could have all been a dream. A loss of consciousness that amounted to no real-life consequence. She is not that person anymore. She does not want to think of that person anymore, whose life revolved around the church and all the people in it.

"I should hope so." Daniel spins her and slips his hand into hers, giving her a quick kiss. "I plan on being married to you for, well, forever, if it's all the same to you."

"Even when we're old and saggy?"

"Oh, baby," Daniel says, wiggling his eyebrows. "That's when the heat will get cranked up. Won't be able to keep my hands off you."

Daniel wraps his arms around Daisy, and she presses her face into his chest, inhaling the mix of his light, citrus-forward cologne, his laundry detergent and the indescribable smell of *him*. It engulfs her, invites her in, and makes her feel more at home in his arms than she has ever been by herself. He is the complementary piece her soul searched for, longed for, since she learned, from her first marriage, that love was not always light, kind, easy; it could curdle into a dark, possessive obsession that left her on high alert, always seeking out a threat when someone came in the name of love. Leo had given her a different kind of warning: love can leave you at its earliest convenience, when something better comes along.

With Daniel, Daisy understands what she could not have known before: that love is an ocean, and the first part, the falling into it, is just a wave that takes its time as it builds, then consumes you as it crashes down. It will recede, then come back again even stronger. The momentum ebbs and flows, but the water never runs dry. It is endless and consistent and, of course, beautiful.

"You are the most wonderful person I've ever known,"

Daisy says, her face still buried in his chest, her voice muf-fled by his jacket.

He kisses her forehead.

"I didn't catch a word of that," Daniel says. "But I'm sure it was life-alteringly beautiful."

"Real shame you missed it." Daisy pulls herself out of his chest so she can look in his eyes. They are light brown with infinite depth. In the twinkle lights, they are pools of molten gold. "It's stupid we can't spend the night together."

"It's tradition," Daniel says. "And tradition does tend to be rather stupid."

"Will you miss me?"

"The real question is, will you miss your phone?" Daniel taps the phone always clutched in Daisy's right hand. "You don't have to give it up, you know."

"No, I do. Right before bed. Katie's taking it from me."

"A clear mind doth a digital cleanse make," Daniel says. "Shakespeare said that, I'm pretty sure."

"I'm pretty sure," Daisy says, pulling him by his lapels and kissing him. "That I love you."

"I'll see you at the altar." Daniel kisses her, more deeply this time, holding her close to him, a move so simultaneously habitual and hot that Daisy regrets their having to spend the night apart.

"I won't be late," Daisy says when they finally break apart.

Daniel blows her another kiss as he walks toward the group of his groomsmen, who are all gathered together, taking pocket shots and shoving each other as they chant Daniel's name. They swoop him into their swarm of drunken energy and lead him down the stairs, away from Daisy.

"Hate to see him go," Katie says, coming up to her. "But love to watch him leave."

"Best butt in town." Daisy turns to her maid of honor.

Katie holds up her phone, recording the moment, smiling widely as she films. Daisy swats away the camera, secretly pleased the comment got recorded. "You post that, and I'll kill you."

"We can't have a homicide on your wedding weekend." Katie puts away her phone and takes out her keys. "Back to the castle, then, princess?"

"Onward."

They drive back in comfortable silence, Daisy's wedding weekend playlist plays quietly from the speakers. The dark highway flies by as she stares out the window, willing this weekend to be everything she's ever hoped for. She'd done everything right. She'd double-checked every plan. She confirmed with every planner and florist and caterer. She'd done well. She'd followed the rules.

Daisy has always been good at following rules. For most of her life, that's what she lived for. Rules, following them and upholding them and never bending them an inch. When she was young, depth was something she let others explore. She is not naturally curious, and the big questions of life rarely plagued her at night. She fell asleep at the spiritual wheel, so to speak, and let others be her guide. Soon enough, her life was governed by many men on many stages who told her what she could and could not do with her body, how she should and should not talk in public and private. Marrying one of those men seemed a natural next step. What was love? God's will. And so she fell in with the Youth Pastor.

The way she fell in love with the Youth Pastor was the same way she'd found religion: through hypnosis. The steady progression over time of mantras devoid of true meaning. *Hate the sin and not the sinner; be in the world but not of the world; it's not a religion, it's a relationship.* They stripped away the *secular* world in favor of Christian capitalism. Once, during a chapel service, a visiting pastor onstage held up a physical CD of Katy Perry's "I Kissed a Girl" and snapped it in half, right there on the stage. Daisy could still remember the loud *crack* as flecks of silver flew everywhere. The man's face was red as he said that the world would do *that* to their souls, given half a chance. Rip it apart like wolves. They had to guard all their senses from sin. They should only listen to Christian music, they should only read Christian writers, they should only watch shows that fell in line with Christian virtues, a concept that, the more he spoke on it, seemed oddly conflated with American nationalism. They could watch *Remember the Titans*, but not *Malcom X*, *The Passion of the Christ*, but not *Silence*. Any movie starring or directed by someone who was not a man was generally off the table. It was difficult, the pastor warned them, but that was their lot in life as Christians: to struggle, to suffer and then, in heaven, get rewarded beyond their wildest imaginations.

Daisy had known the Youth Pastor since she was fifteen. He'd always been attractive, and she'd harbored a crush on him for years, though he was seven years older than her. When she moved back to Houston after college and he reached out to her, it felt like a sign from God. Free from the immaturity of men her own age, she thought she'd found someone to lead her through life, through the spiritual minefield of this world, and usher her into heaven once it was all said and done.

Once she was married, though, she didn't feel lovingly led through life. She felt trapped. His controlling hands, his unyielding mind. He never told her she was smart, only that she was beautiful. Naive for so long, she thought that was enough for love.

For the Youth Pastor, Daisy and her body were a vessel. Sometimes, even now, she wondered if he could remember her face, or if he saw her as a haze, a flash of beauty and promise that were stripped away by her *insubordination*, as he would put it. Her body was to remain nimble, her mind pliable. The fever with which he demanded procreation but denied her pleasure told her everything she needed to know: that he saw her body as a tool for "The Kingdom," that he might use it to sow his seed. "The more babies we have," he told her on their way home from city hall, "the more souls we will save." As if salvation were a competition, and souls were prizes you collected along the way. Daisy imagined the Youth Pastor plucking the souls of their children and placing them in his pocket like they were spare change he'd found on the ground, his spiritual wealth accumulating with each life that ripped through her body.

Daisy rubs her abdomen, a reflex whenever she thinks of childbirth. She never speaks about the Youth Pastor. She reserves that well of shame for her darkest nights. The life she built after two and half years spent constantly by his side, four months as his girlfriend, two years as his wife, when she finally broke away from him: that's what she liked to focus on. The Instagram account she started, The Faithful Foodie. The half a million followers. The restaurants she partnered with. The friends she'd made through it. Even Daniel came from the Instagram's success, after he DM'd her about one of her Sunday posts, the ones she dedicated to sharing her experiences in the church. He commended the vulnerability of her fear and the compassion for herself that she'd shared in reflecting on her experiences. Later, Daniel admitted that, though he found her post moving, what prompted the message was that he, in his own words, thought she was *an absolute smokeshow.*

Daisy smiles at the memory, at Daniel's honesty, at his charm.

"What are you thinking about?" Katie asks.

"Daniel," Daisy says simply.

"I should have known." Katie pulls into the driveway and puts the car in Park.

As soon as they walk into the house, there's a crash in the kitchen. A scream from Clare. A slammed door from down the hallway.

Daisy and Katie rush toward the kitchen, their heels clacking loudly on the hardwood floor. They hear the commotion before they see it: Reghan yelling at Clare, making no effort to quiet her voice, even though they both know Athena is trying to sleep.

"You don't have to post *every second* of your day, Clare," Reghan says as Daisy and Katie enter the kitchen. "And you *for sure* don't need to try the 'disappearing cup' challenge before you know how it works. You don't *actually* drop a mug full of coffee onto the floor."

"Well, then, how do you get that first shot if you're so smart," Clare says, her voice rising well above a whisper.

"Shhhhh," Katie shushes them. No one heeds her warning.

"You literally cut to a shot of you holding nothing," Reghan says. "It's not rocket science."

"Fine, whatever, I'll pay for the mug, it's probably like, what? Forty dollars?"

"The money isn't the point, Clare." Reghan waves her arms for emphasis. "The mug was from their trip to Paris when Daisy was just a kid. She'll never have that memory back now."

"It's a *mug*, not a memory," Clare says. "This is about Nicholas, isn't it? Whatever. You can hook up with him if you want. There are like five guys in my DMs right now anyway. I don't need someone else obsessed with me."

"Are you a real person?" Reghan shouts. "Like, do you even hear yourself?"

*"Daisy!"* Katie says, trying to draw their attention to their presence. "What a fun rehearsal dinner!"

"Is this going to happen all weekend?" Daisy asks, glancing from Reghan to Clare. The two have recently taken any opportunity they can to go after one another. Something about a sponsorship that Reghan was supposed to get, only it went to Clare at the last minute. Clare denies it, but there was speculation that her father got involved, swaying the company toward Clare. Reghan has not forgiven her for it, though she puts on a good show for Daisy's sake. Daisy knew it was a risk, having them both in the same room for too long. But they are her friends. And this is her day. She shouldn't have to compromise.

"Oh, we were just being stupid," Reghan says, flashing a huge smile, showcasing all of her perfect veneers. "Especially Clare."

"Have you seen the 'disappearing cup' challenge on Tik-Tok? I was just trying to—"

"Wedding weekends have no room for arguing!" Katie says, interrupting them both. She whispers to Daisy, "Don't let them drive you too crazy."

"Too late," Daisy whispers back. "Reghan, I've never been to Paris, and we are renting this house, it's not my family's, so I don't know whose mug that is."

"I *told* you," Clare says, hissing at Reghan. "It wasn't a big deal."

"But, for future reference," Daisy says, playing referee between the two. "Best to consider gravity before letting go of any object, especially one that can crack so easily."

"I told *you*," Reghan shoots back.

"Are y'all done?" Katie asks in her yoga teacher voice. Firm, but calming. "I think we should take some time to set an intention for the weekend."

"The intention is to get Daisy married," Clare says. "And I don't like all that hippie crapola you peddle during those classes of yours. We all love Jesus here, am I right?"

"I'm agnostic," Reghan says.

"I like him fine," Katie mumbles.

"I guess," Daisy says. "I mean, Daniel's Jewish, so not him."

"Daniel's *Jewish*?" Clare asks, a bit too taken aback.

"Surprise, surprise, the Baptist River Oaks debutante is anti-Semitic," Reghan says, rolling her eyes. "Do you know anything about Daisy? Or are you just here to get more *sponsorships* you don't deserve?"

"I am *not*, I just didn't *know*," Clare says, the color in her cheeks rising. "And I'll have you know, my father—"

"Daisy, settle an argument for us." Reghan cuts Clare off, sidestepping in front of her to pull Daisy's focus. She flips her long, thick ponytail over her shoulder. It hits Clare in the face. Reghan ignores her protests. "You know Athena's brother? The hottie. With the hair and the mopey eyes?"

"Leo?" Daisy asks. A territorial twinge in her stomach. She ignores it. Leo is not hers. He has never been hers.

"Leo, that's a great name." Reghan faces Clare, who, seemingly dropping the argument from before, nods enthusiastically.

"Such a hot name," Clare says. "And he's from LA, right?"

"God, and he's got those arms, did you see those arms?"

"I tried angling in for a hug but I couldn't find a way in between him and his mom."

"Gotta find a way to make Mollie move, she keeps him close, have you noticed?"

"He's from Houston," Daisy says. The twinge in her stomach twists and tightens. "And his mom hasn't seen him in months, so of course she wants to talk with him."

"Anyway." Reghan waves away her logic. She has no use for it. "Who do you think is more his type? Me? Or Clare?"

"Or is he, like, a super evolved, doesn't-have-a-type kind of guy?"

"Every guy has a type," Reghan says to Clare. "And it's usually me."

"You are so full of shit!"

Clare and Reghan's bickering resumes. They forget they were waiting for an answer from Daisy.

"Want to go sit on the porch?" Katie whispers to Daisy. She drags her outside before she has a chance to answer as Clare and Reghan get after it once again.

Katie slides the screen door shut, drowning out the argument. The wind blows the salt air around them. The ocean crashes. The stars are out but dimmed by the bright light of the full moon, which illuminates the white sand dunes below, covered in sea oats and bitter panicum and protected by an old, weatherworn wood and wire fence, which would surely be knocked down by one great gust of wind.

"So," Katie says, taking one of Daisy's hands in hers, not looking away from the ocean. "What intention would you like to set for the day?"

Daisy glances over at Katie, her dark hair now pulled back with a clip, her face unlined and unblemished. She seems serene, but Daisy wonders if that's the inner calm or the Botox. Either way, it gives her an answer.

"Peace," Daisy says. "I want a peaceful day tomorrow. Peace between those two, for one. Is it too much to want them to stop fighting for my sake?"

"Probably," Katie says, shrugging. "Especially if they start fighting over a groomsman or Athena's brother."

"He'd never go for them."

"You never know. They like to fight. And I don't see them coming to a truce over either guy."

"Well, let's manifest it, then. Peace between them." Daisy considers the concept and adds, "And, while we're at it, peace between Athena and Sydnee."

"Who's Sydnee?" Katie asks quickly, confirming Daisy's suspicion that she had been flirting with Athena.

"Her wife. Ex-wife. She's coming to the wedding."

"Why would she do that?"

"She's my friend," Daisy says. "We've been close for five years. I want her to see me get married. Athena said she was fine with it. But..."

"But she's not?"

"Well," Daisy says, uncomfortable, knowing she enabled the situation by forgetting to take "and guest" off of Sydnee's RSVP card before she sent it. "She's bringing her girlfriend. Her new girlfriend. Who she met while she was still married to Athena."

"Bitch." Katie exhales the word. "Poor Athena."

"So just be careful with her," Daisy says. "She's in a weird place right now."

"I was just being friendly." Katie holds up her hands in innocence.

"Sure." Daisy doesn't believe her, but there's no use pressing it. "Anyway, what were we doing? Intention setting."

"Yes." Katie nods. "You wanted peace."

"Peace and—"

Before Daisy can finish, her phone buzzes in the breast pocket of her jumpsuit. Not yet having mastered the art of staying present, she immediately takes it out. There's a text from an unknown number.

Hey. Congrats.

Daisy frowns. An 832 area code. That's Houston.

"Do you know this number?" Daisy asks, showing it to Katie. She studies it, squinting.

"No, but I haven't memorized a phone number since the '90s."

"It's a Houston area code."

"You probably lost their number along the way," Katie says, shrugging. "Okay, back to the intention."

"I'm just going to respond," Daisy says. "Could be a good connection? You never know."

"Random texts rarely lead to anything good," Katie says. "It's probably someone you went to middle school with who's selling insurance now. Ooo! Or who just went into real estate. I've gotten like five of those in the past year. Market must be good."

Daisy texts back.

Hey! Thanks so much!

Before she can lock her phone and put it away, the typing text bubbles pop up. Katie leans over and sees them.

"Yep," Katie says, nodding knowingly. "Here comes the sales pitch. They always respond right away. They're trying to get their hooks in you."

Daisy's phone buzzes. A new text.

I remember my wedding day.

"See, they start out all personal," Katie says, nodding her head vigorously. "And then they pivot."

"How do you get this many random texts?"

"Old friends, old clients," Katie says. "I should probably

be better about handing out my phone number to strangers at bars, too."

"That's why I changed mine after The Faithful Foodie blew up."

"Well, clearly someone has the new digits." Katie gestures to the phone. Another text appears.

You remember it, too.

The hair on Daisy's neck stands up. Her chest tightens. The edges of her vision go dark, and she can no longer smell the ocean, only the acidic sharpness of too much aftershave and the dense musk of liberally sprayed cologne. Clean, but not fresh, ever oppressive. She feels a phantom hand hold her waist too tightly, guiding her through every sidewalk, every hallway, every crowd at a party. Control disguised as love. Unkindness masked as duty.

She should only feel happiness this weekend. Instead, she feels the darkness of the past. Her phone buzzes again. She has one more text.

In the eyes of God, you're still mine.

"Okay," Katie says. "You made me swear to take it from you before you go to bed. So, one last mushy text to Daniel and then—"

"You take it." Daisy shoves the phone into Katie's hands like it's a bomb about to go off. "I'm going to bed anyway."

As Daisy gets ready for bed, going through her meticulous, ten-step skin care routine, she tries to settle down, to envision her wedding, to imagine Daniel waiting for her at the end of the aisle. How could it not be a perfect day? Everything had been set in motion. She'd double-checked every list. She'd thought through every detail. It is going to be perfect.

She slips into her silk, ivory pajamas. *Bride* is stitched on the breast pocket in pink thread. She turns off the lights. She closes her eyes. She thinks of Daniel, then, of Leo, sitting down the table from her, looking handsome, looking devastated.

He left. For Los Angeles. For his dream. Her heart was crushed afterward. She told no one. Athena was grieving, Sydnee, too, and Deacon had told her a hundred times that she couldn't count on Leo to stay, to be the one, when his dreams would always come first. She didn't want to tell him that he was right.

She hadn't expected him to come. Florida is quite literally across the country from California, and she hasn't seen him since that night. In the car. Outside his parents' house. Eating ice cream out of pint containers with plastic spoons. He talked about his new place in Los Angeles. She asked him to stay in Houston. He took a too big bite of his Chunky Monkey, then Mollie came out to greet them in the driveway. His mouth stayed full. His words never came. He left the next day.

She was alone. She doesn't like to remember being alone.

Instead, she thinks of Daniel, his smile, his kindness, his consistency. He'd never leave her, she knew this much to be true. He'd always stay by her side. That, more than fireworks, more than passion, more than spiked heart rates and improbable dreams, is a love worth holding on to. Daniel has given her so much in their three years together. A home, a comfort, a language between them that no one else knows. A whole world has been constructed between them. It is well inhabited and given great attention. Daniel tends to their world like The Little Prince tended to his: diligent and delighted in all that grew, careful to trim the weeds, preventing bad seeds from sprouting and taking hold.

Daniel is the man for her. She cannot wait to marry him.

She falls asleep thinking of Leo.

# MOLLIE

Daisy's wedding comes as a relief. There had been so little to celebrate in the past few years, so few present moments in which to lose herself. Much of Mollie's days are spent in the past, in reflection. Grief is a patient squatter that never leaves. She's taken back some space for herself, but it will never fully be her own again. Whenever she has the chance to do something different, something new, it feels like a reprieve. A break in the mundane. A way to start again.

Just after dawn, on the day of the wedding, Mollie makes her way down the beach, away from the club hotel, toward the town house where the wedding party is getting ready. Diane, Daisy's mom, insisted Mollie come for every step of the process.

*Think of it as my emotional support,* Diane said when she invited Mollie.

But Mollie knows better. Diane wanted her to have plenty of time with Athena and Leo, a rarity of late, since Leo lived in Los Angeles and Athena hardly spent any time outside of her office. Diane was that kind of friend—a true best friend, always looking out for Mollie, helping her, trying to elevate her life and joy.

It started when Jason died. Diane checked in on Mollie

every week, making sure she was getting out of the house. In that first year, it was essential. Mollie hardly had the energy to leave her room. Most of her friends distanced themselves after the funeral. They wanted to *give her space*, but Mollie knew death and grief were the greatest repellents for people whose brunch conversations couldn't get deeper than reporting what their children and husbands had done and seen in the past month or more. Diane didn't make her talk, but whenever Mollie wanted to, Diane was ready to listen. They'd sit in her living room, drinking coffee in those first six months, and then, when Mollie was feeling up to it, they went to get wine and oysters at a nearby French bistro. It became a weekly tradition that saved Mollie. Or, at least, helped her preserve the part of herself she thought had been so flooded by grief it would never surface again.

The least Mollie can do is to be there for Diane in this chaotic time. She hosted bridal showers, helped find a good caterer and florist, listened whenever Diane needed to vent about every request Daisy made that seemed to be asking just a little too much of her and her husband.

Mollie knows that everything will be elaborate and overwhelming and over-the-top. That's Daisy's style. Sure enough, when she enters the town house, it is already buzzing. The hairdressers and makeup artists are setting up in the living room, hair dryers whirring, airbrush machines firing up, EDM music blasting over the speakers, much too loud for this early hour, but it is effective in shocking awake the senses.

"You're here, finally." Diane greets her at the door with a brief hug, her blond, feathered, cropped haircut, à la '80s Princess Di, is already perfectly shaped and hair-sprayed in place. Her face is still bare, the dark circles under her eyes indicating that she's had little sleep in the past few weeks leading up to her daughter's wedding day. Daisy's last marriage had been hard on everyone. Diane was never told the marriage was happening. The man, one of those church types more interested with the sound of his voice than what anyone else had to say, had done a number on Daisy. She came back to Diane's house almost shell-shocked: by the choices she'd made, the way she'd lived, the patterns she'd fallen into. Diane wants this marriage with Daniel to work, and, in her mind, that means making every detail of the wedding perfect.

Still, through the exhaustion, her smile is genuine, letting Mollie know her presence is more than welcome.

"Wouldn't miss it for the world."

"I wish the Marches would have missed it," Diane says, circling the kitchen, scraping together any ingredient she can find as she prepares a smoothie. "Few more bananas can't hurt."

"Why did you invite them? The kids can't stand them, and those other couples, the whatstheirnames—"

"You know how it is, you invite one couple, then you have to invite the rest of the group."

"Those women are not your friends. The way they talk about our children!"

"I know, I know," Diane says. "But Scott works with their husbands, and, well, you know how it all goes."

Mollie hums, a noncommittal response. Those women were the same ones who couldn't quite bring themselves to visit after Jason died, unsure how to navigate grief or how to invite a widow into their couples dinners. Diane is still tied to the illusion that you have no control over your friend groups, the lie that knowing someone for decades acts as some binding contract for continued companionship, even if spending time with that person leaves you depressed and angry at all the things they said or all the topics they would not address. Mollie knows better. If people cannot show up for her in the present, the past they share has no meaning. Widowhood has at least given her the freedom and power to cut ties with those who can no longer meet her where she is.

"Where's Leo?" Diane asks, not noticing Mollie's lapse into silence, too concentrated on stuffing more fruit into the blender.

"He'll stop by later, I'm sure." Her response is barely heard as the blender shreds through ice and fruit.

Leo was in good spirits when Mollie left him at the hotel that morning. He said he was going to work out and walk into town for coffee before swinging by the town house to hang out with Deacon and Athena while they got ready for the wedding.

Everything seemed normal. With Leo. For some reason she can't shake, though, she is suspicious of his intentions in coming to the wedding. There had always been something between Leo and Daisy, especially on Leo's side, and before Jason died, it appeared to have become something more real and reciprocated. Both Mollie and Jason noticed it. Mollie had wanted to push the point. But Jason, always more calm when it came to matters of their children's hearts, told her to wait and see how it all played out, that Leo would tell them when he was ready. But then Jason died and Leo left and the world moved on. Athena said that Leo ran away from his problems, but Mollie always assumed the loss of Jason shocked Leo into motion. He'd waited and waited and waited. Loss severed his patience and spurred him into action.

When Mollie visited Leo out in Los Angeles, when he'd lived there for six months, she told him that Daisy had started dating Daniel. His reaction was hard to read—he'd always had incredible control of his face. He asked if she was happy, and Mollie said she was, and that was the end of it.

Mollie sensed something simmering under the surface. She feels it still, here, three years later, as if Leo had forgotten the feeling and then, upon seeing Daisy with another man, let it resume inside of himself.

Leo always had a flair for the dramatic. And he's never been great at losing. She has to watch him. He can be so charming and disarming, it is easy to forget he knows exactly what he's doing.

"Just going for the free food, really," Leo said in the hotel lobby, trying to reassure his mother. "I won't even look at Daisy, okay?"

She knows he's lying, but nothing Mollie says will change his mind if he's already made it up. She cannot control her children. She never could. That wasn't her job. Some mothers, the ones she met along the way while Athena and Leo were in school, clung close to their kids, keeping tabs on their every move, their progress in school, the social circles they'd hang around in. Mollie would get emails from them asking if she'd started on Leo's project or Athena's math homework or if she knew who was hosting the party they were all going to that weekend.

"I graduated school a long time ago," Mollie replied, having no patience for helicopter parenting. "And I trust my kids to get their work done and stay safe."

Her responses were never well received. The parents didn't like her, thinking her cold, calculating, even cavalier about the state of her children. Mollie's trust was read as negligence. A mother of one of Leo's theater friends once called Mollie a moron for believing her kids could handle themselves.

"They're built for rebellion," she'd told Mollie. "That's our job."

"What?" Mollie asked. "To give them something to rebel against?"

"To squash it out of them," she said, unsmiling.

It wasn't rebellion, Mollie knew, but an inherent sense of

self that might buck against the conventions set out by a family. She and Jason didn't do everything perfectly, but they did allow their children to explore what made them happy without the oppressive forces of their expectations. Jason had always expected his son to play football or soccer or *something*. Instead, Leo loved to play make-believe in the backyard and dress up in costumes and put on living room plays on rainy days. He was sweet and quiet and sensitive. He had no patience for the shallow mundanity of something so pedestrian as sports. In Texas, in the early 2000s, this did not make Leo popular in school. It *did* force Jason and Mollie to make some assumptions about who Leo would end up dating. They thought about it, talked about it, wrapped their minds around it and eventually came to the same conclusion they'd had since both their babies were born: whatever made them happy, whatever led them true, would always get their unyielding support and affirmation.

After all that work and deliberation, she and Jason were surprised when, in high school, Leo brought over his first girlfriend. They were even more surprised when they realized that he genuinely liked her. She was the first of many. In all their deliberations about who their son would become, they never thought to expand their definition of masculinity. He can dislike sports and still like girls. Who knew?

Athena, however, had always flown under the radar. She was intense. She worked hard. She kept her head down. She never had boyfriends, but she seemed too serious for that sort of high school frivolity. There were no discussions about Athena because Athena was not someone they could totally understand, and that felt like a failure, at least on Mollie's part. That she could create someone so unknown to herself.

It wasn't Mollie's fault. Even Athena would agree to that. There was a wall up for most of Athena's life. An impenetrable presence within her that could not be breached by any level of intimacy. Not by Jason, not Leo, not Deacon, or Daisy, certainly not by Mollie. She kept everyone at a distance. Mollie could feel it, but she didn't understand it.

When Athena came out, the wall started to crack. Then when she met Sydnee, it came crashing down completely.

Now it's back. And Mollie doesn't know if she'll ever break through again. This regression adds another layer of grief. She'd gotten used to knowing Athena. She hopes she'll be able to once more.

"Athena's still asleep," Diane says after she finishes in the kitchen, thrusting a smoothie in Mollie's hands. "Or hiding out. Either way, she'll have to come out soon. It's showtime, can you believe it?"

"What will we do with ourselves after this is over?" Mollie asks. She takes a sip from the smoothie and gags. It tastes like burnt rubber and bad bananas. "God, what is this?"

"Sleep is what we'll do." Diane holds up the smoothie and frowns. "No good? I used one of those supplement powders Daisy's always promoting online." She takes the glass from Mollie and sips, then immediately dry heaves. "God, it tastes like tires!" She takes the glass to the sink, rinses it out, then throws the entire bag of powder in the trash can.

"Where do you need me?" Mollie asks, accepting the bottle of water Diane offers.

"Let's see," Diane says, glancing around. "Well, first—"

"Diane!" A shout from the living room. It's Katie. "Can you come here? We have a little bit of a problem."

"Oh, God," Diane says, bolting toward the other room. "If it's the dress, I swear to God."

Mollie, left alone, goes to the kitchen and assesses the fridge, wanting to whip up some eggs for everyone. The fridge is empty. The freezer, too. Diane used the last batch of fruit for her rancid smoothie. She goes to the pantry. Barren. No food for a whole house of people trapped inside for eight hours.

Before she can think through how to solve this problem, she hears it. A soft knock at the front door. It creaks open. A man's voice calls out, "Is anyone decent?"

The bridal party is busy in the living room, talking through their makeup palette and hairstyles with the stylists. A general air of chaos, excitement and stress occupies them as they focus on the task at hand. No one else hears the knock, so Mollie makes herself useful and answers it.

She has never been one to describe men as *beautiful*, but there is no other way to describe the man she sees when she throws open the door.

He's tall, well over six feet, his long dreadlocks in a twist on top of his head, adding a few inches to his already imposing height. His face is smooth and poreless, with sharp cheekbones and an even sharper jawline. His left eyebrow is pierced, and he has a tattoo sleeve on his right arm. It's an enormous oak tree, the branches running down his arm, toward his wrist, the trunk unseen underneath his black T-shirt sleeve. A dimple forms on his right cheek when he smiles as he watches Mollie staring at his arm, taking in the tattoos.

"Hurt like a bitch, to tell the truth," he says, holding out his forearm. "The leaves were the worst part. Tiny little lines. Never thought it would end."

"It's certainly...detailed," Mollie says. She resists the urge to reach out and trace the branches all the way up his bicep. She shakes her head, trying to reset her brain back to a woman in her sixties instead of the moonstruck teenager she's suddenly become in this man's presence.

"I'm looking for Daisy," the man says, peeking behind Mollie as if the bride might pop out and greet him at any minute. "These are her shoes. From Elise."

He pulls out a pair of bridal white stilettos, the heels of which are bedazzled. They sparkle in the light. Mollie wonders how Daisy plans to walk down a sand aisle in those things.

"Daisy's the bride," Mollie says, doing her best to focus on the shoes so she doesn't gawk any more at the man.

"I'm aware." His smile grows wider, as if he can sense her nerves. Men with his level of attractiveness must know when someone is struck by them, used to their mere presence becoming a spectacle in and of itself. "My daughter picked them up for her in Houston last night. Didn't get into town until late. Claims she needs to start getting ready for the wedding—at eight in the morning—so she sent me down to do her dirty work. Pretty sure she's still asleep. But, I've been up for a few hours, so what the hell. I'm Eli, by the way."

He reaches out his hand.

"I'm Mollie," she says, shaking. His hands are calloused. Mollie feels instantly at ease with his touch. She shakes his hand for too long before remembering to drop it. Her cheeks burn. As if feeling the need to explain herself, she adds, "My daughter's a bridesmaid. I've known Daisy since she was thirteen, back when she was just a little string bean with no impulse control. I'm just here to help out. Though I don't seem to be of much use."

"Well," Eli says, "if you can get these shoes to the bride, I'm sure you'll save the day."

"Never bad to curry favor with the bride."

"Always a good idea." Eli looks at her, and, as if needing to explain further, says, "I got corralled into coming. Something for my daughter's Instagram. She posts pictures of me with *Best Plus One* as the caption. Pretty sure she's trying to get back at the boy she was supposed to invite. Total dud, absolute wet carrot. But she can't seem to shake him. So naturally, I'm here. Because she can't go alone to an event where she was given a plus-one, apparently. All I seem to be good for is running errands." Eli passes the shoes over to Mollie. "Thought I'd get some time on the beach. Make this into a vacation. But not even close."

"Oh, the kids don't think we need any fun," Mollie says. "It's all *Mom, can you do this?* You're thirty-three years old. Do it yourself."

"Jesus year," Eli says, nodding with a sage certainty, as if he, too, understands its significance. "Is your daughter one of the internet people, too?"

"Oh, no, the opposite."

"A cavewoman?"

"Nearly," Mollie says. "An English professor."

"I didn't know Daisy knew any of those." Eli raises his eyebrow in surprise. "My daughter certainly doesn't. Daisy and Elise work together. At least I think that's what they do. Doesn't seem like work to me. They met at one of those travel meetups the internet people do. Turns out they're both brand representatives for some vegan, holistic makeup company. Don't understand a word of it, but they've spent a lot of time working together. Elise tells me to think of it like coworkers becoming friends at the office. Only, their office flies them out around the country to day-drink and take pictures of themselves. Daisy and Elise always do some kind of platform collaboration, that's what it's called, I think. My daughter takes over her Instagram on Juneteenth, Daisy takes over hers the next day for some kind of Pride month awareness shindig."

"But Daisy isn't gay."

"Deacon gets on with her, I think, and some other girl. A lesbian and her wife."

"That'll be my Athena," Mollie says. "Though, it's her ex-wife now."

"I'm sorry to hear that. Is she happier now? After the separation? I know I was."

"Not at all. She's never been worse."

They look at each other for a beat, then burst out laughing. His laugh is booming and not afraid to take up space. It's infectious. Mollie can't help but join in, her shoulders shaking as her voice goes out, her laugh becoming an occasional wheeze. Her sides split and her lungs constrict and she feels, for the first time in years, younger than her age.

"I'm sorry," Eli hiccups himself into composure. "I shouldn't laugh. My daughter would yell at me for it. Says I get too insensitive sometimes."

"Oh, their whole generation is terrified of insensitivity," Mollie says, then, hearing herself adds, "God. I'm ancient. Aren't I?"

"We're relics of a time gone by," Eli says. "Whatever that means."

"Is it bad that I'm relieved? Being young sounds exhausting."

"The way these kids do it." Eli nods. "Well, I'll leave you to it here."

"You'll be at the reception tonight?" Mollie asks. It's too eager, but she doesn't care. A bonus of aging: time is no longer wasted for fear of embarrassment.

"In a tux," Eli says, grinning. "I'll save you a dance."

With a wink, he leaves, closing the door behind him. Mollie leans her back against the wall, clutching Daisy's shoes up to her chest, closing her eyes, taking in the moment, the flirtation, the promise of something good to come. She forgets about the wedding, about Athena, about Leo, about her pain and grief and loneliness, and allows herself the self-indulgence of hope. That something could come out of this night. That she could be more than just a mom. That she could, for the first time in years, start again.

"Mollie!" someone shouts from the kitchen. "Are those Daisy's shoes? We've been searching all over for them."

"Just a minute!" Mollie shouts back, her eyes still closed, savoring this moment that is wholly her own. She lets her mind swirl out of control and into imagination: her and Eli on the dance floor, her and Eli at an Italian restaurant in Houston, her and Eli in bed, legs intertwined, talking about everything and nothing, letting Sunday mornings slip away into afternoons as they sketch out the outline of their lives, tracing their fingertips down each other's bodies, as if they could feel the memories embedded in their skin.

"Really, Mollie." Diane's voice is sharp as steel, and cuts just like it, severing Mollie's imagined life as she swipes the shoes from her hands. "We're already behind today. It's time for the girls to get ready. Can you go into town? Get some breakfast and snacks for everyone to munch on?"

"Of course, Diane."

"Stress, you know." It's the best apology Mollie can hope for. "You walked over? Take my car."

"You've got it." Mollie grabs Diane's keys, tucking away her fantasies for another time. For now, it's all about Daisy. All about the wedding. All about love, and the pictures you can take of it.

In the car, the old Steve Earle song she loves plays on the radio. She cranks up the volume and rolls down the windows, sticking her hand out in the open air, banging the rhythm on the side of the car as she zooms down the open road into town.

This had been her song with Jason. He claimed it for them as soon as he heard it the first time, since he himself had fallen in love with an Irishman's daughter. A Galway Girl, just like the song. He'd play it loud in their tiny, two-bedroom apartment on the rare nights after they had kids, when they were alone, Leo and Athena sleeping over at Mollie's parents' house. Jason clapped along and stomped his feet and twirled Mollie around their closet-corner kitchen, dipping her and kissing her and taking her into the bedroom, where they ripped off each other's clothes and laughed when they couldn't unbutton a shirt or unclasp a bra with the speed their insatiable desire demanded.

Mollie couldn't listen to music for a year after Jason died. Her house went quiet. There was no rhythm left in her. It feels healing now, here, to listen, to remember, to stay held together in the grief and love and memory. How could she ever love another man? She'd had the love of a lifetime, of infinite lifetimes, with Jason. Her throat tightens, his absence leaving her breathless at the most unexpected moments. She wishes she didn't have to think about other men. She had the one she wanted. And now he's gone for good.

She finds a spot in the neighborhood behind the town center and parks. She stays in the car until the song finishes, leaning back on the headrest, closing her eyes, remembering. When it's over, she rolls up the windows and walks toward the market. If Jason were here, he'd hold her hand. He'd talk. He was always talking. It drove Mollie up the wall at the time, but she misses it desperately now that silence has become her most consistent companion. They'd discuss the wedding, but mostly, they'd discuss their children. Leo and his long harbored love. Athena seeing Sydnee. Mollie could almost imagine Sydnee walking along the road in front of her, happy and free, with a market bag in hand.

Mollie shakes it off. She knows from experience that memory plays tricks on you. Only as Mollie gets closer, the person she assumed she imagined still looks like Sydnee. Walks like Sydnee. And she's approaching Mollie with a deliberate path. As if she wants to interject. To say hello.

When they reach her, Mollie takes in the specificity of her, the details that she cannot deny are real: her straight-legged walk, her dense, perfect dark curls bouncing at her shoulders, her broad shoulders and wide, infectious smile that meet her dark green eyes, a welcoming Mollie had grown accustomed to for many years and had been deprived of for the past eight months.

"Mollie," Sydnee says, holding her arms open wide. "I've missed you."

# SYDNEE

It was stubbornness, more than sentimentality, that drove Sydnee to attend the wedding.

For the six months before the separation Sydnee had sat through happy hours and lunches with Daisy as she explained, in painstaking detail, how every second of her ceremony and reception would go down. They discussed flowers and dresses and centerpieces. Daisy stopped meeting with her after everyone found out about Alex, but Sydnee had still put in the hours before, which, despite her best efforts to de-lawyerize her brain, she thought of as billable. She helped make decisions. She gave her honest opinion when it was needed most. She deserved to be invited. And she had earned the right to attend.

Divorce from Athena should not mean divorce from their friends. Sydnee repeated this line many times when she hung out with Deacon and Daisy in those months after the separation. It wasn't often, they were both furious at her. But they were always willing to forgive, to offer up second chances, especially to the people they cared about the most. Sydnee gave them space when they needed it and accepted any olive branch, no matter how small, whenever it was given. Both Daisy and Deacon offered her the same, weary, skeptical look whenever she mentioned that the divorce shouldn't change their relationships. It told her everything she needed to know. Athena did not want them staying in contact with Sydnee. Athena had the friendships first. They should be returned to her in due course, as if memory and years and connection were an asset they could throw in when they divided everything up with their lawyers. Split the finances fifty-fifty, Sydnee gets the house, Athena gets the friends.

But that would not do for Sydnee. She'd watched Daisy and Daniel fall in love, she'd known Deacon longer than she'd known Athena, since they were both in the business school at UT. She'd lived enough life with them to claim them as her own.

"Are you sure it's not weird that I'm here?" Alex asks as they walk through the town square, sipping their coffee and munching on the blueberry muffins they bought from the local market.

"You're my date," Sydnee says. She takes a large bite of the muffin. It's sweet, with a little tang, the perfect compliment to her black coffee. She sips it before saying, "You're invited."

"Didn't you have to beg for a plus-one?"

"No." Sydnee does not tell her that the plus-one was reluctantly given, that Daisy had never really wanted her to bring Alex at all. But, since it's more than likely that Athena's family and Deacon and his family, the only people Sydnee knew well, will keep their distance from her, so as not to upset Athena, it seemed only fair that Sydnee get to bring someone guaranteed to stick with her the whole time. Daisy heard the logic in this and acquiesced, allowing Alex to come, though they both knew it would cost her with Athena. It meant more to Sydnee than she would admit: that Daisy, despite everything, still looked out for her. That she was still her friend.

"Just don't want you to regret it. Coming or bringing me or whatever."

"You're near the beach." Sydnee points in the direction of the Gulf. "Isn't that worth a few awkward hours with free food and booze?"

"I've got my swimsuit on under this," Alex says, gesturing to her puffy jacket and sweatpants. "Polar plunge?"

"You're on your own there."

"Well, you can watch from the beach and save me if I shock my system too hard."

"Deal."

They walk together in silence. The town square is quiet. Alex likes to start her days early, before dawn, but allowed for a 7 a.m. start time after Sydnee begged her to let them sleep in. When she was with Athena, lazy Saturdays and late starts were the norm. It took some adjusting, adapting to the patterns of someone new.

Sydnee hasn't regretted any of it. That's what she has to tell herself, and anyone who asks. Her life has never had room for regret, only forward motion. She compartmentalizes her actions, and the pain they cause the people she loves. That she hurt anyone is not at the forefront of her mind. She acted on instinct—that's how she's always lived her life.

With her marriage, the rationale was easy. She and Athena had grown apart. The writing was on the wall. She only accelerated the inevitable.

Instinct, yes, that had been her god since she was eighteen. Knowing when to stay and when to leave when it came to her parents. Giving them just enough energy so that they could feel her love, but never letting them get in deep enough to derail the path she was carving out for herself.

She carried that into her relationship with Athena. It had been that way since the beginning. She knew when to wait and when to make a move. She knew when to speak and when to stay silent. And when that silence became too constant, she felt the forward motion of her life halted. She had never been good at sitting in stillness. Her instinct told her to take action, and so she did.

At every new milestone she hit, Sydnee thought that she could somehow earn a way out of her restlessness. She thought, especially, once she started making money, that this restless need would cease, that she would finally feel fulfilled. That's the great American language, right? The only true source of self-realization? Not quite. Law school had taught Sydnee many lessons, but nothing so important as this: there is a difference between *having* money and *coming* from money.

No matter how hard she worked, how many tax brackets she moved up, she never could make up for the fact that she grew up in Brownsville, not Houston or Dallas or Austin, with no debutante ball, no coronation into society, no memberships to the country club or yacht club or whatever other club you had to be a part of to be recognized as *somebody*. There was an entire language reserved for the upper echelon of society, a language that many of her bosses and coworkers had been speaking since birth. She could keep up, but she could never relate. Another layer of otherness when the deck was already stacked against her.

On the company's Corporate Tax Law page, Sydnee Valdez stuck out in a sea of Anglican names, her face an anomaly amongst the male, pale, white-haired bosses and colleagues with whom she spent ten hours a day, six days a week. There were other divisions, with more people who looked like her, but Sydnee was good at her specialty, and, if she was going to go corporate, she might as well go all in.

The restlessness embedded itself in the little things, all of which added up, chipping away at Sydnee. Delegating note-taking to her when the executive assistants were on lunch. Having her stay behind on "cleanup teams" after recruiting events. Never remembering her first name, instead, just settling for *Valdez* since they had *a dime a dozen of your first names around here, anyway*. Partners staring at her ass, getting too close behind her at meetings, complaining about their wives' lack of sex drive, then shooting it over to Sydnee, saying, "You get it, right, Valdez?" As if her marriage resigned her to their same inability to enjoy the company of women.

That was another problem. They were never really sure what to do with Sydnee's queerness. With Athena, Sydnee's colleagues could ignore it, pretend it didn't exist. When they saw Athena, if they tricked their mind just enough, they could see any other woman, who looked just like them and their wives.

Sydnee tried to explain this to Athena once, back when they first started dating.

"It's hard for me, too," Athena said. "People treat me differently when they learn I'm a lesbian."

"But," Sydnee pushed back, "up until that point, they treat you like an equal. Because they think you are one. The way you look, it makes them feel comfortable."

"So I should try and make them uncomfortable with the way I look?"

"You're missing the point."

"You're not making one."

It was only years later, after a nationwide reckoning with race that amounted to limited change and an onslaught of infographics on Instagram, that Athena finally understood what Sydnee was talking about. But by that time, it was too late. The issue lingered in every argument, hovering in Sydnee's mind whenever she saw Athena mingling with the partners at her work, so at ease in conversation, never wondering what they would say as soon as she walked away. It was a bitterness that hardened and calloused over time, both in her marriage and in her career.

Sydnee wanted to move into more meaningful work. But she knew that wouldn't pay the bills. Athena had to grind her way as an adjunct in those first few years of marriage, and she could never make more than $45,000 a year, despite working thirty hours a week more than the tenured professors around her. Sydnee's work was soulless, but it rewarded her a salary nearly five times that of Athena's. They were able to buy a house before they both turned thirty, and, at the time, Sydnee didn't care that she was putting up the majority of the down payment, paying the majority of their shared credit card bill at the end of the month, covering the majority of the dinners they spent out together.

She never thought she'd become the type of person who focused so hard on money, to have her mind occupied by budgets and incomes and expenses. But that was real life. Money, bills, moving up. What else was there? Money might not buy happiness, but it did provide stability. And happiness cannot come without a stable foundation. She always tried to instill that in Athena, but it never took. Happiness happens from home, Athena would always say. But how can you have a home if you can't pay your mortgage?

They had changed so much from when they first met during her first year of law school, before she could TA or work in any of the clinics, when she snagged a tutoring job in the student success center. She'd majored in finance during undergrad, but most of her students needed help with Spanish, which she had minored in and spoken since she was a baby, so she spent most of her sessions trying to get hungover frat guys to remember the difference between *tú* and *nosotros*. More often than not, they'd stare at her through bleary eyes, the bags underneath them hollow, their faces unwashed, and ask if she could "just do them a solid and finish it for them so they don't flunk out," or, worse, watch her mouth too intently when she rolled her *R*s, correcting their pronunciation.

Then there was Athena, her favorite student, opening up her world, slowing down her mind, inviting her into the unconditional love of her heart, of her family, of her world. She hadn't stopped to think about it in years. The tide shift that had occurred once Athena entered her life.

When she thinks about their marriage now, Sydnee understands the resentments were stacking up, even before Jason died. They were simmering below the surface, waiting for a moment of release.

Grief provided it, magnifying their issues and cutting off their communication. Athena seemed to think of loss as a scarcity, one that could not be held in equal parts. She took the lion's share and didn't let Sydnee have the scraps. How can love thrive when emotions become a competition? They never really stood a chance once all the walls started coming down around them.

"Where's your head at, Valdez?" Alex asks before wrapping the rest of her sandwich up in foil. She tosses it in the trash. "This chicken biscuit is disgusting."

"We saw them take it out of a freezer and microwave it, what did you expect?" Sydnee takes a bite of her muffin, chewing slowly. Alex keeps things light. It's easy. She doesn't like to go too in-depth, or for conversations to get too messy, or for anything to feel overly complicated. Her marriage to Athena checked each of those boxes. They agreed, when they first started seeing each other, to never mention her. "Just thinking about what I'm going to wear tonight."

"I know what you're going to wear *later* tonight," Alex says, and grabs Sydnee's waist with one hand, using her other hand to go below the waistband of her jeans.

"Stop, someone will see." Sydnee giggles as she says it, pretending to glance around the empty square. This is why they work. The spontaneity, the silliness, the—"Oh, shit." Sydnee jumps a foot away from Alex. "Some lady's walking this way."

It's as if her limbs recognize her before her mind does. Sydnee automatically starts walking toward the woman. Strawberry blonde, shoulders slightly hunched, a slow amble from side to side. Sydnee had seen Mollie walk so many miles. She'd know her silhouette anywhere.

"Mollie." Sydnee says it more to herself, but it comes out as a shout, getting Mollie's attention. She stops and glances up from the grocery list in her hand. Sydnee throws open her arms. "I've missed you."

Mollie freezes and stares at Sydnee like she's seen a ghost. Sydnee feels, for a moment, translucent in the eyes of her ex-mother-in-law. She balls up her fists, squeezing them, the pressure a reminder to herself that she is alive, not a wraith. Mollie, perhaps finally recognizing that she is real, walks quickly into her arms, holding Sydnee close.

"You're doing okay?" Mollie asks as she pulls away, holding Sydnee by the shoulders. "Healthy and happy and all that?"

"Can't complain," Sydnee says. It sounds hollow and forced, devoid of meaning. They have lost the ease with which they used to have their conversations.

"And work? It's good?" Mollie seems to make a conscious effort not to notice Alex standing behind Sydnee, the great reminder of what they lost and how they lost it.

"Soul sucking, but fine." Sydnee wants to take her by the shoulders and explain everything. Her absence, her betrayal, why she had to leave. "Still tinkering with your recipes?"

"A lot can change in eight months, Syd, but not *that* much."

Mollie meets her eyes for the first time. The pale blue is slightly magnified by a layer of tears. Mollie doesn't blink, preventing any from rolling down her cheek. Grief and pain and anger and love. She sees it all in Mollie's eyes. A picture of what her actions have cost.

"Well, I guess I'll see you at the wedding tonight." Sydnee's tone is light. They cannot say what they must. That earnest place no longer belongs to them.

"Athena will be there, so…" Mollie breaks off. Sydnee understands. Her daughter must always come first. Why would it ever be any different? Sydnee hadn't expected to see Mollie again, and therefore had given little thought to what it would be like if they ever ran into each other. It's unexpectedly painful, understanding that they can no longer talk like they used to.

Sydnee prepares herself to say goodbye when Mollie says, "Do you remember that night? A month before Jason… Well, that last month. Y'all were out by the fire, talking. Athena and I were inside the house. Y'all were so intense. I just… What were you talking about? I've always wondered."

"Nothing serious," Sydnee says, remembering the conversation well. It was the last one they'd had alone. Conversations with Jason rarely were serious. At least at first. He'd run his hands through his dense, curly hair and tug on the great, unruly beard he'd needed trimmed. His eyes would flit around the room as he talked, and then, when he was ready to listen, they'd suddenly land on you, and you'd feel like the most seen person in the world. He was so alive, and so present. It made every conversation feel serious, even if they never were. "I was explaining why, in Mexico, we don't use *vosotros*. We got into our colonizer rant."

"His favorite."

"And he said he was planning a trip to Mexico City. With

all of us. Sometime that next year. He'd already gotten fluent, you know. So much better at languages than Athena."

"He worked so much harder at them."

"And he wanted to make sure he had the slang and the casual rules down, too. Said it would all be so much more fun
if I could manage to get my parents down for a visit."

"Oh, that one again. His favorite dead horse to beat."

"Yep. And I explained, again, that they weren't like that.
You know, wanting to see my marriage and my life. They
liked me in doses. The parts they could understand and love.
And he said…" Sydnee trails off. He had said, *I'm so proud to
know the full picture of you, and I'm so proud to call you my daughter.*
But she couldn't say it out loud. Since, if he were alive today,
it would no longer be true. And she always wanted that to stay
true. "He said something nice, as always. And that was that."

"He really thought he could get your parents on board if
they could just meet him." Mollie rolls her eyes, then wipes
them. "He thought the same thing about his parents and me.
But some people just don't change."

They let that hang in the air. Sydnee avoids her eyes. She
can almost hear the unsaid follow-up. *And some people can't
stop changing.*

"Well, it was great running into you," Mollie says, holding
up her grocery list. "But I've got to scrounge up some snacks
and supplies for the house. Can't have anyone fainting when
they walk down the aisle, now can we?"

Mollie hugs Sydnee, squeezing her hard, as if trying to press
all the unsaid words into her. Sydnee reciprocates. When they
break apart, Mollie pats her shoulder, and heads toward the
market. Sydnee watches her go, forgetting about Alex and the
town square and the muffin in her hand. Her mind wanders
to places she rarely allows it to go.

Even after everything, all the silence and the icy attitudes and the fights, when Sydnee allows herself the stillness required for reflection, she knows that she misses Athena.

She had missed her for years. Even when they were still married, when she gave in and kissed Alex after their work event one night in December, after too many sidecars, on the roof of a downtown tower that let them see all of Houston, the sprawling city sparkling in the darkness, unspecified and ethereal, like a sky full of stars spread out on the ground. It was a quick kiss at first, like dipping a toe into too cold water. It shocked Sydnee. Then, it cracked her open with a desire she'd set aside for a day when *things got better* between her and Athena. But better was here in front of her, holding her hips and looking down at her lips with a need Sydnee knew she could satisfy. So before she could rationalize anything, she leaned in and let the floodgates open.

Alex worked in environmental law. It was a cooler faction of the company. Lots of young associates, lots of progressive thinking, in and out of the office. A group of them hung out outside of work and enjoyed mandated corporate celebrations, like the holiday and summer parties, which Sydnee always dreaded. That's where she met Alex for the first time.

It was the summer party at an old River Oaks mansion transformed into an event space. Sydnee took Deacon as her plus-one. Athena hated the parties. They were too loud, too crowded. She preferred to stay home, reading and writing and making little effort to assimilate into Sydnee's professional world. But Deacon loved them. Free food and free booze and swanky event spaces full of pretentious people, all of whom he found riveting in their pompous mundanity, and they usually had a decent live band, which would always be reason enough for Deacon to attend.

The band at this particular party was a folk-country trio, and the mansion was a redbrick monstrosity with white columns in the front, the backyard sprawled for at least an acre by Sydnee's estimation. There was a pool and a pickleball court and a guesthouse the size of every home Sydnee had ever lived in. A catering company cooked ribs and brisket on the smoker, and the air smelled like cedarwood and charred meat. There were buckets of Texas beer on ice. Sydnee was on her third Shiner when Deacon brought over Alex.

"I forgot y'all worked at the same company," Deacon said as he twisted off the bottle cap of Alex's beer, handing it over to her. "Alex and I are on the same softball team. Been meaning to introduce y'all for a minute. I'm going to see if the band will play 'Callin' Baton Rouge' but thought I'd get y'all together on my way over."

"He always does this," Sydnee said as Deacon jogged toward the band. "Tries to make all of his friends friends with each other wherever he goes."

"It's Sydnee Valdez, right?" Alex asked. Her Astros baseball hat was backward, so she had to use her hand to shade her eyes from the sun. Sydnee didn't recognize her from the office. Flaming red hair, pale, freckled skin, small, slightly upturned nose. She wore a black tank top and ripped, whitewashed denim shorts that showed off her thigh tattoo, a pair of wings set against a setting sun.

"Is that supposed to be Icarus?" Sydnee asked.

"And the sun," Alex said, nodding.

"A little dark, don't you think?"

"The sun is bright, actually."

"You know what I mean."

"A lesson in humility isn't dark."

"Falling from the sky is, though."

"He lived better after that."

"Didn't he die?"

"I don't know." Alex shrugged and took a swig of her beer. "I just liked how it looked, if we're being honest."

"Deacon left so fast, I didn't catch your name."

"Alex Grammar," she said, extending her hand. "I've heard a lot about you."

"Good things?"

"Would I talk to you if they were bad?"

"You do have a tattoo of a man dying in the sky on your leg." Sydnee could feel herself flirting, inching closer to Alex, drawn in by the banter. "Could be a sadist for all I know."

"Asking about my kinks already?" She reached out and ran her hand down Sydnee's arm. "Buy me a drink first. Or don't. I like the boldness."

"I'm married," Sydnee said in a rush.

"Deacon told me." Alex cocked her head to the side, smiling. "Do I make you nervous or something?"

"What? No," Sydnee lied. She peeled the label off her beer bottle, needing to do something with her hands.

"Don't worry," Alex said, knocking the neck of her bottle against Sydnee's. "I'm harmless."

And from that moment on, as if she wasn't conscious it was happening, Sydnee was seeing Alex all the time, in the elevators at work, at happy hour events, on the weekends when Athena thought she was working late at the office, and they were alone, and Sydnee filed away all her fear and reservations, focusing only on that forward motion she'd lost for so long. Alex bulldozed forward, her energy impossible to resist. Athena fell away. So did her family, and all the complications that came with it. Jason's death had rewired their lives. The stable foundation they'd all stood upon, united, for so many years, was cracked, leaving them untethered from each other. Leo left, Mollie stayed and Athena became vacant. Sydnee thought, with time, she'd come back to herself. But grief shifts our makeup. Once it seeds itself into our skin, we are never the same. Sydnee was not the same. That restlessness that she'd wrestled with for all of her life amplified its presence in her mind. Athena's grief required stillness. Sydnee's demanded motion. They no longer operated on the same frequency. With Alex, Sydnee found herself in tune with someone else once more. She let herself get drawn into it, muting the dissonant music between her and Athena. She let it fall away completely. She left. She followed her instinct. She never looked back.

Running into Mollie awoke something in Sydnee that she'd refused to recognize for as long as she'd been with Alex. A nagging sense of loss, and, buried beneath that, a hardened, unexamined mass of guilt.

"That was weird." Alex watches Mollie walk away, then kisses Sydnee on the cheek. Sydnee pulls away quickly in case Mollie looks around, not wanting her to see, not wanting to hurt her.

"She was nice. Always has been," Sydnee says. "Even at the beginning—"

"Like, too nice." Alex tries to hold Sydnee's hand again. Sydnee gives it a brief squeeze before dropping it.

"No, that's just Mollie." Sydnee wishes she and Mollie could go out to coffee and catch up, talk about how everything happened. Or, more likely, avoid all that unpleasantness and simply accept each other where they are, discussing what they've been reading or watching or learning from videos on the internet. Mollie was always good at that. Meeting Sydnee where she was, no matter the circumstance. "She was like a parent to me, you know."

"Hey." Alex stops in the middle of the sidewalk. A biker

behind her swerves, frantically ringing their bell as they ride ahead. "I thought we had an agreement. We wouldn't talk about her?"

"I didn't mention Athena."

"Her mother? Really, Syd? That's basically the same thing."

"We saw her. What was I supposed to do?"

"Well, not beeline for her, that's for sure."

"I didn't think about what I was doing." That's the truth. She had seen Mollie and had walked toward her without thinking.

"We work," Alex says, her tone softer as she wraps her arm around Sydnee's shoulders, "in the present. We stop working if you start living in the past. You know?"

"They were a big part of my life, Alex…"

"I have big parts of my life that I don't talk about with you," Alex says. "Because it's easier this way."

"Secrets hidden underneath that leg tattoo of yours?"

"Oh, dozens, that's why it's so big." Alex, relieved that the conversation has lightened once more, starts her list. "Let's see. There was a guy, right, that I used to play doctor with in elementary school. Well, in high school, the examinations *really* heated up, and we…"

As she half listens to Alex unveil her smuttiest secrets, Sydnee wonders if Mollie will tell Athena about running into her. She can picture Athena's face. The intense flare of displeasure. Her eyebrows would lift, and her nostrils would flair and she'd roll her eyes before remembering she was supposed to pretend she didn't care about Sydnee anymore. She'd purse her lips and say, "Well, good for her."

A pang in her chest. How could she still know Athena so well? Such a frustrating, complex, unendingly interesting person. Every time Sydnee thought she understood the full fabric of her, she'd find another thread, leading someplace new.

It was always exciting and enamoring to fall in love over and over again with the same person.

But somewhere along the way they'd lost that sense of wonder. Sydnee knows that. Alex is right. It does nothing, dwelling on the past. It can trick you into sentimentality, into believing in a world that no longer exists.

"Come on," Sydnee says, finally grabbing Alex's hand and tugging her toward the beach. "Let's see you take that plunge."

# ATHENA

Athena had been awake for hours. She hardly slept. Her mind is full of Sydnee, the dread and the hope of seeing her once more.

That Sydnee has moved on—really, truly moved on—makes everything worse. She thinks through the situation. Sydnee is here, in Watercolor, with *her*, so near Athena could run into them in town this morning, with their identical coffee cups and grease-stained brown paper bags. The thought sends Athena's entire body buzzing.

It wasn't always like this. Before Athena fell in love, her life was simple. She woke up every morning at six. She made coffee. She went for a run. She called one of her parents on her way to class during her PhD program, walking them through her lesson plan if she was teaching, or talking through whatever was on that day's syllabus for the seminar class she was attending. After, she'd work through her materials, and, when that was through, attend one of the readings on campus, steeping herself in the budding literary scene controlled and orchestrated by the university. On Saturdays, after she'd finished grading and writing, she went out onto her back porch, cracked open her favorite beer, a Karbach kölsch, and grabbed the book she was reading, just for pleasure. It was a rarity in that time, being able to read something not set on a syllabus, made by her or someone else. She loved this indulgence: her old wooden rocking chair creaking back and forth as she turned the pages, the mourning doves cooing in the trees, the Texas sun shining strong—in the summer, too strong—on her skin, as she relished the chance to sink into a world that was not her own.

A tall boy and a slight breeze: that was heaven to Athena back then. Life was uncomplicated. She didn't know what it was like to fall asleep next to someone every night, to have that presence become a comfort, a weight that her body would become accustomed to. She didn't know the emptiness she could feel in its absence. She didn't even know to call that absence loneliness because, before Sydnee, that concept did not exist. There was only being with people and being alone.

They met during Athena's second year in her PhD program. Athena was expected to demonstrate sufficient skills in a foreign language by their fourth year, but her Spanish was still abysmal. Despite her father's best efforts to teach her any of the four languages he knew—English, Greek, Italian, French—she'd never quite grasped anything other than English. She told her father she didn't have the brain for it. She even found scientific studies to back up this lie. But, truthfully, she didn't practice. And she knew from her decades of athletics that natural talent only takes you so far. If you don't put in the work, day after day, a skill can never form, develop or progress.

When the administration noticed, she called her parents, frantic. Her father pumped her up with assurances that she'd figure out a way to get it done. Her mother, however, always practical, simply said, "Athena, you can't snap your fingers and speak a different language. You have to learn it. You have to study. And you have to ask for help."

So, Athena sought the services of the student success center, desperate for the best tutor they could give her. The best?
That's Sydnee. Always. In everything.

The ethics were blurred, since they were the same age and
Athena was not an undergraduate student. Sydnee needed the
job—her stipend from her scholarship could barely cover the
rapidly rising monthly rent for any apartments near campus—
and Athena needed the help. She'd never had a teacher like
Sydnee. Kind, patient, willing to correct her with a gentleness that had no trace of condescension. Perhaps she could
sense the delicacy of Athena's pride, or maybe she was an
inherently kind person. Either way, they worked diligently
together, twice a week during the spring semester, neither
making a move, not wanting to put the other at any sort of
risk. The sessions were only an hour long, but as the months
progressed, they sat closer to each other, their hands brushing, shoulders resting against one another, the slightest touch
bringing a jolt of electricity. It was like all of Athena's favorite
films: little moments of longing lingering, the tension building with steady progression, with no release in sight.

They got to know one another in increments. They asked
each other how their weekends were, what they were like
when they were kids. But they always kept the questions and
answers in Spanish, forcing Athena to answer simply, her
vocabulary still so limited, as Sydnee patiently slowed down
her speech to make sure Athena caught every word, never
ridiculing, always encouraging Athena's gradual progression
into understanding.

Finally, at the end of the semester, when Sydnee was finished working with the center, they were freed from the con-
straints that held them back for months.

"So," Sydnee said as she packed up her backpack in the

small, windowless study room where they spent all of their sessions. "I heard you're going to Deacon's party tonight."

"I didn't know you knew him," Athena said, genuinely shocked that neither of them had made the connection.

"Every queer person in Austin knows Deacon," Sydnee said. "We dated for a bit. Back in undergrad."

"You did?"

"But I'm gonna be there tonight."

"You will?"

"And, you know. The semester's over."

"Finally."

"And you're going…"

"I am."

"So, we'll see each other," she said, putting on her backpack and moving toward the door. "Outside of this little room."

"I guess we will," Athena said. And, never smooth for any second of her life, especially when she needed to be, added, *"No puedo esperar a mirarte."*

Sydnee stared at her for a moment, her head tilted to the side so that her dark hair shifted to one shoulder, her eyebrows coming together in confusion before allowing a small smirk to tug at her lips. "You can't wait to look at me?"

"Dammit!" Athena slapped her forehead. *"Verte,* not *mirarte.* I always get those mixed up."

"It's cute," Sydnee said, stopping herself from laughing at Athena, still careful to cater to her ego. "I'll see you tonight."

At Deacon's party, they had their first kiss in a coat closet. Pounding hearts and brushed elbows and thighs pressed against each other. So much desire it felt a sin, not for the act of love itself, but for the excess of it. Opulence at arm's reach. Touch as fire. This was their first taste of love. It awoke a hunger in them that they had never known and would never know again. Every kiss was like a communion wafer: never enough to satiate the growing, aching need within.

The next day, they went on their first date. They talked for hours at an outdoor bar in Austin. The patio was full of people, but the world contained only them. Their knees touched and their hands were held, and they laughed and lost their train of thought as they looked into each other's eyes. Athena's stomach dipped. She drank in everything about Sydnee: full cheeks, green eyes, dark eyebrows, even darker hair, thick and full of waves, half tied up into a wobbling bun on top of her head. Her smile was easy and infectious, dimples and one crooked tooth. Her hands were always moving. Nothing about her was stagnant. Athena marveled that earlier that week, she had wondered what it would be like to love someone, and then, on that day, in an instant, as if she'd had the answer all along, she knew.

That seems like a different life now. Almost a dream. She holds the memory in her hand, but it slips through her fingers like water. Unable to be held for longer than a moment, losing dimension with time.

Athena sits up in bed. She hears chaos outside. Everyone's starting the day. She needs to be happy. She *must* be happy. It is a mandate when you accept a role in the wedding party. Your life stops. The wedding takes over. Nothing else exists. What does exist, though, is love, the celebration of it, a collective joy for someone else's happiness. She'd been reluctant to partake in such a thing until she saw Daisy last night, looking radiant in her white jumpsuit, the twinkling lights reflected in her eyes, which were wide with excitement and wonder. There is something spectacular about seeing the people you love fall in love, too, with the right person. Athena's grateful to bear witness. Eight years ago, when Daisy was off their radar, doing the Lord's work, Athena would have laughed at the thought of attending Daisy's wedding, let alone being in the bridal party. If it hadn't been for Sydnee's intervention, Athena might not have ever gotten over Daisy's absence.

She had not wanted to forgive Daisy. She wanted her to feel that same sense of loss and abandonment that Athena had felt in those years Daisy left them for her "higher calling." But Sydnee reminded her of why she loved Daisy, and urged her to give her a chance. Another gift of marriage: Athena's stubbornness was called into question with a loving persistence that, eventually, made her see the world outside the tunnel vision of defensiveness that had dominated her point of view for so many years (part inherent in her nature, part survival instinct from growing up gay in Texas). It made her a better person. Is she worse now that Sydnee is gone? She's been left to her own devices, her own perspective left uncorrected. Could any good come of that?

There's a knock at the door that doesn't wait for a response. Deacon enters with a plate full of croissants in one hand, and two mugs in the other. He closes the door quickly behind him and sits onthe end of the bed. His hair sticks straight up in the back, and he closes his eyes as he drinks his coffee.

"Looks like you've been in battle," Athena says. She notices his mug shakes slightly in his hands.

"It's madness out there." Deacon's eyes are still closed. "Blow-dryers and bad music and way too much estrogen."

"You sound like your dad."

"Maybe he was onto something." Deacon opens his eyes and glances back at the door, making sure it stays closed. "Just need a minute. Before escape is futile."

"No one's come for me yet."

"That's my job, actually. But let's take our time before we head out. It's just…"

"Too much," Athena says, agreeing.

They both sit in silence, listening to the muffled shouts coming from the living room.

"I was thinking about Sydnee," Athena says, unprompted. "And seeing her tonight."

Deacon nods, but says nothing for a while. He straightens out a crinkle in the bedsheets.

"You wanna talk about it?" Deacon rips off the end of a croissant.

"Do you?" Athena asks.

"Not much to say," he says. "Sucks, though."

"I told you she would."

"I just thought—"

"What do you think of Katie?" Athena asks.

Deacon does a double take, his eyes flashing toward Athena, wide with worry. Or is it exasperation?

"Katie is fine. Katie is an influencer. And Katie has a crush on you."

"I know."

"Don't go there, Thene."

"I'm not going anywhere."

"This is Daisy's day." Deacon uses his teacher's voice, slightly deeper and sharpened with the edge of authority. "Don't stir up shit."

"No stirring," Athena says, raising her hands. "Just curious. About your thoughts."

"Well, now you have them."

"Great."

They sit in silence again. Athena tries to move past it. She knows Deacon can't stand her harping on a point. But she can't bite back the impulse. To push. To take things too far.

Athena always did everything in excess. She used too much toothpaste, too much shampoo; she was too intense about the Astros during baseball season, too fixated on Dickinson at all times and too single-minded when she got any sort of scheme lodged in her head. Letting go was a second language she could never quite master.

"It's just that," Athena starts out slowly, easing her way back into the conversation, the way she might into a too cold creek. "If Sydnee's moving on, I think I should, too. Just to show her."

"Show her what?" Deacon asks. It's clipped and cold. He wants this conversation to end, not interested in indulging the impulse.

"That I'm good. That we're good. That I'm with some-one else."

"But you're not."

"She doesn't know that."

"Of course she does," Deacon snaps. "She still knows you. You don't stop knowing a person after eight months."

"How often do you see her again?" Athena asks.

"Who?"

"Sydnee," Athena says. Then, casually adding, "And Alex, I guess."

"Once a month." Deacon doesn't blink. "Give or take. I see you more, if that's what you're worried about."

"So you know Alex?"

"A bit."

"How much of a bit?"

"Does it matter?"

"Not really, I guess."

Athena knows she's pushing Deacon too far. She pulls back, still capable of some restraint. He's been good to her through all of this. She has to remind herself of that, even though a mini storm of fury rises up in her whenever he mentions Sydnee's name. She wants Deacon to choose her, to cut ties with Sydnee and leave her behind, forever. Athena believes there should be *some* consequences for Sydnee's actions. Some pain equal to that which she caused Athena. It seems like she got away unscathed. She kept her friends. She ditched Athena. She got a new girlfriend. They both shared the same loss: the life they had built together, the language they created and the fluency that came with it. But Athena is the one bearing the brunt of that burden. It doesn't seem to slow Sydnee down at all. Is that just luck, or the sum of her worth? Athena is not sure. The question scares her.

There is no one feeling. Constantly, it's every feeling coursing through her at once: anger, pain, and the illusive, ever pervasive jealousy that Athena refuses to name, even when it tears through her and eats her insides, dissolving them like acid, merciless and insatiable. That Sydnee could have it all, and none of it would be shared with her. She never thought of herself as a jealous person, and she clings to that lie like a punctured life raft in open water; even as it pools at her feet, sending her sinking, she wills her mind to think only of all the air she has left to breathe.

The loyalty of her friends should be the least everyone could do for her. But that's not Deacon's way. It's not Daisy's, either. They won't cut anyone off. They hold on to people for as long as they can. Athena should be grateful for that, she knows.

"Sorry," Athena says, not quite looking at Deacon. "For being annoying."

"I'm used to it," Deacon says. But he's smirking, shooting a sideways glance her way. He runs his hand up and down his forearm, tracing the bluebonnet tattoo, like he always does when he's nervous. "I'm sorry, too."

"Don't, there's nothing—"

"No, I just mean—" Deacon pauses. He runs his hands through his hair. It spikes up and stays put like that. "I haven't been completely honest with you."

Athena freezes, the echo of these familiar words ringing in her mind. *There's something I haven't told you...* A Saturday outside in March, in Montrose, at Menil Park. A picnic blanket, a cheese board, a plastic cup full of Sancerre. Athena felt like her life was finally coming back together, that her grief for her father was going from chronically unbearable into incremental waves of devastation. Sydnee wore a bright yellow T-shirt with a small smiley face in the middle, tucked into her ripped, whitewashed jeans. Her hair was up in a ponytail, and she wore no makeup. She was absolutely beautiful.

The memory stings. Athena shuts her eyes. *To make a prairie it takes a clover and one bee, One clover, and a bee.*

"Which poem?" Deacon asks, his voice tender as he observes Athena's silence.

"A bee one." Athena opens her eyes. "What do you need to tell me? I can take it."

"It's just," Deacon sighs. The exhale seems to deflate him. He shakes his head. "I actually think the Katie thing is a good idea. Go for it. You deserve to have some fun."

"Yeah?" Athena asks, perking up at the thought. *The best revenge is a life well lived.* A nice enough saying, but wholly unsatisfying. The best revenge? Getting even.

"Katie was flirting with one of the guys, though. At the rehearsal dinner last night. Nick."

"She mentioned him earlier." Athena waves away the concern. "Basically told me I didn't have to worry about that if I didn't want to."

"So the flirting has already begun."

"On her end," Athena says. "How do you flirt again? I used to be so good at it."

"You were never good at it." Deacon takes an enormous bite of a croissant, sending buttery, flaky crumbs flying around him.

"If that's how you eat on dates, then I'm better than you," Athena says.

"Luckily for everyone, Mel loves the way I eat."

"Who's Mel?"

"Bartender. Live, laugh, lave tattoo," Deacon says, an edge to his voice. Athena, for once, catches it.

"Y'all are serious? I thought it was new."

"Serious, new." Deacon tries to suppress a smile. He *really* likes her, Athena realizes. "They can both be true. I think you'd like her."

"How'd y'all meet?"

"Daniel introduced us, actually," Deacon said, no longer able to stop the smile from stretching across his face, reaching his eyes. "All it took was one date and bam. That was it for both of us."

"So I guess you really *could* teach me how to flirt," Athena says. "Sydnee always said you had a sneaky charm, guess it's true."

Deacon goes completely still and silent. The flush from before is gone. He's pale and wide-eyed, unblinking.

"In undergrad," Athena adds, thinking he's forgotten. "You and Sydnee hooked up, remember?"

Deacon allows himself to laugh. It's shaky, but he seems to come back to himself.

"I've been telling you for years to study my technique." Deacon nudges her shoulder. "But let me know when you start. The flirting, I mean. Need front row seats to this disaster show."

"Fuck you," Athena says with all the affection in the world. She's happy for him. It has been a long time since Deacon settled down with someone. He had to put up with a lot of crap, especially on the dating apps. People asked invasive questions before they even knew his last name or would just match with him to harass him. He eventually found the right platforms to use so he could avoid all that. He had a few flings, but nothing serious.

Athena's surprised he didn't tell her more about Mel earlier, but, then again, who could tell her any good news? She's been a vacuum of joy for longer than she could admit to herself. Is that who she's become? Is that who she's destined to be?

"I want to meet her," Athena says in a rush of earnestness she hasn't felt in years. No cynicism, no irony. It feels odd, but not unwelcome. Like flexing a muscle that had gone too long without use.

Deacon grins and grabs Athena's forearm, giving it a squeeze. "We'll do it," Deacon says. "Back in Houston. After the wedding."

"There's a life outside of this wedding?"

"Not today." Deacon gets up and dusts the crumbs off his legs. He walks across the room and throws Athena her silk robe with *bridesmaid* embroidered on the breast pocket before opening up the door. "Ready?"

"No." Athena gets up and pulls the robe over her pajamas.

"Good." Deacon gestures for Athena to go out first. "Once more into the fray."

Athena's jaw tightens at the thought of all she'll have to do: sip champagne and get her face sprayed by too much makeup and listen to the hairdresser complain about how long and tangled her hair is before they style it. The prospect feels unpleasant.

"Happiness," her father used to say, "is a gift you give other people."

They were planning for *her* wedding when he'd said it.

Athena wanted to save money on flowers. Who needs flowers, anyway?

"The bees," her father said, simply. "And beauty…how could you cut costs on beauty?"

He was a romantic in that way. All of Athena's pragmatism came from her mother. But her father knew how to suck the marrow out of life. He loved that line from *Walden*. When Athena noted that Thoreau wrote it living a few miles from his parents, where his mother could come over and do his laundry every week, her father frowned.

"Who cares about him? The words ring true despite his own falseness. Don't you see, Athena? You don't have to live up to your name so often. All war and wisdom, no softness."

"It's just Thoreau, Dad, it's not that deep."

"Who cares about him?" he said again. "Life is always deep."

"We don't need the flowers."

"Flowers are everything we need," he declared.

He was right. The flowers were overflowing and excessive and more beautiful than Athena could have ever known. The guests loved them. Athena did, too.

Her chest aches as it always does when she remembers her father, then again when she remembers that he's been gone for three years.

She walks toward the door Deacon holds open, trying to loosen her jaw, flexing her cheeks, doing her best to smile, to find the gift of happiness somewhere buried beneath her vast catalog of Emily Dickinson. She'll have to dust it off, wipe off the cobwebs, a gift long forgotten, but a gift nonetheless.

# DAISY

Before dawn, Daisy wakes up, her heart hammering in her chest, her mind full of an unearthly calm. The juxtaposition startles her at first. Is she dying? Her heart giving out while her mind resigns to its fate? She does a quick body scan. Pulse strong, fast, but strong. Forehead dry. Toes intact. Vision clear. She is alive. And she is getting married today.

Her stomach clenches with excitement. She feels like a kid on the last day of school—a whole glorious, sprawling summer waiting for her on the other side of a celebration, usually in the form of a field and fair day. A ritual rite, a necessary joy, before the months of endless possibility begin.

She reaches for her phone on the bedside table before remembering she gave it over to Katie. The impulse, no, the *need* to check her notifications is embarrassing. The pull of her technology is stronger than anything she's ever known. She forces herself to sit in silence, practicing the meditation that Katie taught her. *Today will be magnificent, today will be perfect, today will be...* She rolls out her yoga mat and does a sunrise flow, awakening her body, inviting breath into her lungs as she attempts to find peace and balance before the day begins.

After sunrise, Daisy hears the muffled argument of Clare and Reghan downstairs. They will not stop, she knows. They fluctuate from best friends to enemies with the drop of a coin.

It's their cycle, an unyielding grip of dependency and toxicity that they've trapped themselves in. Katie tried confronting them about it once, but they blew her off, and started making fun of her practice and patience. There is no healing to be had where there is no willingness to grow. Their fighting will continue. Their friendship will endure.

Having Athena here is a saving grace, a stable presence that bridges the past and present. It still blows Daisy's mind that they've known each other for nearly twenty years. They met when they sat next to each other in their Bible class during their first year of high school. Their freshman year, they studied the Old Testament, but Athena and Daisy spent more time passing notes to each other than they did listening to the bone-tired lectures their strict, waspish teacher gave about God's judgment and the punishment that came from it. Instead, they made training schedules for themselves for the fall off-season—Athena, for soccer, Daisy, for lacrosse—and, every day, they'd meet at the track before dawn and run three miles together. The runs were quiet at first, puffing exhales and wheezes, but, once their bodies gained endurance, they'd spend their runs talking. Daisy did most of it, she remembers. Athena was quiet and brooding, but quick-witted and sarcastic and funnier than any person Daisy had ever known outside of her own family. They cracked each other up, and Daisy told Athena about every boy she had a crush on, and they slept over at each other's houses, and their parents became good friends, too, bonding over red wine and good food, and they spent summer vacations together, towing along Leo and Deacon in all their schemes, the younger siblings having little say in their adventures. Together, the world was theirs to take.

Then, they graduated, and it changed. Daisy attended the prestigious Baptist university three hours from Houston, having received a healthy merit-based scholarship that made her overlook the overreligiosity of the school. She'd grown used to it at her high school anyway, had even become fluent in the language of the church in her youth group. But when she arrived at the university, she realized it wasn't a backdrop or a quirk of the school. It was its beating heart, its lifeblood. People took church so seriously that it was hard to make friends without that as a foundation. Daisy had never been one to forge her own path, so, rather than resist and find herself an outcast, she dove into it with the masses, allowing her focus to shift, her language to change, her entire perspective to filter through a lens of belief accented with selective perception. She only saw what she wanted to see, she only heard that which would further her belief in the faith that she'd made her entire personality.

Soon, she was knee-deep in a small, nondenominational, evangelical church that spoke in tongues and had the general claustrophobic air of most successful cults, while Athena went to school in Austin and studied literature and got tattoos and dated women and did everything the people Daisy had surrounded herself with disapproved of with a simmering, seething judgment.

After they graduated, Athena stayed in Austin to start her PhD program, sinking happily into poetry and prose, letting the rest of the world melt away, sharing a small, two-bedroom apartment with Deacon, while Daisy stayed in her college town, working with the church as they planted a new one, before, three years later, she moved back to Houston, joined the Southeast branch of her college church, got with her former youth pastor, eloped and then, two years into the marriage, had her reckoning.

It was a blur, how it all came together then fell apart. It started with purity culture, but it ended with Deacon.

Abstinence was a virtue Daisy held dearer than any other.

It wasn't just the smugness of feeling superior to her friends who could not resist the tug of lust and temptation, though that was a component. Since she was a girl, aided by the lessons in her Sunday school classes and abstinence sex education courses at her private Christian schools, Daisy believed that her body was built for one man, for one purpose: to create a family.

This belief was sacred and unshakable. She didn't kiss any of her high school boyfriends. She hardly let them hold her hand. During youth group, the Youth Pastor pulled her aside one Wednesday night during her junior year and told her that she was one of the most remarkable young women he'd ever had the pleasure of teaching. His eyes sparkled when he said it, his dimpled smile genuine and warm. He reminded Daisy of a young Ethan Hawke in *Before Sunrise*, charming and handsome in a way that felt attainable and unthreatening. It made Daisy feel safe. He told her to watch out for the guys her age. They were always looking for something else. They couldn't quite see what made her special, not like he could. She always remembered that and thought, if I can just find a man like him, to lead me, to love me, I'll never want for anything else in the world.

In college, she was set up with a boy from church who dated her with the intention of marriage. Daisy thought she'd finally found the man she'd been built for, but, one afternoon, she went to order a pizza on his computer and found seventeen still-open tabs of pornographic websites, each one darker, more twisted than the last. Daisy saw images her mind could not erase, but she did manage to beat down the curiosity they arose in her. She broke up with the boy that afternoon, then resolved to find herself an older man, someone mature, who knew how to control his urges and lead her in spirit and in truth—someone like the Youth Pastor.

When she moved to Houston, she joined the women's Bible study at her church and told them what she was looking for in a man. They all came together, placing their hands on Daisy, and prayed for the Lord to send someone her way. The Bible study leader kept one eye open during the prayer, texting the Youth Pastor, saying she'd found the perfect young lady with whom to set him up. When the Youth Pastor read her name, he said he could hardly believe his luck.

He called the next day—called, not texted, Daisy noted with relish. A sure sign of his maturity. They went to a coffee shop that afternoon. The Youth Pastor talked about his goals for their church, the mission trips he wanted to organize, the souls he wanted to save, how he wanted to carve out the infection of sin in our society and replace it with the blood of Jesus. He was intense. He did not ask Daisy any questions. She listened with an awestruck reverence. It was just like in youth group. He was eloquent and thoughtful and sure of himself. His confidence and inability to talk about anything but himself seemed to Daisy a sign of his focus, of his vision. She smiled and laughed and nodded and listened. A perfect audience. He'd always loved that about her. Four months later, they were engaged. A week after that, they were at city hall, eloping. He hadn't wanted to waste any time or money planning a big party. She hadn't wanted to disappoint him, though she'd always dreamed of an enormous wedding. She submitted to his will, as she was instructed by her church. She followed his lead.

The marriage went downhill just about as soon as Daisy and the Youth Pastor got home from their elopement, both eager to consummate their marriage, since they were, finally, after all these years, free to perform the act in the eyes of God.

Daisy was disappointed, but not disheartened, after her first time. It was bound to get better, she reasoned. And maybe if they could have communicated about desires and expectations, they could have worked something out. But the sex was quick and efficient, in and out. Daisy always wound up feeling uncomfortable and cold.

It wasn't that the Youth Pastor was opposed to female pleasure on any fundamental, theological level. He just didn't think it existed. In his mind, the woman was created to bear life. The man was created to sow the seed. His participation was rewarded with orgasm. Hers with childbirth. During the act itself, he believed that, if there was pleasure for Daisy, it always matched his, every time. He was satisfied, he reasoned, so she must be, too. If he knew the word *clitoris*, he certainly did not understand its real-world application.

She probably could have lived with the unfulfilling sex. At that time, she still maintained the belief that sexual desire and enjoyment was a man's priority, never a woman's, though she was starting to change her tune, having spent enough nights sleeping next to a snoring husband with an aching, cavernous need left unfulfilled.

But it was everything else that became insufferable. The incessant talk about himself. The demand that she cook and clean and have dinner warm and ready for him after his late-night lock-ins with the youth group. The deeply unfunny jokes he told and the booming, hollow laugh that burst from him at the end of every punch line, her lack of laughter irrelevant to him. She endured life like this for two more years. Time crawled on.

The final straw was more like a hammer brought down from the heavens. The Youth Pastor told Daisy she couldn't see Deacon anymore. Something about him living outside God's will, something about disapproval. He said it so casually, over dinner, as they ate the roasted chicken she'd spent all afternoon preparing.

"It'll be better for our family," he said. "If we can trim the fat, make sure our children don't have distractions growing up. Make sure their eyes are fixed on what's right. What really matters. So they can love right."

He kept on talking, picking off the skin on the chicken leg, gnawing on it as he talked, leaving nothing to the imagination with his wide-open mouth. He didn't notice that Daisy had gone silent—she was always silent. It was how he liked her best.

Daisy pushed herself away from the table. Picked up her keys. Drove to her parents' house. Found Deacon lying on the couch, watching his favorite comedy show. She plopped down next to him and took his hand, squeezing it.

"What," Deacon said, lifting his head slightly to look at his sister. "You finally splitting on that youth pastor?"

"As a matter of fact," Daisy said, not taking her eyes off the television. "I am."

The next day, she and her dad went to grab all of her belongings. The Youth Pastor stood by, somber, never addressing Daisy or her father. Before she left, Daisy, dipping into the growing rage and fury she'd been harboring for the two years of their marriage, slapped the Youth Pastor so hard across the face he must have seen her fingerprints for hours afterward.

Heartbreak for Daisy had always been reserved for inconsiderate boys and unrequited love. She'd never known it could come from her friends, from her family. Deacon was not happy with her when she moved in with him after she left the Youth Pastor. At first, she thought Deacon missed his space. Then, she realized it was because she'd missed too much. Leaving the Youth Pastor was a step, but it didn't erase all that she had missed: his top surgery; his second puberty; dealing with their parents' friends who just "didn't get it" and made no effort to change that; living in a state whose leaders based their entire platforms on villainizing him and his friends because it scored them points with their ruthless, endlessly unkind base of supporters.

"Athena was my sister. Athena was there," Deacon said once Daisy brought up his coldness. "You were church planting. Teaching people to hate me. To hate Athena and Sydnee and all of our friends. That doesn't just stop being true because you realized it was bullshit."

"I'm sorry." It was not enough, but there was nothing else to say. Even the truth can't carry enough weight to mean something when it's said too late.

"So," Deacon had said after, folding a plain white T-shirt and tossing it on top of a stack with a dozen other identical ones. "Are you here, for real, or are you going to leave and change your entire personality to match the next guy you date?"

With those words began her self-imposed exile from dating. Before she would date again, she would establish a firm ground onto which she could plant her feet, alone, without support or assistance from anyone else. While she applied for executive assistant jobs in downtown Houston, she started playing around with The Faithful Foodie, connecting with local restaurateurs and chefs, taking photos of their food, writing blurbs for their new spots, and, on Sundays, giving herself the space she needed to process her years in the evangelical circles that had taken her away from so much.

During that first year, she'd made an exception to her exile for Leo. He was Athena's little brother. He was free during the day. He had a good eye for photography. She made a thousand excuses for why she kept wanting to spend time with him before she let herself admit that the tingling in her toes and the hammering in her heart was something much more than a platonic connection.

Daisy walks over to her laptop and presses Play on her wedding playlist. There's no need to dredge up the past. The regret from before could stay there forever. Leo made his choice. She could not change his mind. She is here, she is happy, she is in love.

The love she had with Leo was different from the love she feels with Daniel. With Leo, it felt like love. Or, at least the kind of love she'd read about in romance novels and seen on her favorite TV shows. It was all-consuming. It hurt. It was hard. She'd never know when Leo would retreat, when he would leave her at the drop of a hat to drive to Austin for an audition, to pick up another shift at work. He was in, but he was out, too. His mind was always half-focused on what could be. He had to audition for everything his agent sent him, even if it meant missing her birthday, or bailing on their plans, or moving to Los Angeles without consulting her first. When he had the time, though, he focused on her so intensely that it made her feel seen. An illusion of infatuation. Leo only saw the world through his dreams: his dream job, his dream girl. She wasn't sure if she was ever real to him or just another dream come true.

With Daniel, it feels like home, a gentle rush of water that washes through her, rising in her, filling her up. His love is like the brush of his curls on her forehead when they wake up together on Sunday mornings, taking their time before getting the day started, their legs entangled and hands held, bodies close. His eyes are kind and locked on the present. His job is not his life. He works hard, waking up before dawn to head downtown to his job in finance that Daisy still does not quite understand. When he gets home, he leaves it all behind as he loosens his tie and asks about Daisy's day, helping her finish cooking dinner, washing the dishes when they are through.

Consistency had always seemed to Daisy a symptom of

predictability that would inevitably lead to boredom. That's
what had made Leo so attractive to her. His sporadic nature,
his coming and going, her never knowing when he'd show
up, the colossal disappointment when he didn't, the unrestricted euphoria when he did. It left her empty, the energy
it took to hope for him, but she'd thought that was the price
you paid for love.

The consistency Daniel showed her was a sign of his true-
ness, and it never left her bored. It energized her, knowing,
at the end of every day, he'd come home to her. His family
taught him that presentness, the value of time spent together.
They taught that to her, too, bringing her into the fold for the
Friday night Shabbat dinners and the High Holidays, all of
which held so much history and so much connectedness that
she felt enveloped by them, despite not fully understanding
what they meant. It was important to them, so she made it
important to her, too, though she fumbled with pronunciation and the history and the reasons for each gathering. They
gave her the grace she'd been seeking in her own churches
for so many years. It was this feeling more than anything else
that made her agreeable to a religious ceremony.

They'd been engaged for several months before he proposed
it. Daniel was careful. He knew religion could become such
a sore spot with Daisy.

"We don't have to do everything. But, the chuppah, our
rabbi, the hora. It would mean a lot to me."

The rabbi from his parents' congregation had been friends
with the family for years. She'd seen Daniel transform from
stewing, angry preteen glued to his Xbox to passionate, over-
enthusiastic MBA student, to the man he is today. Daisy had
met her a few times at Daniel's parents' house, but she got to
know her better during their premarital counseling. Rabbi
Kaplan was unlike any religious leader she'd ever known: she

encouraged questions, she listened to Daisy's concerns about conversion, she assured her that she'd perform the wedding no matter what Daisy decided.

Daisy would not convert, but she would compromise. They customized the wording in their ketubah, which Daniel commissioned a local artist to design, encircling the contract in pressed flowers and gold-plated olive branches. After they signed it yesterday, with Daniel's best friends serving as witnesses, they put it in a golden frame that will be displayed at their reception. They abstained from any tradition that felt to Daisy as if she were property being handed over to Daniel, for him to take in his possession. She used her voice and she stood her ground and she embraced what she did not understand with an open mind. She listened. She learned. She fell more in love with Daniel as they planned together a ceremony that would work for them both. With their rabbi at the helm and Daniel by her side, Daisy felt that it could all be okay. This was a different marriage. The Youth Pastor was a memory. The religion that held her hostage is distant and long gone. She is ready for it all.

There is still the matter of the mysterious text messages. She's put it out of her mind for as long as possible. But she can't quite remember what they said, or if it was real. She screams downstairs for Deacon and tasks him with getting her phone back from Katie. He agrees without argument. A good foot soldier in the trenches of this day. She closes her eyes and sings along with the music, which she makes loud enough to drown out her own voice.

Back in her church days, prayer was not only a performance, it was a competition. And Daisy could pray with the best of them. She was eloquent and quick, never drawing it out too long, always holding a captive audience. It wasn't for God, she knew, it was for the church. If she had been a man, they'd have asked her to pray every day, but she was a woman, and women could not lead men in anything, so she reserved her prayers for her all-female Bible studies and relished the praise she'd receive after she'd said *amen*. So eloquent, so true, such a great conduit for the Lord to use. In reality, even then, she knew it was about the attention. She wanted to be heard, to be seen. She wanted to win.

Now prayer felt more like a hum coming from her core, a silent meditation of something she could never describe. There was a hope and a yearning tied up in that silence that felt more authentic than any word she'd ever spoken in those huddled popcorn prayers in her Bible studies. It wasn't quite real, yet it was the most real thing she'd ever known. A contradiction, a curiosity, a question. But she trusted it more than she trusted any of those men who told her how she must believe in order to get into heaven—some place they'd constructed in their own imagination, another iteration of *God's will*.

Before the noise, and the rush, and the attention, Daisy lets herself sink into oblivion, calling out into the quiet, receiving back that frequency of old: the reassurance of something wonderful, the strength needed to face the day. After this, she will accept the anxiety, she will allow herself the luxury of stress and panic and worry. But for now, just in this one moment, before it all comes to pass, she wants peace. She tries cultivating this vision of bliss, *manifesting joy* as Katie likes to say. It will be the best day of her life. She will have the best time of her life. She will never forget what happens today.

A knock at the door interrupts her prayer. Her eyes fly open. She checks the clock on her bedside: 8:15. She cannot isolate herself any longer. She inhales, trying to maintain some of the peace she found before.

"Who is it?"

The voice answers, "Leo."

Daisy hesitates. She checks herself in the mirror. No makeup. No anything. Her hair's a mess. Vanity is a constant reflex when it comes to an ex.

"I look terrible."

"So?"

"I—well, okay," Daisy says. "Come in."

# LEO

At Daisy's doorway, Leo lingers for a moment, listening. She's playing a song he doesn't recognize. She sings along, quietly, unselfconscious, as one does when they think they are alone. As she sings, Leo is transported to another time, in another place, when they drove around Houston in his Jeep during the first day of spring. The sky was deep blue, the kind that made you want to dive headfirst into it, and the air was crisp and cool, warm in the sun, that perfect blanket of a temperature that ushered you out of your home and into the world. They blasted music and Daisy sang at the top of her lungs, absolutely atrocious, undeniably perfect, wild and free and alive in every way that mattered most.

The memory gives him courage. He grips the ankle straps of the shoes Diane shoved into his arms and told him to deliver while she shouted into the phone at the caterer. She was so frazzled she hardly seemed to realize who she was passing the shoes off to. Mollie must have told her to keep Leo away from Daisy today. But here he is, on her wedding day, with a chance to see her alone. He takes a breath and knocks.

"What are you doing here?" Daisy asks when he comes in.

"Shoe delivery."

Daisy seems surprised, but not unpleased, to see him.

"Did you meet Elise?" she asks.

"Who?"

"She had my—Never mind. Thanks, Leo." She grabs the shoes from him and pauses the music.

"Oh, don't stop singing on my account."

"I wasn't singing."

She's strangely on edge—jumpy and paranoid, as if cold feet had been intravenously transferred and now courses through her body, setting her limbs rigid and her teeth on edge.

"Second thoughts?" he asks, trying not to sound too hopeful.

"What?" Daisy closes her laptop and puts the shoes underneath her covered and hanging dress.

"You seem a little tense."

"It's my wedding day, what do you expect?"

"Bliss, contentment," Leo lists them out on his fingers. "Unadulterated excitement."

"Ra-ra," she says, miming a cheerleader. "Good enough for you?"

"Need a little more gumption."

"What do you want, Leo?" Daisy asks. She sits on the end of her bed, giving him her full attention.

"I, uh," Leo says, not sure what to say. He always worked off-the-cuff, flying by the seat of his pants, letting improv rule his life. Now, though, it's biting him in the ass. How does he begin to tell her everything he needs to say? "I had a chemistry read. On Thursday. For the medical show you like."

"Really?" Daisy perks up. "Who'd you read for?"

"Can't tell you that." Leo runs his hands through his hair, trying to seem mysterious. "Took the audition because I knew you loved the show."

"Is there any audition you won't take?" Daisy asks. She smiles as she says it, that subtle, small one, the real one that lights up her eyes, not the one she poses with in pictures on her Instagram for all the world to see.

"No, I'm desperate." Leo watches her as she looks at him, still hoping to find some of the same intensity held within her gaze as when she looks at Daniel. It's not there. Had it ever been there?

"Well, you'll get it, I'm sure."

"Probably not," Leo says.

"You have to have *some* hope."

"Some things are hopeless." Leo kicks the heel of his shoe. "Acting, for one."

"It is until it isn't, right?" Daisy says. "Just like dating."

"Gotta shoot your shot while you can."

"I hated all the guys I met on the apps. And then, one day, Daniel."

"I mean, this charm can't last forever."

"And suddenly, all the hope in the world. For men. For love."

"Don't want to be an old man full of regret. I have to try."

"And here we are, on my wedding day."

"And here we are," Leo says, repeating her. "On your wedding day."

Leo studies Daisy. Really seeing her for the first time since he left three years ago. She's the same as ever. Blond bun and bright eyes. She's always most beautiful like this, when she's not worried about being seen, before the makeup and the filters, and the poses. Looking at her gives him the same feeling he'd had back when they were teenagers, and he thought she must be the most beautiful girl in the world, a boyhood crush that carried over, the most consistent force in Leo's life.

"Gotta swing by the groomsmen's house. Deacon left his suit." Leo heads toward the door. "Congratulations."

"I think you're supposed to say 'best wishes' to the bride."

Daisy air quotes the phrase before rolling her eyes. "Congratulations are for the groom. Like, good luck, lady! And great catch, dude! So sexist."

"The patriarchy prevails once more."

"I think that's the opposite of best wishes."

"Best wishes, Daisy." He tips an invisible cap, doing his best to maintain his smile, though his cheeks shake with the effort. "May your future be full of whatever you want it to be."

Leo goes to the door. His hand is on the doorknob.

"Leo, wait."

He pivots back toward her. When he sees her, time stops. It's different from how she looked at Daniel. Tension in her jaw, eyes narrowed, nostrils flared. None of that natural ease and comfortableness she'd had with him. But it's intense. It's all-encompassing. It's real.

How had he gone years without seeing her? The space between them no longer makes sense. They walk toward each other. Daisy throws herself into his arms, wrapping hers around his waist.

"I forgot how you felt." Her voice muffles in his chest. He holds her close. No words, no need. Just this. He buries his face in her hair. Sweet like peonies, stiff with leftover hair spray. It tickles his cheeks. He doesn't mind.

The door swings open. Deacon stands in the doorway. Daisy jumps out of Leo's arms. Everyone freezes.

"I'm getting married today." Daisy's voice is distant, as if she, too, is coming out of that vacuous space, where time and reality have been put on pause. They are back now. Her words pierce him, absorbing into his skin through osmosis. The truth spreads through him, seizing his heart, quickening his breath.

Deacon watches him. Leo doesn't bother to take in his expression. He knows he will only find fury and judgment.

Deacon never liked the idea of him with Daisy. He will find no sympathy here. Leo walks out of the door without looking back.

Once Leo leaves, he hurries down the stairs, grabbing his keys, heading to the car. He doesn't want to talk to anyone. He wants to be useful. To have some purpose today.

He throws himself into the driver's seat and starts the car, closing his eyes, willing any thought of a tear back into the back of his eyes where they belong. He will not cry over Daisy. He'd rather be numb.

But he feels it everywhere. In his toes. His chest. Right behind his ear. A shock of disappointment. An ache. He'd never had his heart broken. He pants, like he just ran very far, very fast. It takes him several moments to gain his breath again.

*I have a Bird in spring, which for myself doth sing.* He repeats this over again, matching his breath with the rhythm of the line. A trick from Athena. Take a line from Dickinson, just one will do, and repeat it over and over again until you calm down. Strange medicine, but effective.

He slaps his cheek—another trick from Athena—and puts the car in Drive. Deacon needs his suit. Leo will get it for him. He will be helpful. He will not cause a scene.

His father would know what to say. Even if he didn't have the answer. He'd say something. He always did.

Jason loved to talk. Leo remembers how it would drive Mollie up the wall. Especially in the summer, after long days spent reeling in Leo and Athena, staving off their boredom, cleaning up after them while they stormed from room to room, leaving trails of toys along the way. He and Athena were wild and full of an energy that could never be burned completely.

When he came home from work, where he already talked with people all day, Jason began talking as soon as he walked through the door. Leo and Athena ran up to greet him, hugging his legs while he gave Mollie a quick kiss. He wanted to know every detail of their mundane day, not letting them leave anything out, starting with Leo, then Athena, then Mollie. Jason was a socialist when it came to lived experience: he wanted everyone to have equal share of every moment.

It made him a great father. Leo remembers sitting on his lap, clawing at his clothes, his ears, his dense, dark beard, tugging hard on it as he talked him through the highlights of his day, which could include anything from a tetherball victory at recess, a bombed multiplication quiz, a fight with a friend, the making of a new friend, and a turquoise rock found on the playground that had now become the most treasured object in his possession.

He took the kids seriously and listened to them, his eyebrows rising in surprise or coming together in sympathetic outrage. He never met an emotion that couldn't live on his face. And what a face he had. Long, curved aquiline nose, small eyes, dark brown, always shining with life, that beard, which hid his remarkable chin and jawline, which Leo luckily inherited. His hair, which Leo did not inherit, receded over time up top, remaining thick and coarse on the sides of his head. His thin lips, chapped, were always ready for a smile. His whole face was easy, never tense, even in stress. Looking at him always calmed Leo down. He missed that instant antidote of a dearly loved, familiar face.

He wasn't perfect, not by any stretch of the imagination. Birthdays were rarely remembered, appointments were forgotten, his promises were bold and vague and rarely came to fruition. But he always showed up when it mattered. And his greatest promise was a well-loved family, which he took great care to curate with every breath. When Sydnee came into the picture and the family expanded, so did he, treating her like his second daughter, always having her favorite drink ready when she came over, putting on the Spurs when they played, even learning enough Spanish to hold conversations in the language—though that was more a gift for himself than for Sydnee, there was nothing he loved more than gaining greater global fluency. Leo knows it would have broken Jason's heart to see the two of them split up. To see Athena so hardened, to have Sydnee leave her in the lurch.

If only he could guess what he would say about Daisy now. Leo had loved her for so long it became a running joke in the family, especially after one Christmas, four years ago, at Daisy's parents' party, when he grabbed the karaoke mic and dedicated a harrowing rendition of "Believe" by Cher to Daisy, pointing directly at her, making an uncomfortable amount of eye contact until he tipped over his glass of eggnog and stumbled around after tripping on the microphone cord.

He'd dated other people, but, in the back of his mind, he'd always held out hope for her. He even put off Los Angeles after he graduated college, secretly thinking, if he stayed around just a little longer, if she got to know him just a little better, she'd finally realize he was who she'd been looking for all along.

Jason, ever indulgent of Leo, couldn't tolerate him putting off his dreams for Daisy. It was one thing, he said, to put off asking a girl to prom in the hopes that Daisy might come into town that weekend. It was another thing entirely to prioritize a wish over the centimeter of a shot you had at your dream.

"If you love her, then love her," his father said. "She might not feel the same. But. You can't lie to yourself. And you can't live waiting for her to love you back. So, focus on your own life, your own career, what you can control. She might change the way she feels someday. But you can't just hang around for her, waiting to find out if she does."

A month later, Jason died, and Leo kept these words close to his heart, a benediction that led him through every decision he made. To move to Los Angeles. To put himself first. To love Daisy and let her come to him in her time, when she was ready. Because it felt to Leo that, from what his father had said, she must come around eventually. Her feelings, once he left, would shift. She'd realize what he knew all along. She'd come running to him.

It's possible, Leo thinks for the first time, that, because they were some of his father's final words to him, Leo believed they held power. That, if he followed the advice, everything he'd hoped for would come to pass. Grief can manipulate an ordinary phrase and twist it into prophecy. But sometimes words are just words, even when spoken by someone truly loved and now lost.

Leo drives too fast toward the groomsmen's house. He blows through stop signs. He blasts his music, trying to make sense of what this means, that Daisy might still love him, that Daisy doesn't love him enough to not marry Daniel. He didn't realize that he'd still been holding out hope for her, a subconscious belief that they were meant to be.

It was probably nothing more than coincidence. But that look. That hug. The feeling of Daisy's face pressed close to his heart. That was no coincidence. That was a decision. It meant something, Leo is sure of it. Maybe fate is a fable, but action cobbles together its own destiny. And there is still enough time for action to be taken.

# DEACON

Deacon walks down the hall behind Athena, preparing to enter the wedding madness, which is in full swing, when he hears his name from upstairs.

"Deacon!" Daisy shouts. "Deacon, come here. Now!"

Athena stares up at the ceiling. She raises her eyebrows. "A crisis already?"

"Right on schedule," Deacon says.

He heads back toward the stairs, taking them two at a time, not wanting to leave Daisy waiting. He knocks and then opens the door. Daisy's pacing around her room, her hair tied back, a wide headband barricading her bangs out of her face.

"Katie has my phone."

Deacon jumps when she spins around. Her white face mask has slits for her eyes, nose and mouth, a jarring sight when he expected to see his sister's face.

"Can I point out," Deacon says, "that you look like a monster?"

"Deacon!" Daisy rips the mask off, her eyes frantic and wide. "My phone!"

"Aren't you supposed to be calm and angelic?"

"I was earlier," Daisy says. "But now, I need my phone."

"Alright, alright." Deacon holds up his hands in surrender. "Are you sure?"

"I just," Daisy says. "I just need it."

"Fair enough."

Deacon doesn't argue. He follows his orders.

On the stairs, Deacon runs directly into Leo. He regains his balance and says, "You're supposed to be getting my suit."

"Special delivery." Leo holds up two white, bedazzled stilettos. "Your mom told me to run them upstairs."

"Oh." Deacon takes a closer look at the shoes. They *are* the ones Daisy plans to wear at the reception. "Okay. As long as this isn't some Trojan horse for your unrequited feelings or whatever."

"Does no one have any faith in me?"

"Remember high school? Prom? Shauna Waters?" Deacon says. "I was going with her—"

"As friends!" Leo interjects, as he always did when Deacon told the story.

"And you swooped in at the last second," Deacon trudges on, not letting Leo shut him down. "Because of your feelings. Even though you *knew* I had a crush on her, too."

"She was straight!" Leo says. "And I really liked her! I just hadn't realized it—"

"Until she was going to prom with *me*." Deacon puffs out his chest. His anger still rises at the memory of the decade-old betrayal. "Once you couldn't have her, you wanted her. Sound familiar?"

"Daisy is different, you know that, Deacon."

"I don't, actually." Deacon points to the shoes. "I've got to go get her phone, so you get those to her, and you get out. I still need you to get my suit from the groomsmen's house. Besides, I'm going to be back upstairs in, like, five seconds. So if you linger—" Deacon gestures to his eyes "—I'll see it. And I've always wanted an excuse to pay you back for prom."

"Real tough guy." Leo shoves Deacon's shoulder, but he's

smiling, that charming, unrelenting grin that gets him out of so much trouble. Deacon can't help but return the look.

"Yeah, yeah," Deacon says.

Leo claps him on the back as he bounds up the stairs toward Daisy. Deacon hopes he can keep his head on straight, but doubts it. Leo does whatever he wants, whenever he wants, because, for Leo, the world revolves around him. It's always been that way. Athena couldn't stand it in high school. He got so much more attention than she did, but he was always better at curating it. Athena held her accomplishments close, expecting others to learn about them from someone else, then celebrate her accordingly. Leo was direct. If he got a part, he'd interrupt any conversation they were having to announce it. If he passed a math test—a true miracle at that time, to be fair—he'd call his parents right away and make sure they had something special planned for dinner. He liked to loop in the world, to invite them into his celebrations, while Athena wanted to ice everyone out, so that they, instead, would invite her in.

Athena. Just the thought of her sends a jolt of anxiety through his chest. He remembers what Mel said. Her insistence. His promise. He had to tell her sometime. He'd come so close when they were in her room this morning. There's no time like the present, but surely the present being the wedding of his sister rendered that saying obsolete?

Deacon shakes his head and lets out two short exhales in quick succession. He needs to focus. For Daisy. For his family. There's extra pressure to make sure everything goes well. Daisy's last marriage being such a disaster means that this wedding needs to be perfect. What better way to start a marriage off than a magical night that no one will ever forget? It doesn't matter that perfect is impossible. They are going to do everything in their power to get as close to it as they can.

When Deacon enters the living room, he's greeted by a wall of sound. Screeches. Clapping. Impromptu karaoke. He clenches his fist, his jaw tightening instinctively. There are many sounds in the universe, but nothing grates on Deacon's nerves more than a group of straight women coming together to celebrate the marriage of one of their friends. It is a specific frequency. A consistent wave of chaos. High-pitched and unceasing, it ebbs and flows with the moment, reducing from a whisper—usually a piece of gossip about one of the other girls—to shrieks of laughter and screamed lyrics to Taylor Swift songs from the early 2010s.

The group is an exposed nerve, sensitive and hyperaware. Hurt feelings are inevitable and always voiced, every slight a drama needing to be played out in full force. There is an incessant need to claim a piece of the bride, to make sure everyone knows how great of friends they are, how long they'd known each other, and how the bride knows them better than anyone else, even—and Deacon is always dismayed to hear this—better than their husbands do.

He steps into the room cautiously, taking in the scene. The makeup station is fully occupied as Clare gets her face airbrushed with foundation, obliterating every line and wrinkle and sign of life, like an actual Instagram filter summoned out of thin air. The living room is crowded with more of Daisy's friends, all of whom Deacon does not know. They gather around Reghan, who holds up a handheld mirror, checking the back of her head to see how well her curls are setting.

"We've got hours to go, so I know they'll fall. But. I just don't know," Reghan says. "They look too tight."

"That's what she said," Deacon says as he slips into the room.

"That doesn't even make sense." Reghan whirls around to face Deacon, sending her too tight curls flying all around her.

"Sure, if she's wearing a dildo and talking to a nonbinary person."

"*Jesus*, Deacon," his mother shouts as she walks into the room from the kitchen. "It's Daisy's wedding day. Can't you just be…"

"Nice?"

"Yes!" Diane says, throwing up her hands, knocking over a tube of lipstick in the process. "Goddammit, look what you made me do."

"That's not nice language, Mother," Deacon says before bending down to pick up the stray lipstick and kiss her on the cheek.

"You didn't come out this sour," she says to him, patting his face.

"Then you made me that way."

She shrugs, not denying it, and he moves on through the crowd of women until he finds Katie on the other side of the room. Damp hair from the shower, she's flipping through the hairdresser's lookbook, trying to decide on a style.

"Shave your head," Deacon says, coming up behind her, making her jump slightly. "It's less work."

"I did consider it." Katie goes back to the lookbook. "But I think I'll go with beach waves. Seems appropriate, right?"

"Very on-brand. I'm sure your pic will get a thousand likes and shares and whatever the fuck."

"Thank you for your vote of confidence," Katie says. "I'll tag you so your phone blows up with notifications."

"You wound me, Katie."

"Just trying to put you on the map."

"I like my digital footprint to remain lost, or, at least, untraceable." Deacon reaches out his hand. "The bride needs her phone."

"Where's Athena?" Katie asks as she searches through her purse.

"Around here somewhere. Taking a shower, I think. Finally peeled her out of bed." Deacon extends his arm further for the phone, but Katie doesn't hand it over.

"Are you sure she wants this? She said she didn't want it."

"I don't know if you've ever heard Daisy shriek," Deacon says, swiping the phone from her before she can withhold it any longer. "But it's pretty convincing. She probably wants to text Daniel. Feels like she'll combust if they don't make contact soon."

"Romantic." Katie pulls Deacon's arm back as he tries to leave. "Hey. You know Athena."

"She's my best friend." Deacon knows where this is going, and doesn't like it. More time spent as a pawn in other people's games.

"What's a good way in?"

"*In?*" Deacon asks, raising his eyebrows.

"Shut up, not like that." Katie struggles for the words. "Like…what does she like? What's her favorite…?"

"Her favorite drink is a tequila soda with extra lime. Her favorite kind of coffee is black and piping hot. Her favorite music is anything without a synth." Deacon takes an overly dramatic inhale. "And, as the entire universe knows, her favorite writer is Emily Dickinson."

"I don't know anything about poetry."

"I wouldn't lead with that," Deacon says, twisting his arm free of Katie's grip. "Now, if you'll excuse me." He waves the phone over his head as he walks away. "My errand boy duties await."

"But I just need a way—"

"Manifest it, it'll come to you." Deacon doesn't bother waiting for her reaction. He can only handle being one person's lackey today. He doesn't need to do more work for someone who can do it themselves. If Katie wants to try to get with Athena, that's her war to wage. Deacon knows one night of flirting did not so easily untether Athena from Sydnee.

Before he can make his way out of the room, Deacon is intercepted by Reghan and Clare, who shove a champagne glass in his hand and ask him to help caption their joint Instagram post.

"You're an English teacher, come on, we just need it to sound good."

It takes them twenty minutes to settle on one—*This weekend is un-beachable*—and by the time he gets to Daisy's room, he sees Leo holding her. Daisy jumps out of his arms. Leo fixes his face, reverting to that bored and unbothered expression that makes him seem handsome and aloof. He doesn't acknowledge Deacon. He walks by him, out the door.

"What happened with him?" Deacon asks after the door shuts behind Leo. "Was he being annoying?"

"Just delivering my shoes." Daisy spots her phone in his hand. "Can I have it?"

"He's not over you, you know."

"Our relationship was complicated."

"Oh, you mean the covert, sneak around, 'don't tell anyone about this,' shady ass excuse for dating?"

"It would have been weird to tell people and then have it not work out. We wanted to make sure it would last before we told anyone. It didn't. So it was the right choice." Daisy's voice shakes slightly as she says it.

"Tell me you don't have feelings for him."

"I told you," Daisy says, averting her eyes. "It's complicated."

"You love Daniel."

"I never said I didn't."

"Leo is not the one," Deacon says. "He's flaky, and he doesn't know what he wants, and—"

"Can I have my phone now?" Daisy cuts him off. "I really need to check something."

Deacon doesn't move. He assesses Daisy. Her eyes dart from his to her phone, a desperate exasperation overtaking her face. When Leo left, Daisy was a mess. She stopped posting on Instagram. She could barely get out of bed. No food appealed to her. All the momentum she'd built after leaving the Youth Pastor sputtered and ceased, her life halting once more thanks to a man. It didn't last forever. It didn't even last for long—one week later, she resumed life as if nothing had happened. But Deacon understood that she had loved Leo in a real way, and he had left and broken her heart. He'd never forgiven him for that. But Deacon had to trust that Daisy's love of Daniel is stronger than any hang-up she has on Leo.

"Here." Deacon throws Daisy's phone on her bed.

"Thank God." Daisy unlocks it and scrolls through the phone. Her eyes are wide and her brows are raised as she sinks into concentration.

"Solving the world's problems on there?"

"No, it's just." She looks up from her phone, her expression impossible to read. "I thought I might have dreamed it. But it was real. The Youth Pastor texted me. Last night."

"I introduced Alex to Sydnee," Deacon says in a rush, as if her confession has given him permission to do the same. It feels good to release it into the air. To stop holding on to it.

Daisy stares at him. She opens her mouth to speak, then closes it.

"When?" she asks.

"Before. Well, obviously, before. But. Basically, I knew Alex through our softball league, and then found out she worked at the same firm as Sydnee, and I thought…well,

who doesn't want more queer friends, right? I thought they'd
hit it off."

"Well, you were right."

"I didn't think they'd hit it off like that!" Deacon paces
up and down the room. Then, he stops. "Wait. Did you say
the Youth Pastor?"

"Yeah." Daisy scrolls through her phone again, showing
Deacon the texts.

He gets a twisted, knotted feeling in his stomach. It doesn't
sit right. "What a dick," he says.

"Must have gotten my number from one of those ladies
from the church."

"Thought you changed it?"

"They have their ways." Daisy's face darkens. "When
there's something they need, they know how to get it."

"Intense." Deacon reads the texts again. In the eyes of God,
you're still mine. "Well, in the eyes of the law, you belong to
no man. Until later tonight." He glances down at his watch.
"It's almost nine. Shouldn't you be drinking mimosas in your
robe and posing for pretend candid pictures?"

"Doesn't this feel like a bad sign?" Daisy asks, taking her
phone back.

"Not really." Deacon thinks it through. The Youth Pastor
was all smoke, no substance. It had been that way since they
were young, listening to his lectures during their Wednesday night youth group meetings, the dodgeball tournaments
that always ended with a sermon. He'd make a big show of
any metaphor he used to articulate the perils of not trusting
in Jesus, but whenever anyone asked him direct questions, or
confronted his line of thinking, he'd shrink and fumble his
words and tell them all to bow their heads and pray. "More
just a sign that you did the right thing. That you're winding
up with the right person."

"Yeah," Daisy says, her shoulders slumping with relief. "Thought I was cursed or something."

"Food's here!" Mollie shouts outside the door.

"Thanks, Mollie, just leave it outside, we'll get it in a second!" Deacon shouts back. A *thump* as the tray is set down. They hear Mollie's footsteps descend downstairs.

"Anyway," Deacon says. "It's all in the past. Y'all got divorced, you know, it's—"

"Daisy, sweetie." Now it's Diane outside the door, knocking without stopping. "It's time to come downstairs."

"One second, Mom!" Daisy takes in the room, trying to find a reasonable explanation for their absence. She glances at Deacon, who nods, happy to be her excuse, and says, "I'm helping Deacon shoot up really quick."

"I hate when you say it like that!" Diane yells. "But hurry up downstairs, Daisy, it's time to get things moving."

"Got it, Ma."

"Anyway, it's no big deal," Deacon says to Daisy once their mother walks away. "It doesn't mean anything. You'll give it power if you focus on it. Think about Daniel. Isn't he the best?"

"The best." Daisy studies her engagement ring. "He's kind, and he respects me, and he makes me laugh, and he sees me, and—" Daisy relaxes into a smile. "He has the best butt in the world."

"Amazing to hear," Deacon says.

"And you." Daisy gets up and holds Deacon's forearms, clutching them hard to emphasize her point. "You didn't do anything wrong. You just…"

"Introduced the loaded gun."

"Excuse me?"

"Chekhov." Daisy's face is a mask of incomprehension.

"Never mind. But Athena doesn't know. Thinks they met through work."

"Well, what's wrong with that?"

"Mel thinks it's lying."

"It's not."

"But it's not the truth."

"No," Daisy agrees. "What are you hoping for here, Deacon?"

"What do you mean?"

"By bringing it up," Daisy says. "You did what you did. And now there's nothing more to be done."

"But Athena deserves—"

"Athena doesn't know." Daisy picks at her cuticle. "And it would only make her angry, knowing you had some involvement in Alex and Sydnee. You know that."

"But we're best friends."

"So are we, but I don't tell Athena everything." Daisy pulls out a bottle of hand cream from her purse and moisturizes the finger she'd picked at. "She can't handle it. Her world is small. Smaller than it's ever been now."

This much is true. Since the separation, Athena had shrunk herself to the size of her office, her head in her research, her heart closed off. It could be frustrating at times, but Deacon would always stick with her, just as Athena had for him.

She had stood by him through every transition in his life, the figurative and the literal. The second puberty, the break-ups, the career crisis in his midtwenties, when he thought he should go to law school to become a public defender because what other option did he have? Besides doom scrolling and anxiety attacks and waiting for the world to close in on him and his rights, his bodily autonomy, his ability to make decisions for himself. Athena had seen his desperation and understood that feeling of helplessness, so she supported him while

he studied for his LSAT, made sure Sydnee answered any questions he had about law school, and then held his hand while
he opened his scores, and, when those scores were dismally
low, looked him right in the eyes and said, "You would be a
terrible lawyer. But you could be a great teacher."

So Deacon got his Texas teaching certificate, while Athena
called in a few favors with the connections she had in administration at the local arts high school, the Houston school
Beyoncé supposedly attended, and he taught his first class of
juniors the fall he turned twenty-six.

He was worried at first. It was a midterm year when he
started teaching, and Texas leaders had morphed themselves to
fit the movement of the moment. Queer and trans bans swept
through the school districts. Though Houston's mayor stood
in direct opposition to all of them, his influence was nothing
in combating the waves of hysteria that swept through local
PTA meetings. Mothers weeping, convinced by the internet
that any educator, specifically those in the humanities, had
an *agenda* to change their children, as if their children did not
know themselves more intimately than they could ever be
known by parents who looked at them and, instead of seeing
a soul, saw the manifestations of their long-held expectations.
Politicians vowed to make schools free from outside influence
and safe from the threat of critical thinking, all the while acting as if teaching their children intolerance and hatred was
the same as protecting them, as if entombing young minds
in the oppressive, never-changing ideologies that worshiped
control, while hating love and acceptance, was the same as
teaching them "good values."

He seethed at the thought of it. Daisy's friends used to
tell him to give everyone a chance. To greet the world with
open hearts and arms and find it embracing him back. It was
different for them. Straight, white, conventionally attractive

women. The world was theirs. And when you rule the world, you have nothing to fear from it.

Deacon knows better, though. Eventually, Daisy did, too. There were people in the world, in his home state and town, who dedicate their lives to the eradication of his rights and existence. He knows there is no changing that. He can move, he knows. But the rent here is cheap, and the food is unbeatable, and his family all live here, and why should he have to leave a place he loves just because someone else tells him he doesn't belong? Stubborn, stupid and perhaps unsustainable as it might be, he is, for the time being, standing his ground. He just hopes the school won't prove to be a breeding ground for that kind of thinking. You never know in Houston where it is safe and where it isn't until you try it out yourself, a constant trial by fire.

Whatever words people use to describe falling in love, that's how Deacon feels about teaching. His students are weird and eager and ready to learn how to make the world a better place. Deacon teaches American literature, and the school let his syllabus shift with the moment, so he adds contemporary novels that speak to every timely issue, the list of which seems to grow as the years go on. Few parents pushed back. Deacon isn't sure if it's because the school focused on the arts, which demanded its own kind of leniency in parenting, or because the students this year had hopped on a TikTok trend that told them to always answer *The Great Gatsby* and *The Catcher in the Rye* when their parents asked what they were reading in school. Either way, it's a pleasure, a strange blip in the hellscape of Texas teaching.

Deacon always carved out a week to focus on Dickinson, and he'd bring Athena in to lead a discussion at the end of the week. It was extraordinary, seeing an expert in their field at work. Athena talked with confidence, moved through discussion with dexterity, captivated his students' attention (no easy feat, he knew). Her mind was a marvel, and he loved being in such close proximity to it. He didn't want to lose any closeness, even if it meant hiding the truth from her.

Athena is his best friend, and Deacon desperately wants to do right by her. With Mel's prompting, his guilt has gained a life of its own. It was his fault, he knows, that Sydnee ever met Alex. Though he cannot, in all seriousness, take the blame for Sydnee using that introduction to cheat on Athena. That choice was on Sydnee, and Sydnee alone. He fears, though, that Athena will not see it this way.

"It's not wrong to keep it from her?" Deacon asks, desperate for someone to tell him that it's okay to hide the truth, to bury some secrets.

"I don't know what's right or wrong." Daisy stands up, pulling the clip out of her hair so that it flows down by her shoulders. "You can tell her someday, I guess." She picks up her white silk robe and slips it on, then opens the door. "But today is my wedding day, Deacon. So it sure as hell better not be today."

# ATHENA

Left alone by Deacon, Leo and Mollie, Athena wanders into the living room, where someone terrible has taken over the aux cord, blasting an awful EDM song with an unrelenting bass and beat that repeats in a seemingly endless loop. It spikes Athena's anxiety, her back tightening and her neck stiffening. The sound is inescapable, at once meaningless and pervasive.

"You *bitch*!" Reghan screams, sprinting in from the hallway, Clare hot on her tail.

"I'm just trying to *help* you, I don't want your T-zone becoming oil city when we're taking the pictures!"

The makeup and hair people are busy going over their books, making sure they understand the day's assignment. Reghan and Clare continue to scream at each other on one side, while the bass drum pulses through the speakers on the other, shaking the glass coffee table in the middle of the room.

Katie peeks in from the porch, and, seeing Athena stranded in no-man's-land, rushes in to grab her arm, dragging her back outside, where she slides the glass door shut.

"They won't stop *fighting*," Katie says as she drops down into the deck chair and lets her arms splay out in exhaustion. "All over the stupid sponsorship."

"I don't speak influencer..." Athena sits down in the chair

next to Katie, propping up her feet. The view of the ocean from their seats is unobstructed, and the clouds part just enough for the sun to start warming her shins.

"A brand partnership deal," Katie explains. "It was a big one, too, some kind of national health food store. A lot of money on the line."

"Isn't Clare, like, a baroness or something?" Athena asks.

"Essentially. Oil heiress, River Oaks royalty, however you want to say it. But she likes winning. The money is just a bonus."

"She and Reghan seem so close on Instagram."

"That's the whole business," Katie says. "It's a curation game."

"You seem good at it." Athena remembers what Deacon said about having a little fun. She shifts away from the ocean so that she can focus her full attention on Katie. The only thing she can remember about flirting is maintaining eye contact. She stares at Katie's eyes. They are a shocking shade of hazel, with gold and green flecks all around. When the sun hits them, they have an almost radioactive glow.

"Are you okay?" Katie asks, looking right back at Athena. "You're not blinking."

"Oh, I was just—"

"You think I won't expose you?" Clare bellows from inside. "Give me one reason not to!"

"Because you'd probably get confused and end up uploading one of your unfiltered nudes!" Reghan shouts back. "Yeah, I've seen the folder on your phone!"

Katie gets up and bangs on the glass door, screams for the two of them to shut up. She sits back down, massaging her temples. "Jesus. Weddings are only fun when you're not in them. I'm starting to get a headache. I'm desperate. Tell me something good."

"All I can think of right now is Bradley Cooper singing that line in the Lady Gaga movie."

*"Tell me somethin' good,"* Katie sings in an overdramatized, faux-baritone country voice. "But really. Something good. Please."

"Well," Athena says, "Sydnee is here. In Watercolor. With Alex."

"I know Sydnee." Then, seeing Athena's confusion, adds, "We've hung out. With Daisy. But I don't know Alex."

"Her new girlfriend," Athena says. "They met while we were still married."

"Oh, shit." Katie's eyebrows rise in surprise, though Athena is certain Daisy must have told her all about the divorce. Athena notices no frown lines on Katie's forehead, and she instinctively feels for her own. They are entrenched and extremely visible. "I can't believe she'd do that."

"Daisy gave her a plus-one. I said she could. We didn't expect her to take it."

"Of course she took it," Katie says, shaking her head. "People take every inch that they're given. And then they still want more."

Athena shrugs, knowing she's right, not wanting to admit how right she is. Even in her family. Leo takes all the time and space and money he's given to pursue his dream. Her mother takes every bump in the road and forges ahead, creating with it a new opportunity and an endless source of optimism. Athena takes her silence and never relinquishes it. They all took everything they could from Jason, and even when he's gone, they still long for more: more advice, more memories, more time together that they no longer have.

Did she take too much from Sydnee? Athena can't contemplate such a thing. Not yet. Not when her fury gives her so much purpose, when *victim* feels a role so much easier to inhabit than one that would require analysis. She took what was given. Who doesn't, in a marriage? It's a give and a take, isn't that what they say? For better, for worse, in sickness, in health. Vows said years ago, now void.

"When was the last time you had sex?" Katie asks abruptly.

"Excuse me?" If she'd had a drink, Athena would have spit it out.

"Sex. Last time. With Sydnee?"

"I don't talk about this stuff." Athena glances back into the house, hoping something in the living room can save her. Reghan and Clare are still fighting, and Deacon is nowhere to be found. Athena is trapped.

"It's just physical," Katie says. "I bet your Dickinson did it all the time."

"Unlikely," Athena says, a reflex of correction. She remembers she's supposed to be flirting. She clears her throat and, inexplicably, lowers her voice an octave. "I mean, there was Sue. And a few mysterious men."

"Sue?"

"Her sister-in-law." Athena clears her throat again, the lower register not quite agreeing with her vocal chords.

"Damn, Dickinson was a messy bitch, huh?"

"Well, their friendship predated the marriage." This wasn't flirting. It felt more like a lecture. She should say something smooth. Or do something with her hands. Why did her body suddenly feel untethered from her mind? Heavy limbs refusing commands. In a panic, Athena reaches up and takes her hair out of its bun, letting her long, frizzy, split end ridden hair hit her shoulders and run down her back. She twirls it in her finger, trying to tame its wildness as subtly as she can.

"Forget about sex. When was the last time you had a haircut?" Katie asks, looking Athena up and down.

Athena's messy dark mass of hair stands in stark contrast to

Katie's, which is perfectly smooth and curled, kept clipped up high on the back of her head, an intentional messiness that is both effortless and stylish.

"Um…" Athena thinks. It had been a while. Since the separation, she'd let some grooming go by the wayside. Her eyebrows, always dark and a bit unruly, had merged in the middle, she'd go well over a week without washing her hair, and her skin care routine, once a seven-step, rigorous nightly ritual, had devolved into simply washing her face with bar soap. Her hair, though, she hadn't touched since before her father died. Almost three years. She tossed it up in a bun every day, so she rarely thought about its length. But it now reaches the middle of her back, devoid of volume or shape. It is lifeless deadweight.

"You carry a lot in your hair, you know." Katie inches closer to Athena, reaching out to touch it. "I could cut it for you, if you want."

"What?" Athena asks. She pulls back slightly, not used to such an intimate gesture. "Now?"

"No time like the present," Katie says, cheerfully. "I saw some scissors in the bathroom. I thought about cutting my bangs last night. That was after three glasses of wine. Luckily, the impulse was resisted. But for you…"

"Who looks like such a gremlin?"

"Gremlin adjacent, perhaps." Katie gives Athena's knee a gentle squeeze. "You can't move forward if you carry around the past."

"Which lives in my hair?"

"Which is *held* by your hair," Katie says, as if the distinction should make a difference.

Athena runs her hands through each scraggly strand. So much of the external world had not mattered to her in grief. She was mired in mud, barely able to put one foot in front of the other. Maybe this is perfunctory. And it will not change a thing about her life. But there is something enticing about it to Athena, this one small step.

"Daisy will kill us," Athena says, twirling her hair around her finger, tugging at it so that it pulls on her scalp. How much more pain could come from this length? She starts to think of her head as a garden untended, weeds that have overstayed their welcome. She itches to remove them from their roots.

"Daisy will survive."

"Okay," Athena says. "But if we're going to do it, we have to do it big. A true chop."

"Is there any other way?" Katie asks, already on her feet, heading back into the house to get all the supplies she needs. When she comes back, she has shampoo, conditioner, scissors, a set of clippers and a bowl. She grabs the hose from the back of the deck and brings it over. Athena eyes everything with mistrust, but nothing more than the clippers.

"Are those…?"

"Oh, yeah," Katie says, grinning. "Time for your new life to begin."

Athena's new life begins on a backless, wooden stool, on a birchwood porch, wet with morning dew, as waves crash down hard on the sand, the yellow warning flag flying high on the beach. It's safe to swim, but be careful. She stares out at the water as her hair falls down around her. She takes it in, the ocean, all its natural beauty, letting Katie do whatever needs to be done. She has released control. She focuses only on her breathing, the rhythm of the tide.

*Find the sea, Athena, you're built from the sea.*

Before she came out, Athena's world was external. Her internal life remained hidden from her consciousness, the truth too controversial for her unprepared mind. Private Christian high school did not help. Nor did her family surrounding themselves with people who were predominately white, upper-middle class, with varying proximities to Christianity. In these circles, there was a set of expectations that young women were supposed to follow. You will go to college. You will do well. You will meet a man. You will start a family. You will become a mother. You will help your sons become great men. You will help your daughters become great mothers. You will become a grandmother. You will die, quietly, hopefully, in your sleep, at a ripe old age. You will go to heaven—if you have followed these rules.

It was a different time. The world was smaller. If Athena had been born even five years later, her entire adolescence might have been completely different, more attuned to her body, certainly more aware of the world around her. But she was a late-age millennial, old enough to remember the world without computers, the feel of a VHS clicking into place within a VCR, the joy of discovering new music in a record store, buying an entire album just so she could listen to one song on repeat, but young enough to remember the hold Facebook had over her peers in high school, then Instagram in college, everyone developing an obsession with pictures and uploading them for feedback from the world.

Growing up, Athena was afraid of what she'd find if she ventured too far into the unknown. She was not a pioneer, nowhere close to an early adapter. She played it safe, closing herself off, drinking in the world around her, taking in every detail she could in order to occupy her ever racing mind, trying her best to dam it, prevent it from going too far inside herself, lest she discover that truth which she already knew, and feared above any other. She could not be a lesbian, not then, not when she still adhered to the order of the world set out by... God? He was always in the mix. Some of her parents' friends might say it was Ronald Reagan. She was never sure who orchestrated the plans. She only knew she had to fall in line. To do that, she had to fall away from herself.

The seagulls. The waves. The salt air. The breeze blowing cool, but not cold, swirling little tornados of her hair around the deck. Katie's hands on the back of her bare neck as she guides the clippers behind her ear. Her hands are soft and steady. Athena relaxes into them.

"Do you ever think," Athena says, almost absentmindedly, forgetting to be hardened and defensive, "that you'd be a different person if you were born just a few years later?"

"Hmm," Katie says, holding the clippers away from Athena's head as she thinks. She brushes the back of Athena's ear as she reaches for the scissors. "I'd probably be on TikTok instead of Instagram."

"But you," Athena says, attempting to look at her. Katie clamps her hands firmly on Athena's temples and holds her head straight. "Do you think you'd be a different *person*. Like more free or something."

"I've always felt free." Katie brushes the hair from Athena's shoulders. "And now, you will, too."

"What do you—"

Before Athena can ask, Katie hands her a handheld mirror. She gasps.

Her hair is gone.

Not gone. But different. Sheared at the sides, at the back of her neck, with tufts of hair, cut short, curling up on the top, still damp.

"It'll look nicer when it dries." Katie watches Athena closely, waiting for her reaction, her eyes narrowed. "Oh,

God, this was impulsive, wasn't it? No take backs, though, so you better like it."

"I look like Abby Wambach," Athena says in awe, still staring at herself in the mirror. "I've always wanted to try this."

"Darker hair, but cut's the same." Katie grabs her phone and snaps pictures and, considering Athena's approval consent for broadcast, opens Instagram, chooses a filter and starts filming her creation. "Why'd you wait for a rando to do it for you?"

"You're not a rando," Athena says as she runs her hands up and down the back of her head, the buzzed hair tickling the pads of her fingers, pleasure shooting through each one. "Sydnee liked it long. I guess I thought I did, too."

Katie stops recording, not taking in a word Athena says as she focuses on her phone. She shows Athena the video, an artful shot of Athena's head, with the ocean sprawling out in the background, *Cut by Katie* as her caption. She doesn't mute the audio, Athena's musings catapulted into the void without any thought or consideration given to them.

"Do you like it?" Athena is suddenly self-conscious. The initial exuberance has worn off, giving way to absolute panic. "It's short."

"It's trendy." Katie holds up her phone for a selfie with the scissors.

"I study a poet who's been dead for nearly 150 years, current trends aren't really my thing."

"Just repost my story on yours and see what your followers think."

"I deleted Instagram," Athena says, wondering if she should redownload it now and start crowdsourcing self-esteem.

It's not the worst idea. As she leans down to check her phone, it buzzes. Her entire heart drops into her stomach.

It's from Sydnee.

You could have done this years ago, I wouldn't have cared.

This is their first point of contact in almost eight months. Athena checks around her. Is Sydnee somehow in the house? Daisy wouldn't do that without telling her, would she? As if Sydnee can still read her mind, she texts again.

Katie's story. I saw it. I like your new hair.

Athena hates how much she loves this. She holds the sudden, unreasonable burst of hope at bay. There will certainly come a day when Athena won't take every word and message from Sydnee as a sign. A day when she can sit quietly with the memory of what they had, maybe on a screened-in front porch, maybe with a new partner by her side. When she can't remember the sound of Sydnee's voice, or the way she laughed, or the way her skin felt, soft, even with its bumps and bruises, against her cheek. When her heart will stay steady, its rhythm unbothered by the presence of a beloved because she will no longer be that beloved, just a person, from a time before.

But for now, for today, Sydnee is still a miracle, a heartbreak, a missing piece of—if Athena would allow herself to get so sentimental—her soul. Because of this, she spends too long thinking of a response, forgetting to take in the wind, the ocean, the external world. Her hair is new, but her life has not changed.

# MOLLIE

Mollie carries up a tray of food for Daisy, but when she reaches Daisy's room, the door is closed. She knocks. No one answers.

"Food's here!" Mollie shouts.

"Thanks, Mollie," Deacon says, his voice slightly muffled through the door. "Just leave it outside. We'll get it in a second."

Mollie stands still, slightly indignant. It took time and effort, didn't they know, to prepare a plate. She thinks of barging in, like she used to do when Athena and Leo ignored her in high school, but that had never led to anything good for any of them, so she lets it go, setting the tray down in front of the door.

When she gets back downstairs, Mollie finds herself alone with Reghan and Clare, who have tired themselves out of yet another argument, their yelling simmering into subdued silence as they sit on either side of the couch, checking their phones. As she walks in, Clare, eager to start talking again, jumps up, mimosa in hand, beelining for her.

"Ms. Mollie," Clare asks, sipping her mimosa through a straw. "Who was that tall drink of water you were talking to earlier?"

"Total zaddy, Molls, good for you." Reghan does not glance up from her phone as she says it.

"Zaddy?" Mollie asks. This weekend has taught her that she doesn't understand the internet, or any of the languages it uses.

"Y'all gonna get together tonight? Little romantic wedding meet-cute? Ooo! Ms. Mollie you deserve this!" Clare walks over and squeezes Mollie's arm, her acrylic nails pressing into her skin. Mollie rubs the spot once she pulls them away, making sure she didn't leave any marks.

"He's going with his daughter."

"Message him and ask if he wants to meet up before." Reghan scrolls. "That's what I did with Nicholas."

"You did *what*?" Clare asks, appalled. "We had a deal."

"And I had a sponsorship."

"Oh, grow up, Reghan, I swear to God—"

"Mollie, it's easy. Just find his Insta, add him and then DM him. Y'all can make cute little plans for tonight. It'll be fun. Little flirtation before it all begins."

"I'm sorry," Clare says, tossing her long red hair over her shoulder. "But we agreed that Nicholas was out-of-bounds for both of us."

"I'm trying to find this baseball game. Nicholas was talking about it. Need to see what the fuck he means."

"You hate baseball."

"Nicholas is, like, obsessed with this clip," Reghan says. "A no-hit something? A big hitter? Oh, no-hitter. Here it is."

Reghan sprawls out on the couch, playing a video at full volume. Clare flips the bird as she storms out of the room, but Reghan doesn't notice, focused as she is on understanding what Nicholas loves so much about this sport.

A baseball announcer breaks down the pitch selection. The crowd boos when the umpire misses a call. A fastball hits a leather mitt with a satisfying *pop*.

Mollie walks into the kitchen, away from the noise. The sound of baseball always triggers the memory. A strange soundtrack for the end of the world.

It was a Tuesday in October. Athena was at their house for the Astros game. It was the playoffs. "*Postseason*," Athena corrected her. The air was cool, but not cold, still humid as Houston always insisted on staying. But the sky got that bottomless blue that signaled fall had arrived in Texas. The door was open. The breeze blew in the living room. The pregame show announced the starting pitches and lineups for each team. Mollie was never sure of the round, but she knew it was before the World Series, and it was the final game. The winner moved on, the loser went home.

"Game seven," Athena said, always quick to correct her, in life and in sports. "Against the Yankees—God, I hate the Yankees. Does it get better than this?"

"Nope," Jason answered from the bar area. He was making drinks. "When we win, this will be the best day of our lives."

"Second best," Athena said. "World Series or bust, remember?"

"How could he forget," Mollie said, rolling her eyes. "It's all you two talk about."

"Is Sydnee coming?" Jason shouted out. "Or am I just making three?"

"A trio, please," Athena shouted back. "She's still working."

"*Tres bebidas. Con tequila o ginebra?*"

"Excuse me?"

"You really need to pick those Spanish lessons back up, Thene," Jason called out. "It'd mean a lot to Sydnee."

"Sydnee doesn't care, Dad." Athena flipped through the channels, trying to find the Astros game. "So, what was the question?"

"Tequila or gin?"

"Gin," Athena and Mollie called out at the same time. They looked at each other, their eyes lighting up with laughter. "Jinx!"

They almost didn't hear him fall. But how could they not. A thump. A crash of glass. A limp hand hitting the hardwood floor. The laughter froze on each of their faces. Mollie saw the fear flash through her daughter's eyes. Her first instinct was to hold her. But then she went into the bar area. Saw Jason sprawled out, spread-eagle, on the floor. Her heart stopped. Her legs were jelly. She willed herself to stand. They called the ambulance. Everything was a blur, the lights and sirens and silence in a cold, empty hospital waiting room.

Jason was in surgery for hours. Leo came to the hospital shortly after they arrived and sat between Mollie and Athena, staring up at the TV. The game was still on, but he didn't care about sports. Neither did Mollie. That was for Athena and Jason. The Astros won with a walk-off home run in the bottom of the twelfth. Athena didn't react, just glanced up at the mob forming at home plate, then checked her phone. The surgeon came out to the waiting room. Jason died on the table. The aorta burst. There was nothing more they could do. Mollie went to the bathroom. She threw up. *Time of death, 11:37.* She had seen enough medical dramas to know how they said it. Defeated, matter-of-fact, done. She wiped her mouth with the back of her hand. The fluorescent lights flickered. She refused to look at herself in the mirror.

They were still in the waiting room, shocked, when Sydnee arrived. Her hair was tossed into a bun, flyaway hairs haloing her face, her eyes wide, tears already forming. Leo got to her first, wrapping his arms around her, whispering the worst words any of them had ever heard. Sydnee slumped into a chair, her head in her hands.

Athena glanced at Mollie, expression vacant, pale face, hollow eyes, dark circles beneath them. Then, over to Sydnee, eyes still strange and lifeless, devoid of their signature sparkle and shine. It scared Mollie, but not as much as it should have. She didn't know it, but that was the last day she'd see Athena's eyes light up for many years.

"You were supposed to be there," Athena said to Sydnee. Her voice was faraway, cold and caught in her throat, but it still carried across the room. Leo and Mollie shared a look. His green eyes closed as if he knew what was to come.

"He wasn't supposed to die!" Sydnee said, face still in her hands, voice cracking.

Something fractured for everyone that day. An irrevocable fault line. Mollie tried to put them back together, but the pieces didn't fit the same after Jason was gone. It was another wave of grief, to realize her presence was inadequate, always shadowed by her partner's absence. She felt it in herself, too. Who was she without him?

Since the world ended, every day, Mollie took small steps to build herself a new one. It was smaller, this brave new world, but it became more fulfilling with each passing day. Her life took its time restarting. She was surprised by the pleasures that came back first. Baking transforms into a saving grace. An early morning walk becomes a companion. The world shrinks and slows and wraps around you, a consuming comfort. She'd felt sorry for widows and their suddenly shrunken worlds before she became one. But the smallness was a gift. It encouraged little steps every day. Short distances. Crumbs that could sustain. Just make it out of the bed. Make it to the kitchen. Make it around the block. Say something out loud at least once a day, even if your voice strained and your vocal chords felt useless. Call Athena. Call Leo. Let them cry. Don't let them hear you cry.

She never forgot Jason, but sometimes she did forget that he wasn't alive. The jolt and shock and pain that gave her every morning started to reduce with time. After the first year, it would happen only a few times a week, then a few times a month, then a few times a year. Three years had been an eternity and no time at all. A black hole, bending time and space and spitting her out the other side without warning. She is present and in the past, her memory of the life she'd had before as clear as the day in front of her. She is with Jason and without him, a cruel limbo, a purgatory. That's what loss is: the space between the *before* and the *after*.

Daisy's wedding provides temporary relief from the quantum physics of her grief. Mollie's happy to run errands, to follow orders, to bear the brunt of Diane's anxiety-fueled anger if it means, for a weekend, she can steep herself in another person's life. She's even happier to be here after Reghan's idea to find Eli on social media.

They'd suggested Instagram, but Mollie doesn't have one of those. She kicked it old-school, on Facebook. She'd gotten great at stalking, a skill she'd gained in mourning. She had an uncanny ability to find people on the social media app. All she needed was a hometown, and she could track anyone down. Old high school friends. Ex-boyfriends. Estranged cousins who ended up being knee-deep in alt-right conspiracy theories. Like a detective, not everything she uncovered was pretty, but it never stopped her from getting to the truth.

Eli is an easy mark. She goes to Daisy's profile, locates his daughter, Elise, on her friends list, and the first tagged picture on her profile is from him. She adds him as a friend, and for good measure, sends him a direct message. She starts typing, then pauses. What to say? She types out a few options. Hey handsome. Ahoy there sailor. Hey good-lookin', remember me? Before settling with a simple **Great meeting you today.** She rereads the message, wishing Diane were downstairs to help her. She's on her own, though, and she doesn't want to waste any time. This has to be good enough. It's simple. Straightforward. And true.

She hits Send, and resists the urge to throw her phone across the room.

She walks back into the living room. Clare and Reghan have resumed their argument over the groomsman. Then, Athena comes through the sliding glass doors from the porch. Mollie gasps.

Her hair is *gone*.

Chopped short at the sides, with length left on top. Her hair hasn't been this short since she was born. It takes Mollie a minute to register her daughter, but how can she not know those shoulders, that slightly slouched posture, the head on a constant swivel, looking every which way, taking in every detail around her?

Since the separation, she's withered away. Her broad shoulders had always been sculpted and strong and sure of themselves. She kept them back, kept her head held high. Her coaches always called her "a big girl." Mollie hated the term, but Athena seemed to arm herself with it. Bigger, better, not afraid to take up space. She projected sturdiness, had since she was a kid, playing on the block with Leo and the other boys, just as strong as them, just as fast as them. Equal in every way. She never doubted that she belonged, that she was built to move and run and be free. Mollie knows none of that came from her and Jason. Athena was born with it. They just stayed out of her way and let her live.

Now, though, after Sydnee, after Jason, Athena seems diminished. Not smaller, but not the same, either. Deflated, somehow.

But at least the hair makes it seem intentional. For the first time in a long time, Athena stands up a little straighter, holds

her head a little higher, as if the shedding of her hair has reju-
venated some lost part of herself. Mollie loves it. She goes to
embrace her daughter, but, before she can, Daisy runs down
the stairs. When she spots Athena, she stops. Balls her fists.

Mollie expects her to scream. Instead, her voice gets quiet,
dropping an octave lower than usual.

"No fucking way." Daisy points at Athena's head. "Why
would you do that? Today?"

"It was long, and I—"

"You could have waited. One. *Day.*"

"It was my idea." One of the bridesmaids, *Katie*, Mollie
remembers, steps in front of Athena, as if she can shield her
from Daisy's anger. "She needed a change."

"A change? A trim, maybe. But, a change?"

"It's not like it's the end of the world," Katie says.

Mollie grimaces. That was the wrong thing to say. Anything that goes wrong for Daisy today *is* an apocalyptic ending.

"You better manifest to your hippie-dippie universe that
she still looks good in lavender silk," Daisy says, her voice
raised, but not quite yelling, barely maintaining her composure. She addresses Athena. "I know you hate weddings,
Athena, but this—"

"I'm gonna take a walk." Athena steps out from behind
Katie. She doesn't look at Daisy, or anyone else. She runs her
hand up and down the back of her neck. "Come back a little
later. Let you cool off."

"You can't just—"

"Let her go," Katie says.

Athena flies by them both. No one tries to stop her. She's
out of the door in seconds. Daisy glances from the door back
to Katie. Then, without another word, she grabs a bottle of
champagne and pours herself a glass, walking out to the porch

with her arms crossed, her lips pressed tightly together, as if holding back all the incisive words she'd like to say. The hair and makeup artists go after her to make sure she's okay.

Katie and Mollie are left alone. They make eye contact. Katie lets out an awkward laugh, breathy and unsure.

"Guess I shouldn't have cut it so short." She walks over to the bar and puts ice into a specialized party cup etched with Daisy's and Daniel's initials, along with their wedding date. She squeezes lime over it, then pours in tequila. Too much tequila. Mollie doesn't judge. "Think I'll go find Athena. Give her a little pick-me-up."

Mollie watches her go, trying to remember if her own wedding had been so stressful, with such high stakes. But she only remembers the good part. Walking down the aisle. Jason in his tux. His smile, and his eyes brimming with tears that he let fall freely. They danced and they drank and they didn't care about the details. Jason's family wasn't there—they refused to come and see him throw away their legacy by marrying a girl like Mollie. Even the sting of that, though, feels distant and dull, like her memory of childbirth, the pain faded away, leaving only the lightness, the joy, the promise of what was to come.

A ping from her phone. Mollie checks it. A message from Eli.

Hey there. My daughter already ditched me for her friends, so I'm flying solo. Pregame the ceremony tonight? Beach club bar? Around 4?

She closes her eyes before the tears can come and steadies her breathing. Sometimes she gets so lost in memory that she forgets. Jason exists only in recollection. She is a widow. That chapter of her life—their life—has closed. She needs to turn the page. But the pages are stuck together, too heavy to flip forward. It's easier to stay on that last page, rereading the same paragraphs over and over again. She has them memorized, but seeing the words still brings comfort.

She reads the message again. She knows she should go. She likes Eli. At least the five seconds she saw of him. In those five seconds, she felt more connected to him than any man she'd met in the past year, when she finally forced herself to put herself out there, test the waters so to speak. She always came home alone, unbothered, because the men she met were no threat to her loneliness.

It feels different with Eli, and that scares her. Their instant connection feels like it could be real, if she gives it the chance to become so.

It's not a betrayal. Jason would never stand for her to think of it that way. He believed in life's momentum, in swimming with the current. Resistance is futile. Change comes as it comes. It's better to work with it, to not let yourself get swept away.

She repeats it again: this is not a betrayal. She sends a thumbs-up emoji back to Eli. He replies quickly, It's a date!

Jason's face comes more clearly to her mind in unconscious moments than when she tries to summon it. She remembers his smile, the crinkle at the corner of his eyes, which were dark brown, the same color as Athena's. The flyaway hairs on his scraggly beard, the way the bridge of his nose curved, his forehead getting larger as the years went on, his hairline receding against his will. He would press his forehead into Mollie's, close his eyes and hold her close. She was most at ease in those moments. Jason was not a perfect man, Mollie knew that, but perfect wasn't the point. He was her home, and his arms around her felt like sinking into the couch after a long, taxing day. No anxiety, no tension. She could just be.

Eli's message is still open on her phone. She will go. She will try. She will take one step forward, away from the past, into a new life.

This is not a betrayal. So why does it feel like one?

# ATHENA

Athena should have foreseen this. Her hair, now short and sheared, did not fit Daisy's vision for her perfect day. Her bridesmaids were supposed to be homogenous and symmetrical. A cropped haircut threw off the entire vibe. Or, at least, that's how Daisy put it.

It seems ridiculous to Athena, but weddings force your hand: you are not allowed to be anything other than an object perfectly placed on a predetermined stage. Your life, for a day, freezes. You are a player, you know your lines. There is no room for reaction. There is no elasticity in a moment.

Athena leaves, giving Daisy space and allowing herself room to breathe. She wanted to fight back, to argue, but she will not make this moment about her.

It's cold outside. The northern wind is weak, but still sends a chill through Athena. She considers going back in to get a jacket, but she knows better than to test Daisy. Out of sight, out of mind. That will calm her down.

She crosses the two-lane highway. The houses lining it are stacked high so that the ocean remains hidden, heard but never seen. The wooden panels of the homes are painted in pastels, one lavender, two blue, one yellow, where Watercolor got its name. All bright and welcoming, with wraparound porches full of plush furniture and large umbrellas and gas grills. The South is full of ghosts, but, perhaps here, they feel they can ward them off with their color-coordinated million-dollar second homes in their monochromatic communities.

Athena wanders down a random street, breathing in the cool air, letting it shock her lungs. The shouts and squalls of children on the backs of their parents' golf carts pass her by every now and then. The ringing of a bike bell echoes from a few streets over. A bass bump from a bad Top 100 song plays from the roof of a nearby house. There is no silence in this place. The ocean forbids it. Something must always be roaring. Here, for better or worse, you are never quite alone.

A pastel pink house lined with barren rosebushes makes Athena stop to study it. Come springtime, the flowers are sure to be a riot of red, their subtle sweetness catching in the wind, intermingling with the salt, heavy air and heat. *Nobody knows this little Rose... Only a Bee will miss it—Only a Butterfly.* Athena searches around for one of them, but there is no rose, no bee, no butterfly. November holds all blossoming and fluttering things at a distance. A shame. Athena could use the company.

Roses always remind her of Jason's funeral. Her father had not wanted one—*Too depressing, when I die, throw a party, but do not, God help y'all, throw a funeral.*

They attempted the party. Mollie filled the house and backyard with red roses, Jason's favorite. They played his favorite songs. But the thing about death is that it touches every corner of every room. Happiness is a gift you give other people, yes, but death is a dreary guest and rarely receives any gifts at all.

So they had their grotesque hybrid party/funeral in the backyard of Athena's parents' house, where she and Sydnee had their wedding. There was Texas beer and wine and a table full of gin and tonics. A group of dark-haired women brought over a bottle of ouzo and placed it gingerly on the end of the table, each clutching the black shawls around their shoulders closer into their chest, as if trying to hide, make themselves smaller.

The Greeks had arrived. Athena had never met her aunts, or, at least, had never remembered meeting them. She had heard stories about them—the rice pudding one burned before their father's birthday one year, the pranks the other used to play on Jason before school, the tender words the oldest would speak to him after he got his heart broken for the first time in the eighth grade, it had always stuck with him, her unironic empathy for a youthful heart, the indulgent listening to his fear that he would never find love again, that thirteen years old was all he was promised, and the rest was a sea of loneliness waiting to swallow him.

Athena didn't know if her father had reached out to his sisters after he married Mollie. Another question left unasked, never to be answered.

One of the sisters broke away from the others and walked toward Athena.

"I'm Georgia," she said with a strong, steady voice as she held out a shaking, liver-spotted hand. "The oldest of us, as I'm sure you can tell."

"You look great," Athena said, a reflex of reassurance.

"I look old." Georgia waved away the comment with a flick of her wrist, the gold bangles on her arm banging against each other. "But I am sorry. For your loss. For…our absence."

Athena couldn't think of anything to say. She was engrossed by this woman, whose eyes were just like her father's, whose nose curved to the left in the same way as her own. It was strange seeing her heritage etched so clearly across a face she had never known.

"Jason was a good boy," she continued, nodding. "Always so sweet. So full of love."

"He was a good father," Athena said. She wanted to prolong the interaction for as long as she could. It was as if some of her father lived on for a moment, in the right light, with the right expression on Georgia's face.

"Your mother looks well." Georgia glances over at Mollie, who kept shooting furtive glances their way. "She didn't expect us."

"It's been a while."

"Family is family, no matter how long an absence lasts."

"He talked about you," Athena said, awkwardly, as if she could heal what had broken between the sisters and her father. "How you always listened to him, how you helped him through tough times."

"The world is always ending when you're young. And Jason's world ended every other day. His heart was big. He gave it away too freely. To those who didn't deserve it."

Georgia again shot a look over at Mollie, her jaw flexing as she clenched her teeth.

*Dying is a wild night and a new road.* Athena went over the line in her mind. Why couldn't this situation shift and start anew? Death paving the way for new life. The years of separation had dragged on for too long. Surely Georgia felt so, too. This could be the new start they had all been hoping for. Athena wasn't ready to let her father go completely, and Georgia and her sisters were part of the genetic thread that tied him to this earth. They had to stick together. To keep his memory alive.

"Maybe we could all—" Athena started.

"It was good to see you, Athena," Georgia said, gently, cutting off her olive branch before it could extend. "I loved your father. May his memory be eternal."

She walked away, swaying slightly as she gathered her sisters and clutched one of their arms for support. They walked away, huddled together in all black, like the Three Fates bound together for eternity, leaving the mortals behind, never giving them a second thought.

Sydnee crept up behind Athena, snaked her hand into hers.

"What cauldron did they come from?" Sydnee asked, pointing at the sisters' backs.

Athena felt laughter rise up in her, ready to burst. But before it could, she choked it down. She set her teeth. She let the joy warp and transform into fury. Athena, unwilling to face her despair and sadness and grief, latched on to this newfound rage with the desperation of someone drowning.

"Read the fucking room," she said, her voice dripping with all the malice she felt in her aunts' gaze as they looked at Mollie. Athena glared at her wife, her beloved partner, and relished the wide-eyed shock her words induced. It felt like power, control, certainty. It took up every inch of space inside of her, this fresh wave of anger. It left no room for tenderness. No room for love.

Perhaps for Emily Dickinson, dying could create a new road. But, for Athena, death only paved dead ends.

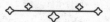

Athena's cheeks burn. She doesn't like to think of how she acted in that first year after Jason died. How she lashed out at Sydnee. Gave her such little ground on which to stand. She slaps her cheeks and buries the memory.

At the far edge of the neighborhood, where the houses end, tall pine trees open up to a boardwalk. A large sign at the opening bans bikes and golf carts. It's for foot traffic only. Athena follows it, letting herself be swallowed by greenery on all sides: wild weeds and seagrass blowing in the breeze,

dense bushes with sharp, protruding branches, and the om-
nipresent pines above her, their needles scattered everywhere.
She slips on a pile of them, but manages to maintain her balance. Instinctually, she checks to make sure no one saw it.
She is alone. Perhaps, in Watercolor, where there can be no
golf carts or bikes, there will be no people.

The boardwalk leads to an enormous lake, the water dark
and still as glass. The overcast sky reflects on it, the clouds
moving above and below, a doubled horizon. On the other
side of the shore, small and distant from where Athena stands,
a forest of pines and greenery extend out, undisturbed by the
near-constant vacation developments that surround the area.
Athena holds her breath, wondering if this is what the world
was like before bulldozers and cranes and capitalism stormed
through and ripped it apart.

A crack behind her. Athena turns sharply to her left. At
the edge of the water, through the woods, a deer emerges.
A doe, with a white-spotted nose. The doe stays still for a
moment. After the area is assessed for danger, it walks slowly
toward the water, dips its head down, drinking in its fill. As
it laps up the water, a small ripple runs from the shore to the
center, sending the lily pads up and down. It's subtle. A little
hiccup in the otherwise still abyss.

The deer moves from the water toward the shore, grazing
on grass, patiently eating, no rush to get its nutrients, there
is no threat here. Athena thinks of all the classmates she'd
known who'd invited her on deer hunting trips throughout
the years. She's grateful, now, watching this beautiful, lithe
creature, that she never took them up on it.

The wind picks up, and Athena folds her arms into her
chest, trying to stave off the chill. As she does, she can almost feel the wide hands of her father, calloused on the inside
of his palms, rough but tender, with his short, square fingers

wrapped around her shoulder, pulling her into him. She remembers burying her face in his chest when he hugged her. He smelled like bar soap and worn leather, sometimes with the faintest hint of tobacco and cherrywood if he'd been smoking a cigar. The scratch of his stubble when he kissed her cheek. The dark, chocolate eyes boring straight into hers when she told a story. The baritone hum that perfectly harmonized with whatever song played over the speakers. The plucking of a Spanish guitar on long winter nights in the backyard by the fire. The clapping together of those great, inviting hands when everyone sat down together at the table, prompting him to happily declare, *This is heaven!*

Memory has no rhyme or reason. There is no logic in ghosts. They all visit on their own time. They don't need an invitation. They own all the keys.

The doe snaps up its head at the sound of a twig breaking. When the footsteps hit the boardwalk, the doe freezes. Athena expects to see Deacon.

It's Katie. Her hair is still damp, not yet done. Daisy will be furious that she's escaped before the glam squad could get to her, and Athena's impressed that she'd risk that rage just to come see her. Athena points to the deer and puts a finger to her lips. Katie walks carefully, slowly, until she gets to Athena.

"Thought you could use this," Katie says, handing Athena a cup. "Tequila soda. Extra lime. Just like you like it. Right?"

"Thanks." Athena takes the drink. The acidity of the lime hits her tongue before the rush of agave and the burn of alcohol, watered down by a miniscule splash of soda water. The tequila catches her throat, sending her into a coughing fit. Her cheeks flush immediately.

"Oh," Katie says, watching Athena's eyes water. "And extra tequila."

"Thanks for the warning," Athena says through coughs.

"I can take that back if you want."

"No, no." Athena drains the rest of her drink. The taste reminds her of grad school in Austin and Sydnee and every memory she never thought she'd want to throw away.

Athena shakes the ice in the cup, needing to do something with her hands. Katie pulls out her phone, opens up the Instagram app, and takes a video of the deer in the distance. When she's done, she captions it, *Nature is healing <3*.

"You know, a moment still exists even if you don't capture it with your camera." Athena chews on a piece of ice. "It's not like a tree in a forest with no one around."

"But my followers deserve the content." Katie posts the story and shrugs. "It's my job."

"To live in a moment and then capture it," Athena says. "Ruthless."

"It's not trapped, it's shared."

"So it's a zoo."

"It's the internet."

"Same thing."

"You look hot." Katie reaches up and runs her hands along the side of Athena's head. It sends chills down the back of her neck. "With the new hair."

Athena checks behind her.

"I'm talking about you," Katie says, softly punching Athena's shoulder.

"Thought you might have been talking to the deer or something. She's looking good today."

"She does have great legs."

"You did a nice job."

"Do you feel lighter now?"

"Physically or metaphysically?"

"Both?"

"Both," Athena says, nodding. She throws her head back

and forth, as if tossing her phantom hair over her shoulders. She's starting to feel the tequila heat up her cheeks and lighten up her mind. "No more past-life weight, or whatever."

"Well, good. You deserve some lightness, you know. After everything you've been through."

"And what do you think I've been through?" Without the booze, this presumption would prickle underneath Athena's skin, an itching irritation. She didn't drink much after the separation because she didn't want to lose her edge. She wanted to feel every slight, to stay cognizant enough to react when necessary. But, now, the tequila numbs the world around her, making everything lighter.

Katie is pretty in the sunlight, which comes strong through the clouds. The light splits across her face, casting half of it in shadow, the other half in gold. The eye in shadow seems a light brown, while the sun makes the other come alive with color, honey flecked with green, full of depth. Athena notices the laugh lines around her eyes, the slight curvature of her nose, hooking to the left, and her right eyebrow, which is raised slightly higher than its pair. There is beauty in the asymmetry. Even the background highlights her attractiveness. The water, unmoving and dark, a mirror to the sky. The doe grazing in the forest. The warm weather violets wilt and sink into the greenery behind them, discards from a season long gone, adding an unexpected pop of color, a final gift in their death.

"You've been through plenty. Divorce, death." Katie lists them off on her fingers. "Adjuncting."

"Forced to be a bridesmaid in another straight wedding," Athena says, pulling Katie's hand close to hers, lifting up another one of Katie's fingers, making sure she counts it.

"Takes some guts," Katie says and clasps her hand in Athena's. They hold hands for a moment. Hers are soft and small and uncalloused, well manicured. A spark of connection shoots through their fingers. Athena lets go, her head hanging down, not sure what to make of feelings for someone who isn't Sydnee. It'd been years since she had a crush. Even then, when she had them, she became clumsy and awkward and unsure. The discomfort was familiar and not unwelcome. Athena never thought she'd feel the tug of attraction again. It is good to know that she is not completely wrecked, that some parts of her are healing.

Katie and Athena stand shoulder to shoulder on the boardwalk, saying nothing, gazing out at the water. The clouds are clearing up, blue peeking through the grayscale sky. The silence between them is comfortable.

"You know," Katie addresses Athena. "I am more than the moments I capture."

"Aren't we all?"

"I mean," Katie says, bumping her shoulder into Athena's. "Don't count me out just yet."

Athena continues staring out at the still water. She inhales the salt air. She can't see the ocean, but it's everywhere. She exhales and considers this. What would it cost her, really? To let in someone new?

"What would you say," Athena asks, "to more tequila?"

"We'll need it when Daisy sees you again." Katie takes Athena's arm and presses her palms into it. "And remembers your haircut wasn't a stress dream."

They walk back to the house, bumping shoulders and brushing hands as they go. Athena sneaks glances at Katie, her calm expression ever steady and never changing. Was it a facade? Or had all her yoga classes taught her something true about inner peace?

Back at the house, Daisy brushes off their apologies and leads them each to a chair to get their hair and makeup done. She silently seethes, clearly on edge, as she gestures to the clock in the kitchen: 1 p.m. Pictures are in two hours. They are cutting it close.

Before she gets to the chair, Mollie pulls Athena aside.

"You really pissed off Daisy." Mollie runs her hands through Athena's hair. "But this is great."

"You like it?" Athena asks, delighted. She never tired of any moment where she could gain her mother's approval.

"Love it." Mollie holds her by the shoulders and evaluates her, glancing up and down. "You finally butched it up!"

"I feel like that's offensive?"

"It's a fact!" Mollie says. She cocks her head to the side as she studies Athena, inhaling with a hesitancy that suggests she has something to tell her. Something Athena won't like.

"What is it, Mom?" Athena asks. "Is it Leo? Did he do something weird?"

"No, no, your brother is fine." Mollie lets out a shaky laugh. "It's just, when I was in town—"

"Athena, goddammit!" Daisy shouts from across the room. "Get your ass in that chair!"

"Go, go, go." Mollie shoves her forward, and steers clear of Daisy's path as she heads toward the door. "Gonna get myself ready. I'll see you at the ceremony! Don't trip!"

Athena waves to her mother, wondering what she had to say, but knowing there is no time to find out now. She settles into the chair next to Katie, letting the hair and makeup artist size them both up. They take more time with Athena than they do Katie, indicating a blemish here, a stray hair there. If Daisy has her way, there will be no pore in sight, no baby hairs out of place. It's a show, after all, a wedding ceremony. The stage is set, and now it's time for the costumes to come on.

It's not so bad, Athena thinks as she searches for a natural palette in the makeup stylist's lookbook, putting in the effort to separate this day from any other. It makes it special. She's hard on Daisy for her perfectionism and unyielding desire to execute her vision to a T, but, like the backstage of any play, there's an energy in the air, a buzz before everything begins. It marks the moment, the final hours before Daisy begins the rest of her life.

Athena watches Daisy bustle around the kitchen, sipping a mimosa through a straw, waving her hands frantically as she talks with her mother, gesturing to her still unstyled hair. Her frustrated face is the same as it's been for as long as Athena has known her. Scrunched up nose, wide, wild eyes, mouth opening and closing as she holds herself back, damming up the rant that rests on the tip of her tongue. It's the same face Athena saw the time the box office worker wouldn't give them tickets to an R-rated movie because he didn't believe Daisy was actually seventeen, and the time Athena wouldn't give Daisy her chemistry homework to cheat off of ten minutes before class started in high school, and the time the boy who took her to prom showed up in a crush velvet tux even though she had specifically requested that he refrain from doing so.

*My friends are my "estate." Forgive me then the avarice to hoard them!* Another commonality Athena found with Dickinson. She held her friends close. When they slipped away, it devastated her. Those years without Daisy had been hard. She never admitted it to anyone. Not even Deacon. There was a vacuum. Anytime she heard a piece of gossip about one of their high school classmates, Athena had to crush the instinct to text Daisy. She lost access to their shared memory bank. She worried it would remain vacant forever. It seemed, in those years she was gone, that she'd lost her to a religion and the men who controlled it. Though she resisted her return with coldness—she could not control her need to punish for the pain that was caused, and she made little effort to control that childish instinct—she was glad to have her back. In time, after she started to trust Daisy again, Athena understood the pain she had endured, and the resilience it took to break free from the world she was almost lost to. It was in that moment, when her ire made way for empathy, that she was able to fully forgive Daisy.

As she swivels in her chair away from Daisy, Athena acknowledges, for the first time, the honor of being asked to be here by Daisy's side. To see her off as she embarks on this next great adventure. Athena lets the gratitude flow through her, thaw those stubborn parts of her that want to make this all about her and her misery. It's not a transformation, but it is an invitation: to enjoy this moment for what it is instead of rushing it along.

A hairstylist draws her hands through Athena's new cut. Before, Athena's thick hair would take thirty minutes to blow-dry, a never-ending, agonizing process that often left her hair frizzier than when it started. Now, the styling is, for the first time in her life, easy.

"I'm gonna change your life today," the hairdresser says, bringing out four bottles of product. "You will live and die by these."

First, and most important, the wide-tooth comb, which she uses to brush her hair straight back. Then, the pommade, the oil, the volume enhancing mist and the hair spray, in that order, all worked into her hair in quick succession. She combs it back once more, finding the part on the left side of Athena's head. She gives it a quick blow-dry.

"All done," she says, handing Athena a mirror.

Her dark hair is tall and artfully wild, staying in place no matter how hard she shakes her head to the side. She runs her hands through it, and they get caught up in all the product and hair spray. It looks good, though. Like she was meant for it all along.

"See, I didn't do so bad, after all," Katie says, giving Athena's hair a sidelong glance.

A makeup artist starts spraying foundation on Athena's face. She sits still, unable to talk much, and allows Katie to take the lead in their conversation.

As she sits, immobile, her face painted by a stranger with even stranger products, Athena remembers what it's like to listen, to ask questions, to learn about a person from scratch. Katie was born in Shreveport, but moved to Houston when she was six, beginning kindergarten with no friends and a curious mind, shy but brave enough to reach out, to ask the person next to her in class if they wanted to play. They did. From that moment on, she had the sibling she'd always wanted—she was an only child—and she and her best friend were still close. They survived middle school, where their hormones went haywire, and they fought about boys and grades and bras every other week. They mellowed out in high school, staying close, always hanging out together, so much so that more than a few people thought they were secretly dating. The rumors flattered them, but the love remained platonic and true, romantic in the way that all great friendships can be: a place where two people can come together as their full selves, serious and silly in equal measure, and be accepted without a second thought.

Katie also went to UT, but she hadn't known Athena or Deacon or Sydnee. She hardly knew anyone, since she spent most of her undergraduate career driving back and forth from Austin to Houston, taking her mother to MD Anderson for her chemo treatments. Breast cancer. Stage three. Aggressive. Curable. But not for her mother. It spread too fast. She died during Katie's senior year.

"If I'd been married then," Katie says, focusing her eyes

straight ahead, "I probably would have driven my partner away, too."

"I didn't drive Sydnee away," Athena says, defensive. "She chose to cheat."

"Well," Katie says. "You're a better woman than I was in grief."

Her mother's death began a dark and troubled time in Katie's life. With one semester left, she dropped out of UT. She moved back to Houston for her father. She didn't want him to be alone. She spent her days in the house, while her father went to work. They ate takeout for dinner. They talked very little. They watched sports and late-night shows, then went to bed with few words said between the two of them. Katie passed the time in bed or on the couch, her eyes glued to various screens. She was numb. The memories blur together. All she remembers is a consistent, unyielding buzz in her brain, a white noise that never faded and muted everything around her. She was walking through the world without gravity. It took a long time for her feet to touch the ground.

Then, her best friend started taking her to weekly yoga classes. She hated it at first and skipped them half the time. But after a few months, she felt herself expanding with every breath, the intentional inhales allowing her space to fill her lungs and catch her breath. She started going every day, even without her best friend. After a year, she got certified as an instructor. She created her Instagram page. She gained an enormous following. She focused on grief and yoga, how healing could come through movement, how the teachings of Eastern philosophy gave her the freedom to move through every wave of grief. The natural cycle of pain that mimicked every cycle of the natural world. An ebb and a flow, a push and a pull, balance and imbalance, inhales and exhales.

"The pain doesn't stop," Katie says, as if reading Athena's mind. "But it does ache less often with time."

It occurs to Athena that Katie doesn't have a crush on her—or, if she does, that's not the sole reason for her interest. Grief is a lonely plane of existence. It rules with a cruel, cold fist, clenching everything around you, cutting off your oxygen, and all other sources of life. The grip loosens a little when you talk with someone else also in its hold. Athena feels it in herself. That pain which she felt she could only share with Dickinson, alone in her office, with the dim, fluorescent lights, she now wants to share with someone else, a living and breathing someone else, who can respond in real time instead of cryptic, beautiful, maddening lines.

"I hear my dad in the ocean," Athena says, her eyes still closed after the makeup artist finishes airbrushing her face.

"What does he say?"

"Find the sea. You're built from the sea."

"My mom talks to me through birds," Katie says. "Chirps and songs and melodies."

"They never leave us."

"Or we never leave them," Katie says.

"Stay still, girls," the makeup artist instructs them as she reaches for the lip liner.

They lapse into silence. Keeping the company of their ghosts.

# SYDNEE

They spend their day in luxury. Alex took her polar plunge in the morning, and, far from hypothermic shock, found the Gulf's water to be an even-keeled cool, nothing like the Atlantic she'd spent so many summers dipping into off the coast of South Carolina. After, they had brunch and Bloody Marys in town, feasting on buttermilk biscuits and gravy, bacon, eggs, and a steaming plate of cheesy grits, with a side of home fries for good measure. Alex made friends with the waiter who told her about a gallery just off the main road, where young Southern artists displayed their work. They spent an hour and a half there, taking in the different mediums. Alex discovered a particularly moving mixed-media piece from an artist in Birmingham, and, wouldn't luck have it, the very artist was in that day. They chatted for, what Sydnee felt, was a little too long. By the time they finished, Alex had two enormous canvases underneath her arms, and it was already time to go back to the hotel and get ready for the wedding.

"Think I need a drink before this," Alex says after lint rolling the sleeve of her navy blue blazer. "Shots? Beach club bar?"

"Tequila?" Sydnee asks. It's the only liquor she can stand.

"Always."

"Then you got yourself a deal."

The beach club bar is relatively empty, except for a handful of beleaguered-looking parents who have left their children to fend for themselves in the resort pool.

"Guess that's what lifeguards are for?" Sydnee asks as one of the parents slams back a double whiskey.

"Sydnee?" Someone asks behind her.

It's Leo. In a suit. His hair is parted down the middle so that his bangs drape on either side of his forehead. He pushes them out of his face. He's tan as ever, his green eyes downcast as he rubs the back of his neck, clutching a twenty-dollar bill in his other fist. He seems awkward and unsure. The feeling is mutual.

Sydnee hasn't seen him since last Christmas, and even then, the visit had been brief. He didn't stay in Houston long. He said he liked LA during the holidays. The tips were better, the gym was emptier, and he didn't have to stare into the grim and gaunt faces of his mother and sister, the grief still clinging on to them, holding them tightly, never letting them go, even three years later. Sydnee always thought Leo ran from his own grief, but maybe he ran from the bereaved, their pain and stagnation too much for him to handle. Or maybe he worried it would spread to him, locking his knees and putting his ambition on hold. Sydnee couldn't blame him if this were the case. She'd felt that heaviness. In her last year with Athena, their home felt encased in molasses. Every movement was slow, every conversation full of long pauses between sentences. It can suffocate you, all that stillness. Sydnee had almost forgotten what it was like to breathe freely.

"Mom dragged me on her date," Leo explains, still standing behind Sydnee and Alex. He does not look at Alex and barely makes eye contact with Sydnee. Alex has her head down, twisting the empty shot glass in her fingers. Sydnee resists the urge to reach out her hand and reassure her. There is no reassurance here. Leo would not take kindly to an introduction. He flags down the bartender and orders a shot of tequila. He sips it, always careful with booze around Mollie, never letting himself get out of control. "Blindsided me. No warning. She's just as bad as Athena when she flirts."

"Athena's flirting?" Sydnee asks, surprised. From everything she'd heard from Deacon and Daisy, Athena had taken up her mourning protocol after the separation, locking herself away in her office with Emily Dickinson, only coming out to socialize when she was forced by Mollie or Deacon and Daisy.

"But Mom's worse because she won't admit that she likes this dude. Just calls him her *new friend*."

"Well, good for Mollie," Sydnee says. "She deserves to be happy."

"Just wish she wouldn't discover her happiness while she insists on gluing me to her side."

"I see." Sydnee can't stop herself from squeezing his shoulder. Old habit. "It's still all about Daisy for you, huh?"

"It's not like I'm a liability." Leo finally shoots back the rest of his shot and flags down the bartender, sees their empty shot glasses, and orders three more for all of them. "I had a crush, like, three years ago, we dated for, like, two seconds, and then I moved to Los Angeles and that was that."

"But the Christmas party," Sydnee says. She and Athena had charged themselves with calling Leo out on his bullshit whenever possible. That much handsome needed a firm branch of accountability to hold his ego in check. "When you had too many whiskey sours. Then switched to eggnog. And you—"

"No need to dreg up the past, Syd." Leo pulls out cash to pay for the drinks as soon as they come over. He passes each shot around. They down them. "These are on Mollie, by the way. She always gives me cash when I see her. Worried about me."

"We all are, Leo, always." Sydnee pinches his cheek. "Our baby boy all the way out West."

"Yeah, yeah." He slaps her hand away, smiling, but still not quite looking at her. A pang in Sydnee's chest. This used to be so easy. She doesn't know what she expected. She'd made her decisions. The time to come to terms with that had passed Sydnee by without her realizing it. She'd been too busy—with work, with Alex, with anything that kept her moving forward—to realize how drastically the divorce would shift her life.

Leo sees Mollie walking out with her *new friend*, giving him a hug before he leaves the club. "Shit. She's gonna forget about me if I don't grab her. Good to see you, Syd, and you." He gives Alex a curt nod before rushing back to his mother, taking her arm in his, and guiding her toward the boardwalk.

"Good kid," Sydnee says, watching them walk down the path, each talking animatedly with their hands.

"Do you miss them?" Alex asks, her eyes flickering from Sydnee to Leo and Mollie.

"Define *miss*."

"Don't get cute."

"I mean it," Sydnee says. "Do I miss the family of it all? Sure. You know mine's all weird and closed off."

"Do you miss them?" Alex repeats. On her nose, there's a little blot of sunscreen that needs to be rubbed in. Sydnee reaches up to do it for her, but Alex swats her hand away. "I don't need you to comfort me."

"I wasn't, I—"

"I just want you to be honest with me." Alex ties her hair back into a low ponytail. Another patch of sunscreen is visible on the nape of her neck. Sydnee resists reaching out this time. "And yourself."

Sydnee thinks about it. She'd known Athena for a decade.

So much had changed in that time. Her life was different when she first met Athena. Back then, the highlight of her week was Mondays, when she would buy tickets for the Powerball draw, and in the few hours before the numbers were announced, she spent her time daydreaming what she would do with all that money. Buy a house in the Heights for herself, a house for her parents back in Brownsville. Fly first class. Rent a Tuscan villa. Save for retirement. Retire outright. Pay off her student loans. Pay off her friends' student loans. Go to doctor's appointments without calculating how much her health would cost her when she got to the receptionist's desk. Get her cavities filled. Fill her pantry. Fulfill a thousand frivolous whims. Start a foundation. Make a difference. Be somebody. As the minutes ticked down until the draw, she'd hold her breath, allowing herself to hope. She'd wonder, every time: Is *this* the American Dream?

She never won. Eventually, Athena made her stop wasting money on tickets. Then, she got a job of her own that paid more money than she could have ever imagined. That kind of financial security was its own kind of lottery. She let the tickets go, and all the dreams that came with it.

That was too far back, though, before Athena's family came into the picture. She'd thought, at first, that Athena had been exaggerating at how close she was with her family. That was the sort of thing you saw on sitcoms, not in real life. For Sydnee, family was silence and dysfunction, everything staying above the surface. There might be an iceberg underneath the water, but they would never talk about that.

Her family, from Mexico and staunchly Catholic, did not approve of her dating women. While she was not cut off in the same way that Jason was, she worked hard to ensure she was financially independent from her family and their narrow views of love. Money can make people do desperate things, and she was not willing to compromise any part of her life in order to gain assistance from her parents. Sydnee worked mornings at Shipley Do-nuts and nights as a bartender and days as a teacher's assistant to make it through college and, eventually, law school.

When she finally met her family, Sydnee understood that Athena wasn't lying. Their family was close. Jason had stitched them together so tightly with his unwavering devotion that they never needed more family. When Sydnee came along, they welcomed her into the fold, making room for her in every tradition, every holiday. Everyone loved Sydnee, but especially Jason, who couldn't stand to see anyone shut out from a family, as he'd been shut out from his.

*I know what it is to lose family in the name of love,* Jason told Sydnee after the fourth or fifth time they'd met. *You're one of us now.*

And so she became. She now had two families, and, whenever she was with them, felt something she'd always yearned for, but never knew how to find.

But that was before. Now, Jason is dead. Athena hasn't spoken with her in eight months. Leo could barely look at her, not in the way he used to, nor could Mollie when she saw her earlier. It isn't her family anymore. They aren't the same. She'd broken the trust they built for years. Her cheeks flood with heat, a shame trickling through her for the first time. She sets her jaw and bites the inside of her cheeks, grounding herself in the pain, not letting herself succumb to regret.

"I don't miss them," Sydnee says.

"This was a bad idea." Alex gets up from the bar, pulling out her phone.

"What?" Sydnee asks, confused.

"The wedding, my coming." Alex types quickly on her phone before nodding. "Yeah, I'm not going to that wedding."

"Alex, come on. I had to talk to him. He came over! He was my brother for, like, a decade."

"That's great. You didn't do anything wrong."

"So now we're just not going to the wedding?"

"I think you should go. Alone." Alex shifts in her seat, rubbing her eye with a vigor that suggests her frustration with the situation has been simmering all day and finally been given permission to be released. "They're your people."

"They're not…"

But this time, Sydnee cannot deny it. They *are* her people. Had been for almost a decade. She loved her own family, but they had set their severe limitations on her life. They would always see her, always welcome her home, but only if she were alone. Athena and Deacon and Daisy and Leo and Mollie and, of course, more than any of them, Jason, they had been her family. They helped fill in all the gaps left by her own kin. With them, her world had felt, for the first time, complete.

Her hesitancy is all the answer Alex needs. She walks out toward the street, Sydnee close behind her. Desperate to change her mind.

"Got myself a table at a fancy restaurant in Rosemary Beach." Alex shows Sydnee the menu. "They have lamb lollipops and a rooftop. I'll be fine."

"But you're my date." Sydnee isn't sure what to make of this pivot, if it will cost her later.

"Going to a wedding with your ex and your best friends and everyone's families?" Alex calls an Uber. "You hear how ridiculous that sounds, right? This was a mistake. I didn't think it through."

"We're supposed to go through all the chaos together. That's what a relationship is, right?"

"Well," Alex says slowly, looking down the street for her car. "Maybe this is a sign. For us to slow down."

"It's been almost a year."

"And you were married for about four months of that." Alex flags down her car. "Just think about it. Opening up the relationship. Making it more casual. Could be good for us, don't you think?"

"Well, I know that's what you think."

"Sydnee, you don't know what you want."

"You can't tell me what I want."

"True," Alex says. She squats down to check the car's license plate, making sure it's hers. "For Alex?" she asks when the driver pokes his head out of the window. "Have fun. I'll see you afterward." She kisses Sydnee on the cheek, then dips into the car.

"That your sister?" Sydnee hears the driver ask before they drive away. She looks around her, as if some stranger passing by could give her a sign, tell her what to do. No one pays her any attention. She's on her own.

It's thirty minutes until the ceremony starts. She closes her eyes and sets her resolve. Going alone feels vulnerable and frightening. Alex offered her some protection, an assurance that people wouldn't come up to her and bombard her with questions about the divorce, about the rumors, if it was true that she had really had an affair. With enough booze, every person in there can become Barbara Walters, coming at her with hard-hitting questions, leaving tact behind until they get the answers they want. She craves a simplicity that will not be granted to her this evening. She braces herself for the impact of that.

If she hadn't left Athena, this weekend would have been different. She'd have been in the wedding, spending the day inside the town house with Daisy and Athena and the rest of the bridal party. She'd have all the freedom to talk with Deacon and Daisy and whomever else she wanted to, because her presence would elicit no more attention than anyone else in the room. She would be engulfed by the warmth of close friends and family coming together to celebrate, to revel in the joy of marriage, the commitment of it, the seriousness of it, the fun of it.

Instead, she is alone. Not even Alex stuck around. No sympathy waits for her, she knows this. She's always known it. How had she let her life become surrounded by all of Athena's people? Deacon and Daisy were still her friends, but there was a wall there between them that had not been there before. After Sydnee left Athena, she talked with Daisy about it, how trapped she felt by her marriage, how everyone she loved was interlocked with the one person she was trying to leave. Athena had become someone else, someone meaner and angrier and darker than before.

Daisy had held her hand, listened to her vent, and said, as kindly as she could, "All of those feelings are valid. And we still love you. You're still our friend. But, Sydnee, why did you have to cheat?"

Sydnee sucks her teeth and pulls out her phone. She wasn't ready to answer the question then, and she's certainly not ready to answer it now. She pulls up the walking directions to the ceremony. She follows the route. She hopes she makes it in time.

She arrives at the ceremony a few minutes before it starts. A plywood aisle runs from the boardwalk, over the sand, to the ornate chuppah waiting at the end. It's covered in green vines—jasmine, the little white flowers blooming out of season, a miracle—with a billowing sheet on top of it. Almost all the seats are filled. She slides into the back row, in the far corner, waiting for the ceremony to begin.

A string quartet plays. The groomsmen walk down the aisle after Daniel's grandmother, the sole grandparent, makes her way to the front row. The men take their places in a line outside of the chuppah, on the left side of the aisle, a reversal from the Christian tradition Sydnee had become accustomed to. Daisy will like that, Sydnee thinks, the separation from her life before, a concrete way to begin again.

Daniel walks down the aisle with his parents on both of his arms. His mother on the left, his father on the right. He leads them underneath the chuppah, greets the rabbi up front, shaking her hand. Daniel watches the bridesmaids walk down. Daniel smiles at them all, patiently awaiting the arrival of his beloved bride.

Athena comes next. She doesn't see Sydnee, so her smile does not falter, her head stays held high. It had been months since she'd seen Athena in person. She forgot the details of her: the reluctant smile, the almond-shaped eyes, the way her hips sway to the side whenever she walks, no trace of grace in any step, but a wonderful sight to behold all the same. From the line of groomsmen, Deacon gives her a thumbs-up and a wink. That, more than anything, makes Sydnee's heart burst: with love, with regret, with longing for the world before.

They had been doing better. She and Athena. The end of the tunnel seemed to show flashes of light. Sydnee believed the healing had come at last. She welcomed it. She was ready to move forward. To learn how to live with Jason's absence together, to forge a path out of grief and into the next stage of their lives. Athena had started her book proposal, part literary criticism, part memoir. The work invigorated her. Sydnee thought, at last, that she was getting her wife back from a long, dark hibernation.

Then, the rejections started coming. It was, even to Sydnee, an avalanche of noes. They had been form rejections, and easier to stomach, until the final one arrived. The editors at the press she had been most hoping to work with had added a small note of explanation to their rejection. Sydnee still remembers it word for word.

"Death and Dickinson," it seems to us, is an unimaginative, and frankly, infertile ground of inquiry to pursue, as it has been examined so exhaustively throughout the years. Though we commend your use of personal narrative to propel this investigation along, stories of grief, like "Death and Dickinson," are so ubiquitous it cannot be said to be remarkable enough to take the chance on this hybrid work. Thank you for considering us. Happy writing!

It was like a relapse. Athena retreated once more. The spark that had revived her was extinguished. She shut off from everyone again. She didn't want to talk about the rejections. She didn't even want to talk about Dickinson. She did not want to be touched, she did not want to be held, she did not want to be acknowledged in any way. Sydnee was, once more, alone.

She tried to stay strong. To be a good partner. But she missed sex. It was more than just getting off. Sydnee never thought that would be the case. Especially for her and Athena, who, for the first few months of dating, couldn't get enough of each other. Even after the frequency of their need died down with the years, there was still an intensity when they came together, a connectedness that made Sydnee feel grounded in Athena. The eye contact, the closeness, the wordless communication.

When that stopped, Sydnee felt cut off from Athena. Her heart couldn't remember what had linked them in the first place. She came home to a silent house, she left a silent house. The woman she'd married became a ghost, relegated to dark rooms and white noise. Sydnee needed more substance in her life. And Alex was there, waiting for her to come.

Sydnee started talking to Alex more after she got back from visiting her family in Brownsville, that last Christmas before everything fell apart. Athena said it didn't bother her that she couldn't join, that she'd spend whatever time Sydnee was away working on research and cleaning the house and hanging out with her parents. So she went to Mass, and she helped her dad and grandmother make *pozole rojo* in the kitchen, and she sat down on the couch with her uncles and aunts and cousins and watched the Cowboys play on Sundays before driving back to Houston, where Athena would simply ask, "How were things?"

Alex was different.

"That's so fucked up," Alex said, the Monday after Sydnee got back from Brownsville. She'd explained the strange dynamic between her wife and her family. "Why doesn't Athena care?"

It was simple, strategic and wildly effective. After Alex voiced the question, Sydnee couldn't get it out of her head. Why didn't Athena care? How had she never cared? In the years of knowing Sydnee, Athena had never once expressed a desire to get to know her family. She forgot Spanish almost as soon as she graduated with her PhD. She suggested that Sydnee spend holidays with her family, away from Athena. She was supportive, but it was almost too much. It was kind and understanding and it infuriated Sydnee. She wanted Athena to care. To recognize that this scenario was fucked up. She wanted someone else to step in for her, use their voice where she felt muted by expectation and an inability to explain what was considered inconceivable.

Alex was not the answer. But she was a way out. It wasn't right. It was cruel, even, Sydnee knew. But it was the choice she made, over and over again, a habitual betrayal that sanded down the vows she'd promised to keep until the end of time.

The rebounded grief after the rejections led to their marriage's disintegration. It happened even before Sydnee met Alex, and then increasingly so afterward. Sydnee hadn't realized she was doing it, all the little things that broke down their connection. She stopped listening when Athena talked about her day. Sydnee asked, because you're supposed to, she's not rude, never rude, but she tuned out as soon as she heard the first long-winded *Well, it started out like crap...* She filled in the blanks because she'd heard the story before: it started out like crap because the coffee filter broke in the lounge of the English department. Coffee at home wasn't an option because, if you'll recall, we still haven't gone to get grounds at the specialty store we like because taking one step inside hits both of us with a wave of sawdust and mulch that make us remember Jason in a way neither of us can quite process while going on an errand, which, by definition, should entail every numb, mundane, boring task, evoking little to nothing within either of us. We could go to H-E-B and get coffee from there, but every time we're out, we both forget. So the house remains without coffee, and now the workplace does, too. She went on. Sydnee checked her watch, lamenting that this was not the end of the story, that the misery had somehow found a way to extend beyond the caffeine crisis and into the minute world of Emily Dickinson's envelope poems. Another name scratched out by Mabel Loomis Todd, another railing rant against the homophobia of the early nineteeth century (which, like, *duh*, Sydnee wanted to say, exasperated at having to hear one more well-made point articulated, verbatim, for the thousandth time, robbing it of all marvel and meaning). Sydnee knew that if she hadn't known this woman for a decade, she would find her the most fascinating person in the world. But now, because of time, she'd become redundant. Old news. Sydnee hated that phrase, even more so associated with *her*. She could not stop associating that phrase with her.

Sydnee got so well practiced in filling in the blanks, she stopped knowing what the answers were. She lost the nuance, the little lines of hope Athena would throw into conversation, not quite willing to draw the attention to it herself. A pre-tenure review meeting that went well. An article accepted for peer review. A new line found from Dickinson that contained the word *split*. By the time Sydnee tuned in for long enough to hear something good, Athena had already clammed back up, unwilling to expand where she would not be received.

But at the wedding, as she sits in the audience, the golden hour lighting up everything about her ex-wife that had always been beautiful, she remembers the late nights spent on their couch, cuddled under the quilt Athena kept in every house she'd ever lived in, white and blue and hand stitched, it looked like a Greek flag transformed into a checkerboard. It was from one of her grandparents—Sydnee always assumed on Jason's side because of the colors, but she'd never actually asked. Underneath it, they'd watch movies and discuss them afterward, getting into heated debates about plot holes and structure and cinematography while drinking whiskey on ice and taking bites from a cherry dark chocolate bar.

The little, silent intimacies woven into their body language over time. Hands held in the car and walking down the street, shoulders bumping as they moved. Athena tracing Sydnee's arm and collarbone when they were alone, absentminded but still tender. Coming home after a long day of work to the smell of sautéed garlic and onions, a white wine chilling in the fridge, and Athena greeting her with that wide smile, which she saw so rarely in those last three years. It was a gift, the joy of your beloved. Sydnee had taken it for granted.

The crowd rises, and Sydnee tries to logic away the longing. They are at a wedding. The divorce papers are final-
ized. They never had closure. They will never get closure.
The list goes on.

Instead of Canon in D, the string quartet shifts to an indie-
pop song. Sydnee recognizes it as the one song that lands on
every single one of Daisy's playlists. It is the greatest summa-
tion of who Daisy has become in these past few years: someone who prioritizes meaning over tradition, who puts her
desires over that set out by any institution. As Daisy moves
onto the aisle from the boardwalk, the crowd shifts, gasps,
reacts. Sydnee cranes her neck, trying to get a good look as
Daisy steps into the golden light of the setting sun.

# LEO

Leo should have known Mollie had a plan. She never drank before big events. Pregaming, she always said, was a vile ritual invented by college students who weren't old enough to show up to a bar and buy their own drinks. Her distaste for it may have had something to do with a UT parents weekend, when Leo, having come home from a wrap party at three in the morning the night before, stopped by a Tri-Delt tailgate on the way to lunch with Mollie and Jason. He needed a hair of the dog, and his co-lead in the play had told him to stop by the tent if he had a moment. Their showmance had finally commenced at the party, where they sat in a corner, making out for the better half of the night. They were both too drunk to do anything else. It was the gentlemanly thing to do the next morning, stopping by her tent, and if that came with one, two, three beers…?

It had come with six beers, causing Leo to stumble down the road toward lunch, thirty minutes late. Jason ordered him an espresso, and Mollie spent the entire meal chastising him about knowing his limits and respecting them accordingly.

"Leo, son, you've got to learn to hold your booze, especially in front of your mother," Jason said. He fished a loose Advil out of his back pocket. "Take this and sleep it off."

It was easy for Jason to say. He was built like a middle line-backer, always steady no matter how many beers he'd had. Leo had been, at the time, scrawnier, shorter and an extreme lightweight. His father could never understand how a few drinks could get on top of Leo.

"More mass, less drunk," Leo would tell Jason, patting his stomach, whenever he brought this up.

"Less mass," Jason would fire back, poking Leo's chest. "Fewer drinks. How about that for an equation?"

It was sound advice, but, being in college and harboring an unending desire to prove his father wrong, Leo continued to pregame, especially before meeting up with his parents, which prompted Mollie to establish strict rules for the family. No drinking before events, especially if that event is going to have drinking at it. No preparty gin and tonics for Jason, no Karbaches for Athena, no, well, anything for Leo. Even after he graduated and stopped spending his weekends drinking all night, his mother still upheld the rule, figuring that, as soon as it was dropped, Leo would take advantage of it.

But now, before Daisy's wedding, an event guaranteed to have bottomless booze, Mollie readily accepts a martini at the beach bar from her *new friend*, a tall, handsome man with an easy smile who touches Mollie's arm too much for Leo's lik-ing, and Leo understands that he is the plan, this covert date, as good a reason as any for Mollie to drink before an event, and not care if Leo does, too.

The man is nice to Leo, introducing himself as *Eli*, but Leo knows when a third wheel needs to cut loose, and, luckily for him, he sees Sydnee at the bar, with *her*. He doesn't even care. He'll give his mother ten minutes of flirtation and imbibing. As he leaves, he hears his mother say, in an alarmingly sul-try voice, unlike any he's ever heard her use before, "So you probably have a lot of practice picking up women in bars."

He practically runs away, praying for the first time in years to let him hear nothing more. He joins Sydnee at the bar, happy to see his ex-sister-in-law, even if she's with *her*. Leo talks without thinking, doing his best to maintain casual conversation, not wanting to learn too much about Alex, what she thinks about this wedding, or her drink, or anything else in the world. He fights the urge to take Sydnee by the shoulders and shake her. She had love with Athena, even if it had seemed lost. They could have found it again, if she'd just stuck it out through the storm, made it to the other side. Some people didn't get their shot at love. This wedding is a constant reminder of that. But he says none of this, speaking about nothing of consequence and focusing on himself, leaving when he spots Mollie saying goodbye to *Eli*, picking up her purse and heading to the exit, too, like she forgets that Leo is with her. She denies this when Leo catches up, but he knows better.

Mollie makes sure they get to the ceremony thirty minutes early. Leo suspects this has something to do with wanting to save a seat for her new man friend. He doesn't bring it up. He wants her to go for it, if that's what feels right. She gets skittish if she feels pressured to do something, especially by her children. Leo lets it lie. Why shouldn't she have a little fun?

Sydnee is right. Mollie does deserve this. After all the grief and all the distance, it will be nice for her to have someone close.

It was strange, Leo thinks once more, to see Sydnee with that woman. He'd been polite, a great actor, he marveled at himself. But her face infuriated him. The protective instinct of any sibling kicked in as soon as he saw her touch Sydnee's arm, trying to get her attention, trying to move her away from him.

He faces Mollie, about to tell her about Sydnee, but she's

craning her neck toward the boardwalk. Her hair is pinned up in a loose knot at the base of her neck, bobbing back and forth as she pivots her head, and she's wearing more makeup than she's worn since Jason's funeral. This *new friend* has already made an impact. Leo shakes his head, proud of his mother's ability to pick herself up and move on. He could learn a thing or two from her.

The early arrival leaves too much time to kill. It leaves Leo antsy, but time is what he needs. He thought it all through. Nothing fancy, don't draw attention. Keep it simple. Maybe he should have done it earlier back at the house, asked Deacon to wait outside, while he told Daisy to run away with him back to Los Angeles. He checks his father's watch. Was there still time for that kind of gesture? Could he be brave enough to try it?

"You're very handsome," Mollie says, noticing his bouncing knee as he sits hunched, staring ahead. Her tone is so humiliatingly mom-like it completely erodes the compliment. "And, you know, there are a lot of nice girls here for you to—"

"Mom, you're making it worse."

"How am I making it worse by making you feel better. Leo, what you have to understand…"

His mother talks. That's how she gets when she worries. Nonstop warnings, stream of consciousness. It had only stopped once, briefly, the year after Jason died. None of them were up for talking much. They had silent dinners in the living room that used to come alive with life, Sydnee and Jason arguing about some detail in the local paper, Athena making fun of Leo, Leo dishing it back, Mollie trying to keep the lid on all of them, reminding them to be kind to one another, to listen, to watch the volume of their voices.

The night before Leo left for Los Angeles, they had one of those quiet dinners at Mollie's house. Leo had been staying there for the past week, his lease up in Houston, his new one waiting for him in California. It was six months after Jason died. They were all still unsure how to be a family without him. Sydnee attempted to make conversation. She made jokes, and Athena shot her hardened looks, and Leo understood then what Athena should have known all along: that she was strangulating the joy out of their relationship, leaving little room for it to breathe. Being around it was claustrophobic and unendurable.

He called Daisy. She picked him up. They drove to H-E-B and got pints of Blue Bell ice cream, then parked in the driveway of Mollie's house and talked, eating straight out of the pints with their plastic spoons.

"Do you have to go to Los Angeles?" she asked. Her voice was steady, but a film of tears coated her eyes.

"Do you want me to stay?" Leo watched her closely. He held out his hand. She took it for a moment, running her fingers along his, tracing the tips of his fingers, where the cuticles were raw and gnawed. She pulled her hand back and dipped into her pint, taking a too big bite of ice cream, buying herself time.

"Yes," Daisy finally said. "That's selfish of me, I know. But I want you to stay. With me. For us."

He hadn't expected that. He leaned away from Daisy, reclining in the passenger's seat, sucking on his spoon, thinking. He could break his lease. There were always auditions in Austin, he didn't have to go to Los Angeles. He could make a way for them both, Daisy and his dream.

Leo thought of what his father would say. His memory was still so fresh then, and his loss still so shocking and cruel. He could almost hear his father's voice saying, *Focus on your own life, your own career, what you can control.*

He knew what he had to do.

"I have to go." He said it to himself as much as he said it to her.

"Are you—"

"If I don't go now," he said, holding her hand up to his lips. "I'll never try."

She pulled her hand away. Looked down at her lap.

"I can't wait for you." She wrapped her hands around the steering wheel, clenching it so tightly the knuckles pressed out against the thin skin. He wanted to reach out for her, but she seemed suddenly far away, too distant for him to reach.

"I waited for you," he said, his throat tightening, straining his voice.

A beat. Daisy twirled the spoon in her fingers. Her eyes were downcast.

"I'm glad you did." Before he registered it, her hands had flown off the steering wheel, grabbing his face, tugging him to her. She kissed him hard, and he tasted her tears as he kissed back. He held her cheeks, which were soft and wet and warm. She drew away just as quickly as she had let him in, and that was the end of all that he had ever hoped for.

"Leo, Leo," his mother says, her voice maintaining that lecture cadence that she always used when he was young and hadn't done his homework yet. "Are you listening to me?"

Before he can summon an exasperated look to throw his mother's way, Leo's phone rings.

"I'm getting a call, Mom."

Leo rushes out of the aisle, back to the boardwalk, away from the beach. It's his agent.

"Leo, buddy," his agent says as soon as he picks up.

"I'm about to walk into a wedding."

"I'll make it quick." His agent clears his throat, the way

he always did when he prepared to talk shop. "So, talked to the guys at the network. You got it."

"Shut the fuck up." Leo stops walking, gobsmacked. On a day when all the cards seem stacked against him, this is the last piece of news he expects to hear.

"Still gotta hammer out a few details with the contract, but I'll send it over later when it looks good."

"Holy shit."

"They loved your edge, said it was a no-brainer. Go celebrate, Leo, you earned it, buddy."

Leo had learned, living in Los Angeles, that "edge" was a label given to someone people couldn't quite pin down. If you were androgynous, you had an edge. If you were a butch lesbian, you had an edge. And if you were from the South and seemed well-informed or well-read, then you had an edge. This ambiguity had never worked for him before, so he is happy to take whatever he can get from it.

He'd gone to the chemistry read the day before he left for Florida. His hopes were not high. Since accumulating more rejections than he could count, his expectation for success had reached negative levels. He went into auditions, and, almost immediately after they were over, forced himself to forget they had happened. If good news did come, it was a pleasant surprise. If the news was bad… Well, he'd already forgotten about it, hadn't he?

The show is a medical drama that has gone way past its expiration date. Leo doesn't care for it, but what does that matter? He doesn't need anything groundbreaking, he just needs a shot. And Leo will take any of those he can get.

The role is simple. He'll play a convict getting treatment at the hospital. One of the lead characters will treat him. A similar storyline had played out in the show a decade ago and it seemed high time for the writers to dig back into the past and bring back what they could. Mostly, Leo has to sit in a hospital bed, handcuffed to the rails, giving long monologues about justice and liberty and anarchy ruled by a lack of impulse control. The scenes are overindulgent, but the audition had been a chance for Leo to tap into the swirling abyss of chaos he felt within himself at times when he lacked any control in his life.

The callback was a chemistry read, so he got to meet the actor. Leo gelled with him right away. Always a good sign. Leo used his Houston accent, the subtle elongation of vowels, to give his character a distinct sense of self. It was a bold choice, the casting director said, since they'd written the character as an Oregon native. But they liked the Texas angle better. Any chance to dunk on the Lone Star State was welcome in their writers room.

Leo glances around him, so shell-shocked by the good news he almost forgets where he is, and why, moments before, he'd felt so devastated by the past. The groomsmen gather on the boardwalk down the way, each messing with cuff links and adjusting hair, an impulse of vanity before standing in front of a crowd.

Leo runs over to them and grabs Deacon. "Deacon, where's the bridal party?"

"They're over there in that shed area." Deacon narrows his eyes. "But Daisy's not with them. If that's what you're—"

"Thanks, dude, good luck up there." Leo doesn't wait for Deacon to articulate his skepticism or suspicion. He has no time for anyone else's fear. The feeling in his chest, the hope brimming and bursting, must be shared. He needs to find her. To tell her. To have her see.

When he gets to the shed, he peers in the window to find her standing with the rest of the bridesmaids.

He barges in.

"Leo." Athena's voice is sharp and panicked. "Daisy will murder you. I'm serious. She's already so on edge."

"She's in that little bridal shed, it's fine." Leo glances around. "Come here." He pulls Athena outside. The wind blows strong and cool, no longer sharp with chill. It's finally warmed up, after all.

"What's wrong?" Athena asks. Her eyes are wide with worry. Her alarm reminds him of when he was in high school, constantly failing all of his math classes, teetering on the verge of flunking out of school.

"Nothing," Leo says. Ahead of them, down the sidewalk, guests file into their seats, clutching their shawls and clinging on to their hats as the wind rises up. They are far away, though. He and Athena are alone. "It's just. Do you remember that day? When I was eight, you were eleven. Out in the backyard. In November."

"Leo, what are you—"

"Just—do you remember?"

It was the first crisp, cold day of the season. A college football Saturday. The University of Texas game was on in the living room, and the back door was open to let in the breeze. They could still hear the roar of the crowd as Leo took Athena's hand and led her outside so that she could spot him while he practiced the back handspring his friends from school had taught him that week. The grass was cold, the ground was hard. The air kept its chill, the sun covered by an overcast sky. It finally felt like autumn, Thanksgiving only a few weeks away. A break from school, from the confines of hallways and homework and huge boys who liked to push him around when they were bored after school. They called him words he did not know, and when he asked about them, his cheeks burned and a strange shame started in his cheeks, flowing down to his toes. It filled him up, then left him vacant, a raw, gnawing absence. He didn't fully understand what it all meant, but he knew it signaled him out as different, and different didn't make you many friends.

But alone at home with Athena, he felt safe and fully free to be himself, in all the depths of his eccentricity, which was really just unselfconscious creativity. He and Athena had spent their whole childhood exploring every corner of their backyard. Their little square of paradise. Bushes lined in front of the fence, full of secret hiding places. They took tree branches and twigs and leaves and built themselves a fort inside the bushes, a fortress from the world. They would sit together, their legs crossed, their foreheads pressed into each other, vowing to always hide this place and protect the secrecy of it. No one else could enter. They formed the AL Alliance, aptly named by Athena, and their great binding allegiance was that they would never, ever leave each other behind. No matter what happened, they would always come back for each other.

That particular November day was one of the last they spent in their fortress. Athena would soon outgrow this fantasy life, her attention focused on her friends and learning how to morph herself for this new phase of living, prepubescent anxieties and fixations with fitting in and staying cool, leaving her no room to indulge the imagination of her younger brother.

But that would happen later. What Leo likes to remember, what he comes back to in these years living away from his family, is that final time in the fort.

"Let's be fairies," Leo said, still young enough to play make-believe, but old enough to know he could only do this at certain times, when he was at home with Athena or at a trusted friend's house. He'd learned the hard way how ruthless boys could be when you acted outside the norm: football, baseball, basketball, video games, and, because it was Texas, guns, hunting and camouflage.

"Okay," Athena said. Her hair was slicked back into a tight ponytail. She didn't like any loose hair falling in her face. Her cheeks were ruddy from the cold, but her eyes were wide and alive with light, an idea sparking. "But we lost our wings. We have to find them."

"So we can't fly?" Leo said, bummed. He liked whizzing around the backyard, running so fast the wind whipped through his hair, the air stinging his lungs. If he focused hard enough, he could make it feel like he was flying through the air, in some other world, his feet lifted off the ground, his body untethered by gravity. No one would beat him up. No one would call him names. They wouldn't even come close to catching him. He'd soar away from them all.

"They're not gone forever," Athena said, as she traced the back of her shoulder blades, the place where her wings had fallen off. "They're just lost. We have to find them, Leo. We have to find the magic."

They set off in the backyard in bare feet, searching through every bush, checking every flower, grabbing fistfuls of grass and checking every blade. From inside the house, Jason shouted at the TV, mad at some call made by the referees, but they did not stop their search. The wings could be anywhere, on anything, hiding in plain sight. No organic matter could go unsearched. Magic left traces, they both knew. If they could just find a clue...

"Leo! Leo!" Athena shouted from the bushes closest to the garage. "In here!"

Leo stopped in his tracks and sprinted over to her. She was crouched in the bushes. Her head was tilted to the side. Her brow furrowed. Her face was sad and full of meaning, as she pointed down to two sticks buried in the bushes.

"There's only one," Athena said, taking him seriously.

"You take them," Leo said, trying his hand at chivalry. "It should be you."

"No." Athena shook her head. "I'm too big now. They won't fit me. But you. You've got it. For always. The magic will always live in you." She took two sticks from behind the bushes. "Turn around."

Leo did as he was told. He felt the sharp edges of the sticks tracing his shoulder blades. Athena murmured a few words, giving every other syllable a harsh inflection, like she was casting a spell. Leo never got baptized, but he imagined it felt like this. Still air. Silence. The weight of rebirth held in another's hands. The surrender to renewal. Leo felt the enormity of the task at hand. He savored every scratch of each twig. He was becoming someone new. Someone strong. Someone brave.

When Athena was finished, she tapped his back three times with both sticks and let them drop to the ground.

"Wings?" Leo asked, stretching out his arms wide, moving them back and forth, feeling the magic spread from his back to his fingertips. Wings. Freedom. Power. It all coursed through him. He forgot his life at school. He forgot his shame. He let all the imaginary forces in his body unleash and fill him up. Before he could start running, Athena grabbed his shoulder and put her hands over his eyes, shrouding his world in darkness.

"Fly," she whispered close to his ear, her hands too tight around his face as she covered his eyes. "Go fly, go far, don't ever stop or look back. You're strong here, Leo, you're so strong. So fly. Fly."

He tells the story so quickly that he's panting once he's finished. Athena's eyes are narrowed, her head tilted to the side as she listens. His heart sinks.

"You remember, don't you?" He feels an urgency that he does not understand. "You gave me the wings."

"You loved to fly," Athena says. "So fast, too. Very aero-dynamic."

"You let me have the wings," Leo said again.

"There was only one pair."

"I'd been having some trouble at school."

"Boys are jackasses, aren't they?"

"But you gave me the wings," Leo says. He's not entirely sure why, but he needs her to understand this, as if this is the one, crucial point of everything. "You never let me win. But you did that day."

"That wasn't a win-lose game. It was just pretend."

"But you…" Leo trails off.

"What is this, Leo? Is this about Daisy?"

"No, it's about me."

"Okay."

"I miss Dad." Leo lets that hang in the air. "Why's every-thing different without him?"

Athena pauses. She chews on the inside of her cheek. It used to drive him crazy, seeing her do that, but now, he feels nothing but a rush of affection. It's so specifically her. Dis-gusting, yes, but singularly Athena. He loves it. He loves her. Her quick wit, her drinking too fast and too loud, her face, so much like their father's, and her smile, so much like his own.

"He made us whole," Athena says. "And now we're…"

"Broken?" Leo asks.

"No," Athena says, her voice thoughtful and faraway. "Just…incomplete, I guess. A fraction of who we were."

"I got the part." Leo looks away from her, not able to say it straight on. His excitement and need to see her enthusiasm match his is almost too much to bear. "For that show. My agent just called."

Athena stares at him. No response. No reaction. Leo braces for a sarcastic remark or something to undercut the moment. Instead, Athena pulls him in for a bone-crushing hug, then, once she releases him, kisses him on both cheeks.

"Leo," Athena says. Her voice cracks. "I'm so proud of you."

"Yeah?" He's still braced for a crass comment or quick-witted put-down.

"Dad would be, too. Have you told Mom?"

"I'll do that later." Leo clears his throat. "She's kind of focused. On this man."

"Ugh, gross."

"What I said when I saw you flirting last night with Katie."

"Okay, whatever, Mr. Hollywood, I'll probably have to suffer through seeing you kissing beautiful movie stars on-screen any day now." Athena gestures to the renovated garden shed, painted white with ornate roses carved on the front door, the perfect place for a bride to stand in wait. "Daisy's probably coming out soon. You should go sit down. But." Athena hugs him again. "I'm just so proud of you."

"It's not a big part or anything—"

"It's the start. Those are always small, right?"

"Guess so."

"Go," she says, gently. "See you at the reception."

Leo makes his way back to the beach. He finds his seat. Sure enough, his mother is sitting next to the man he saw earlier at the beach club bar. He gives him an awkward wave and plops down on the other side of his mother, taking her program, pretending to read it, waiting for everything to start.

His pulse pounds in his ears. The thrill of the news runs through him, the validation he felt from Athena, always his toughest critic, allows him to savor this small victory. He glances down at the program and sees Daisy's name. His throat tightens, and some of the excitement halts, a clenching in his chest that makes it hard to breathe. It's happening. And there's nothing he can do to stop it. He had the chance to tell her. But he chose to talk with Athena instead. It was not lost on him what that decision had cost him. The time for action has ended. This is happening, whether he likes it or not.

The worst part is watching her walk down. He knew it would be. He wants to close his eyes, ignore the entrance, but this is the one part he can't miss. As the string quartet plays Daisy's favorite song, she approaches the edge of the board-walk, her arm in her father's. He wears his dress blues, imposing as ever, his ruddy, pockmarked face stoic, but his head is held high, proud as can be. They make their way from the boardwalk to the sand-dusted plywood that serves as their makeshift walkway over the beach.

Daisy is magnificent by design. Her dress has lace sleeves down to her wrists, and a high, lace neckline. Leo doesn't know any of the technical terms. He only knows that the golden hour light hits her in such a way that she glows, effervescent, not of this world. An angel among them adorned with pearls and satin and lace.

She glances his way. Her full cheeks are red, and her eyes are hardly visible for how hard she beams. The picture of joy. The picture of light. Leo watches her walk down until he can no longer see her face, though the image of it will stay with him forever. This, more than anything, should give him closure. But he only feels his heart expand, bursting at the sight of her so happy, even if it's not with him. He would never admit it, but he knows, in the most sacred part of himself, that this is the truest sign of his love.

Leo stares out at the water, tuning into the ocean instead of the rabbi. *Find the sea, Leonidus, you're built from the sea.* The wind carries the whisper of his father's words, and he believes that he is here, tethered to something, anything, perhaps the ocean itself.

What is lost today can never be recovered. It is time to let go of that dream that had kept him company for so long: that Daisy would always wait for him, that he could leave whenever he pleased and return to find her as he left her, in love with him and ready to start their life together. He doesn't know how to move on. Time will teach him. Of that much, he is sure.

For now, perhaps, it is enough to hold on to the hope of this new opportunity. A television job. A real paycheck. A three-episode arc. He clutches on to the promise of the opportunity like some hold on to their prayers, pressed close to his chest with loving, tender hands.

# DEACON

The groomsmen's house smells like feet.

Deacon can't understand this. The men had only occupied the space for a day, and already, they've managed to mark their territory. Stale beer and pizza and a third, more elusive smell that reminds Deacon of his fourth-grade classroom after recess.

It's a shock, coming from the bridesmaids' place, where shampoo and perfume and a seventy-dollar candle filled every room with a sweet, comforting scent that he'd enjoyed throughout the day. Though tensions ran high, it had kept Deacon calm, the lavender and eucalyptus wafting in from every corner of the house.

"You made it!" Daniel comes into the living room, already wearing his tailored tux and white bow tie, complete with a black cummerbund. His curls are styled and contained, but they still fall over his eyes. He swipes them out of his face as he shakes Deacon's hand. "We're just finishing up the Tisch. You made it for the best part."

He gestures to the table the groomsmen have just abandoned as they circle up together in the living room.

"It smells like a locker room in here." Deacon takes the bag of chips, eating a handful. "Need smelling salts or something just to stand around."

"We did some damage." Daniel gestures to the kitchen, which is scattered with empty beer cans and open chip bags. "It's not that bad, is it?"

"It's worse. But if it makes you happy, I'm happy. Whatever Danny wants for his special day."

"Yes, it is famously the groom's time to shine. The prince's day."

"Don't let Daisy hear you say that."

"Of course not," Daniel says. "I'd like to live to see my wedding. Oh, almost forgot."

Daniel grabs a black silk yarmulke from the side table and tosses it to Deacon, who puts it on, pressing it down on his head so that it doesn't slide off. After, Deacon adjusts Daniel's bow tie, which has gone askew, and takes a moment to take him in. He's so handsome. His dark, curly hair is long enough to tie in a tiny topknot (something Daisy has expressly forbidden today), his jawline is just as chiseled as his sharp cheekbones, his big, soulful brown eyes are clear and bright, and his thick, dark eyebrows that almost meet in the middle are raised in an unconscious, earnest excitement.

Daniel always poses perfectly in every picture Daisy posts, and, more importantly, he knows what angles to use when taking pictures of her. For an influencer, there couldn't have been a bigger win-win.

There's so much for Deacon to love, too. Daniel is strong, steady, sarcastic and kind. He's everything Deacon ever hoped for in a brother-in-law. Before, when he imagined who Daisy would marry, he feared it would be one of the sports-obsessed, emotionally vacant men they were surrounded by in their schools. The boys who had been told for all of their lives that they were special, born for leadership, destined for great things, and had believed it because the world gave them no reason not to. The consequence was always a god complex and a lack of personality.

Or worse, he feared she'd wind up with another man like the Youth Pastor, who wore judgment in gentleness's clothing, parading around their goodness without giving any thought to love.

How had she wound up with the Youth Pastor in the first place? Still a mystery. Deacon would not bring it up today. Why dredge up the past when the present was so full of promise?

Daniel is perfect for Daisy. If he were more sentimental, he might say that their marriage is meant to be.

"Deacon," Daniel says, holding out his arms and bringing him back to the present. "Fix my cuff links, would you?"

"Hands shaking too badly?" Deacon takes one arm at a time, threading the iron cuff link through and clasping it on the other side.

"A bit." Daniel shows him his other hand. It's steady as ever. "Just thought my brother should put on the finishing touches."

"Well," Deacon says, finishing the second sleeve. "I'm honored, bro."

"Broski."

"Bruh." They clap hands and pull each other in for a brief hug, patting each other hard on the backs, as if they could transfer all their affection through the force of it.

"Alright, boys," Chad shouts from the center of the room. "Let's huddle up."

"Oh," Daniel says, looking from Chad to Deacon, his brown curls swaying back and forth as he does so. "You're going to hate this."

"I'm going to—?"

"Deacon, Deacon, Deacon." The guys chant his name.

Daniel shrugs, giving Deacon an apologetic smile. "Think of it as an initiation." Daniel walks over to the huddle, chanting his name louder than the rest, encouraging him over as they switch up the song.

Deacon joins. Instead of standing around the circle, he's shoved inside of it. He gets a brief flash of panic—that this is a trap, that these overgrown frat boys are about to beat the shit out of him—before he feels himself hoisted in the air, lifted by each groomsman. The secondary photographer, who had been packing up her bag, glances up and immediately grabs her camera, frantically snapping pictures, capturing each millisecond of this strange ritual.

The speaker is cranked all the way up. The song picks up from a soft voice singing over an acoustic riff. It builds. And as it does, with the drums taking over, with the bass keeping rhythm, with the guitar shedding all tenderness and shredding instead, the guys toss Deacon up in the air, singing along to the song at the top of their lungs, screeching out that they've never been so alive.

Then, they drop Deacon down in the center of their circle, jumping around him, still singing. "New York City is Evil," they shout along, then respond with lyrics of their own, "Texas Forever!" Deacon, alarmed, amazed, joins in with them after his shock wears off—he knows the song, he knows the words—and by the end, he's jumping with them, screaming with them, a part of them in a way he never felt possible.

As the song slows at the end, the guys lock arms, grabbing Deacon out of the middle so that he's connected with them, his arms resting on sweaty backs and shoulders. He glances around. The guys sing softly, their eyes closed, finishing out every word with a fervent sort of worship. Deacon had only seen that expression before in church. The ruddy cheeks, the raised eyebrows, the eyes closed tight and tense, their heads bowed. Whatever this is, Deacon realizes it's sacred to these guys. And they let him in. They made him a part of it. Belonging starts, not with understanding, but with an invitation. Their brotherhood is now his, too.

When the song ends, Daniel passes out a round of shots to everyone. Whiskey for most, water for those who no longer indulge. Deacon takes his whiskey. They all raise their glass.

"To the best guys, to my brothers," Daniel says.

"To Daniel, to Daisy," everyone shouts back in unison. They knock their drinks back. Deacon shudders as his goes down, and he feels the whiskey heat him up immediately. He chugs a glass of water. Grabs his jacket. And meets the crowd as they file out toward the ceremony.

When he remembers this day, the wedding will always come to Deacon in flashes of white. The white sand beach. The white flowers around the chuppah. The cream-colored yarmulke on Daniel's head. The flower girls in white dresses, tossing white rose petals out onto the sand, stopping halfway down the aisle to squat down and dig in it. The bride, Daisy, in her white dress, floating down the aisle, her smile wide enough for all the crowd to see.

Deacon watches his sister, and he remembers Halloweens when she dressed in a bridal gown, a veil obscuring her face, her knees scraped and bruised underneath the skirt, hiking it up as she ran from house to house to get more candy. He remembers dusk, the cicadas blaring, the breeze fluttering through the magnolia branches in their backyard as they rolled around on the grass, their bare feet covered in mud, their gaze going skyward, trying to find planets in the twilight. He remembers the closed-door years, when they both holed up in their rooms, disconnected from each other, preoccupied by their own problems, believing them to be singular and wholly unique. Spring days in Houston as adults, walking down Westheimer, sampling the thrift shops, popping into Poison Girl for whiskey and beer at the end of the day, their feet tired and their arms full of bags filled with clothes. His heart is full as he sees her see Daniel for the first time, her eyes alight with love and promise. Deacon doesn't cry, but he feels his heart swell with love and pride that his sister has found the person with whom she will spend her life. He understands, now, the beauty of weddings and the significance of bearing witness: to always remember this day, when they exchanged their vows, and came together to celebrate their new life, in the presence of all the eyes that love them.

By the time the family finishes taking pictures—they opted to wait until after the ceremony, so Daniel could see Daisy for the first time when she walked down the aisle—the reception is in full swing. The band plays jazz while everyone eats, which Deacon does quickly and with great gusto, starving after a day spent waiting on Daisy.

"Hey, handsome." Athena comes up with a beer for him, holding her own tequila soda. She shakes out one of her legs, wincing. "Remind me why I agreed to wear heels?"

"Because Daisy asked you to," Deacon says. "And they make your legs look good."

"You're just buttering me up."

"You look good, I'm serious," Deacon says. "Go out on the dance floor, show off those gams."

"People will wonder if I've lost it."

"You have, haven't you?"

"Whatever." She takes a healthy sip of her drink, looking down at his feet, kicking her shoe against his. Deacon knows she's about to get earnest. She always has to brace herself for it. "You've been so good to me."

"Slow down there, cowboy, or you're going to accidentally say something nice."

"I'm serious," Athena says. She puts her drink down on the table beside her and pulls both of his hands into hers. "I couldn't have made it through this year without you. The kind of friend you've been... Always sticking with me, putting up with me."

"That's what friends are for." Deacon's pulse quickens. Did Daisy tell her? Is she trying to fish the truth out of him? This has to be a setup, right? Athena hasn't been this kind to him in years.

"When I found out about Alex, I didn't think I'd be able to breathe, let alone make it this far. Through the breakup and the...well, everything else." Athena pauses. "You and Daisy. You were there after my dad... And, your parents, too. That's what family does, right?"

"We're family." Deacon's chest tightens. It's true. They are. And he's kept this one great secret from her.

"I've just been thinking about it. How much you mean to me. It all started when..."

Their friendship began on the soccer pitch for varsity tryouts during Deacon's freshman year of high school. Athena was a senior. She'd been voted team captain. She was good. Defensive central midfielder. Quiet, but magnetic. Hardworking. She could read the field quickly, make split-second decisions about where to redirect the ball. She made plays. She scored goals. She was tough as nails. Everyone wanted to play like her, even on the boys team. She didn't care about any of that, though. All Athena wanted to do was win.

He'd known about her because of Daisy. She and Athena were closest back then, before Daisy went off to her Christian college and became insufferable for half a decade. It was different. He was different. Shy, uncomfortable, wired and wanting. He didn't like being noticed. In the hallways, he'd hunch his shoulders as he tied his backpack straps together, pulling hard on the ends so that it pressed into his chest so tightly he could barely breathe. He found quiet corners in the courtyard of the private prep school and scrolled through his phone or finished his homework while he blasted dissonant metal music that matched the dysphoria he felt inside himself. The perfectly manicured lawns and clean brick pathways that connected the overly large campus together melted away in his little corner. He was in his own world. He liked it that way. Solitude and Clif Bars and Diet Coke. He didn't need other people.

With soccer and Athena, though, everything changed. He suddenly wanted to be seen, by Athena, especially. Deacon wanted her to notice him, wanted her to make something of him, wanted her to transform him into something other than invisible.

There was an aura about Athena, something in her presence that made it seem like if she saw you, really took the time to take you in, she could invite you close, into her charm and confidence, stick her hand right through your chest, solve the riddle tangled up inside of you and rearrange all the parts to make them fit. Everyone around Deacon seemed to shapeshift with the moment or the crowd they were with. Athena was solid. Formed in marble, unmoving. Deacon longed for that stability, for that sure sense of self. If he could not have it himself, he wanted it in his proximity.

He worked hard during tryouts. When Athena offered to stay late with the freshmen to help them practice, Deacon stayed, too, though his legs ached and his sides split and his stomach gnawed with hunger. Homework could wait. Chores could wait. Every need he'd ever known could wait if it gave him a few more minutes with her.

The crush was intense. Once he made the team, it only got stronger. It took hold of Deacon the way no other had before. He burned CDs for Athena, he read every book she recommended, he soaked up every word she had to say.

"You're such a stalker," Daisy said to him when he made her drive to the coffee shop so they could pick up Athena's favorite coffee order before school.

Perhaps at the behest of Daisy, Athena finally took note of Deacon's desperation and started spending more time with him. It was a dream come true for Deacon, who was convinced this would help them fall in love with each other. He watched Nora Ephron movies on loop in order to prepare for his own personal rom-com.

But the more time they spent together, the more Deacon's crush faded into the background. He learned that Athena was human, with quirks, and unlike those Nora Ephron movies, they did not deepen his affection for her. She was serious. Incredibly competitive. Prioritized school and soccer above anything else. She'd just read Dickinson for the first time and wouldn't stop repeating lines from poems and letters she loved. She rarely asked questions, and whenever Deacon offered up any thoughts or observations of his own, Athena had zero follow-up questions, her mind elsewhere, an evasiveness that, from far away, was mysterious and alluring, but up close, was nothing more than dismissive. She did not, it so happened, possess any power to help him clear up the murky waters that drowned out his true sense of self. She was not a key. She was Athena, through and through. Specificity only makes a person gain or lose magic. There is no in-between. Deacon quit the team the next year. He saw Athena often—their families had grown close in the years that Daisy and Athena had become friends, especially their parents, who bonded over vintage cabernets and Billy Joel and a shared sense of humor.

Athena and Leo started tagging along on their family trips to Florida. Outside of their family obligations, though, Deacon saw little of Athena. That, he thought, was that.

It wasn't until years later, when they were both at UT, that they reconnected through a mutual friend, at a senior's house. Deacon was nineteen. Athena was twenty-two. Deacon ignored Athena when he walked in. College was for new starts, and he didn't need reminding of the brief but all-consuming crush from when he was fifteen. He was cooler now. Confident. In control.

But then the tequila tasting began, and they both pretended to know the difference between *reposado* and *añejo*, shooting back the stuff way too fast to pick up on any nuances that made it special, handcrafted, one of a kind. For them, all it did was burn. The seniors talked about the notes of vanilla and oak, while Deacon and Athena secretly chased each shot with a can of Sprite and a lime wedge, getting less sly as the night went on. After the fourth one, they locked eyes from across the room after they finished their soda chug. Athena's face broke open into a smile. It was completely green. A lime slice wedged in her mouth, little pulp flecks sticking to the edges of her lips, her shoulders shaking as she laughed at the two of them.

"Who let us in, anyway?" Athena said when she walked over to Deacon.

"Their fault for not knowing we'd be too dumb to know the difference." He handed Athena another shot and poured himself one, too. "At least it's not mescal. That stuff tastes like a campfire."

"And burning rubber," Athena said.

"Amen." Deacon lifted up his Sprite can to hers. With the clink of aluminum, their friendship began.

It was love like neither of them had ever known. After that

night, they were inseparable. Daisy had ditched them both for her evangelical life at her college down I-35. They weren't abandoned by her, but they were ignored. Years would pass before she came back to them in full force. In her absence, Deacon and Athena became best friends, filling for each other the void Daisy had left behind.

Being together was like becoming a child all over again, with sharper senses and keener minds. Little voices and absurdist scenarios that no one else understood took over their language, making them insufferable to everyone but themselves. They talked late into the night, sipping spiked seltzers and smoking weed, fluctuating from unstoppable fits of giggles to all-out paranoia, fearing their spines had fused to the couch and they'd never leave the room again. There was a fuck-everyone kind of freedom in their friendship. If no one else liked it, who cared? Athena helped Deacon with his shots of T, Deacon helped Athena calm down enough to finally ask out the girls she liked, and they both became more fully themselves with each other. Their friendship was their great sustaining force, even through the rough times: when Daisy got with the Youth Pastor and stopped talking to both of them altogether, so consumed with her new relationship and role in the church; when Deacon ditched Athena for a solid six months to date a WNBA player; when Athena shut herself away while she worked on her dissertation and refused to reach out to anyone when her stress was mounting and threatening to turn her inside out; when they both got unreasonably irritated with each other the year after graduating undergrad and living together for the first time, constantly snapping at one another and fighting and not mentioning what they were really mad about—a mac-and-cheese pot left in the sink too long, uncleaned, the clothes sitting in the dryer for days on end before they were folded.

There was much they had overcome. It felt impossible that anything could break them. But the impossible happens when the right place and the right time meet together with their inexplicable force and rip through life as it was known before.

As Athena talks, reflecting on their friendship, Deacon thinks of Mel. What she expects from him. How she needs him to step up for her, for them, and stand in the truth.

In six months, he and Mel will move in together, an old town house in Montrose with an iron gate covered with ivy and Texas jasmine, and in the springtime, it will bloom with a flood of white petals, the sweet perfume hanging in the heavy, hot air, a gift every time they go out and come home. They will rescue a black Labrador from a local shelter, and they will name him Winnie the Pooch. They will spend Saturday mornings taking him out on long walks around the neighborhood, stopping at their favorite café for coffee and breakfast tacos and freshly baked dog biscuits. They will learn to always bring water on walks for Winnie when they go out in the summertime, and they will buy booties for his paws to protect them from the boiling hot tar of the Houston pavement. They will fight over where the plates should be put in the kitchen, and how many showers one person should take per day. They will learn how to live together. Autumn leaves will crunch under their feet, few and far between, but enough to make them grateful for the changing seasons. They will host Thanksgiving at their house for their friends who can't spend it with their families. The next day, they will buy a Charlie Brown Christmas tree and fill it with more lights than it can handle, making the tiny, twiglike branches sag and shake and eventually snap off as the weeks go on. They will hide presents underneath the tree. One will have a ring inside, his grandmother's. One sapphire surrounded by small diamonds, a gold band. Deacon will get down on one knee. Mel will say yes. There will be another wedding. There is always another wedding. Vows exchanged on that day will be upheld for the rest of their lives, which will be rich in love and joy.

Deacon knows none of this, but he can sense it. The life hanging on the line with Mel. He wants to be the person she believes in, full of strength, even in hard moments. He must risk the impossible. He has to give the truth a chance.

"Athena," Deacon says, interrupting her, pulling her farther away from the crowd so that his words don't get lost in the steady roar of voices. "There's something I haven't told you."

# ATHENA

After everyone gets ready, taking a painstaking amount of pictures of the process, the bridal party files into a renovated garden shed off the boardwalk by the beach, where they wait for the wedding ceremony to begin. They cannot be seen by guests before the big reveal. That would take away some of the magic.

Daisy is ushered to another area, where she will read a letter written by Daniel. A photographer will capture every second as she absorbs the carefully chosen words of her future husband. With any luck, they'll get a few shots of her eyes welling with tears, but not quite spilling over, a delicate withholding of the floodgates that is sure to photograph well.

In the shed, Reghan and Clare—no longer fighting—take over the conversation. It is, as always, vapid and endless, revolving around the drama featured in the latest reality dating show or the beef between one Housewife or the other. Athena breathes, trying to bury the annoyance that spikes at the droning conversation, reminding herself why she liked Reghan and Clare. They both took in Daisy when she needed a community after her church friends shut her out. Never judgmental, always open-minded, they allowed Daisy to be fully herself, to learn and grow and heal and thrive. For that, no matter how much they might annoy her, Athena will always be grateful for them.

Luckily, Leo saves her from enduring much more. He seems dazed as he tells her about the part he got, bringing up a story from childhood, bringing up their father. It's strange, Athena realizes, they never talk about him together, not without Mollie. Maybe they'd just needed some good news, as if they could not summon his memory until there was something worthy of it.

Once Leo leaves, Katie comes outside. A gust of sea breeze blows back her perfectly curled hair, stiff and thick with hair spray.

"So much hair spray, it's barely moving," Katie says, tucking a piece behind her ear.

"Another benefit of the haircut." Athena tilts her head to the side, free from the mass of curls and clips and products that would have most assuredly added several pounds to her already-heavy head.

"Something I wanted to show you," Katie says as she unballs her fist to reveal a stone. It glows with two tones of green marbled together, the lines swirling and intricate, forming a mesmerizing pattern. "Malachite," Katie explains. "The stone of transformation."

"Transformation?" Athena asks.

"My dad got it for me. After my mom died. He found it in a thrift store in Austin. The salesperson talked him into it. I've kept it with me every day since."

"Cool." Athena's not entirely sure what to say. Stones and astrology and crystals are something she makes fun of more than something she tries to understand.

"I want you to have it," Katie says. "Give you some good energy. Some healing."

Katie's face is the picture of earnestness. Her eyes are wide ovals of emerald, swimming with hope, her lips, thin and painted a cranberry red, part slightly as she exhales, waiting for Athena to respond. That her father had given her this, that it had afforded her so much healing in grief, is not lost on Athena.

"Lord knows I need it," Athena says. She looks out at the water. On the beach, the yellow warning flag has changed to purple. Jellyfish and other creatures creeping into the water.

"I like you a lot, you know," Katie says. Athena can feel her gaze, intense and focused. Athena stares out at the beach. "It's been fun spending time with you today."

"Yeah." Athena does not want to make any promises she cannot keep.

"Flirtation doesn't hurt anyone," Katie says. "You know that, right?"

"I guess."

"I know you're still healing." Katie's voice is gentle as she transfers the stone into Athena's hand. "But whenever you're ready, you give me a call."

As their hands brush, Athena feels that same shock of feeling from earlier, on the boardwalk by the lake. It takes her a moment to recognize it as desire. She'd been devoid of the stuff for so long. It feels wrong, and then Athena remembers, with a jolt, that it's okay. That she's single. It's strange. A grief, a comfort, an opportunity, all at once.

Katie leans in and kisses Athena lightly on the cheek, then squeezes her shoulder and goes back into the garden shed.

Athena runs her thumb along the malachite. The edges are rough and unpolished. She holds it up to the sky, so that it catches the fading sunlight. It sparkles and gleams, as if it contains some magic within, a conduit of wonder. If transformation were to come from this little stone, Athena could use it now more than ever. She places it in her dress pocket and pats it gently, letting the stone knock against her hip. She returns to the shed with the others. They all wait in nervous silence, ready for the ceremony to begin.

Finally, at five after five, an aggressive, no-nonsense wedding planner ushers the party out of the shed, muttering that they're five minutes behind schedule. They form a line and head toward the beach.

A string quartet plays. Every wicker seat is filled. A burlap runner over plywood makes an aisle in the sand. The rabbi is at the center of the chuppah, smiling at the bridesmaids as they make their way down, the prayer shawl over her shoulders blowing slightly in the wind. Daniel beams at each one of them, his eyes already welling, his hands behind his back in anticipation as he stands up on his toes, trying to sneak a peek of Daisy before she comes down.

Just before Daisy walks out from the shed, the string quartet switches to a rendition of an indie song by an artist Daisy loves. When the chorus picks up, Daisy steps to the back of the aisle, clutching the arm of her father, who wears his army blues. The guests rise and turn around. Daniel cries and smiles and drinks in the vision of the rest of his life.

The wind picks up during the ceremony. It's hard to hear the rabbi. She has to repeat several lines for the benefit of the crowd. Daniel gazes at Daisy, locked in, his eyes glowing with excitement and love, listening to the words he's already heard, the repetition unnoticed or insignificant. Maybe that's love: seeing the beloved with brand-new eyes every time, no memory of what has just occurred, a sort of blissed-out, drunken state of infatuation that erases your very consciousness and forces you to focus only on what's in front of you. They exchange vows. They say *I do*. Daniel stomps on a glass. The crowd goes wild.

The wedding party and family stay behind on the beach for

pictures. What should only take five minutes, ends up taking an hour and a half, with Clare and Reghan demanding the photographer get every angle possible: their shoes, their shoulders, the back of their heads. It's a nightmare. Athena's irritation creeps up once more. It's exacerbated when Katie comes up to her, moments before they walk up to the reception, to inform her that the bridesmaids voted that she should give the speech during the reception. It was supposed to be Reghan, but her phone fell in the water when she was trying to take a video on the beach, and now her speech is gone, and she can't possibly go without a script. Since Athena's an English professor, and therefore good with words, they decided she could do a better job off the top of her head than anyone else. Athena tells Katie that all she has to say about love right now is that it will wreck your life and betray you at the first opportunity. Katie says that even that is better than anything Reghan can come up with on her own. Athena is trapped. There's no way out.

The reception is just off the beach, up behind the sand dunes in a grass enclave by the beach club. There's a tent with party lights strung up on the ceiling. The dance floor is made up of stone tile, and a buffet line forms at the back. People rush between the food and the open bar, settling into their round tables, enjoying the soft music the band plays. Athena sees Sydnee for the first time as she sits in the corner farthest away from Athena's table. Red dress, hair down, makeup perfect. *Dammit*, Athena thinks, disappointed that she has the audacity to still look hot. Despite herself, Athena checks around for Alex, too. She doesn't see her. Maybe she's gone to grab drinks. Or maybe, Athena allows herself a flash of hope, she didn't come at all.

Athena is feeling good. Daisy seems happier than she has all day, relieved to finally get herself to the celebration, with no

more time to worry about what can go wrong, or if the flowers are right, or if Athena's new haircut will single-handedly
ruin her entire aesthetic.

But then Deacon pulls her aside at the reception, and he
tells her.

He stares at her, his blond hair gelled, his light eyebrows,
almost translucent, knitted together in concern. His eyes are
narrowed, waiting for her reaction, like he's afraid she is going
to explode.

She says nothing. Just walks away. Leaves him standing
there. Mouth agape. He does not deserve to be absolved, if
that's what he was seeking. Alone at a table near the bar, she
drains her drink and gets another.

She could have gone her entire life not knowing. It was
better, thinking they had met through work, that it was fate,
or destiny, or whatever force predestined horrible outcomes
to fall upon people. That Deacon had introduced them...

A small voice in her head protests. *What does that change?*

It changes her imagination. How it all went down. She
could have stopped it. She could have pulled Deacon aside
and said, *Never tell anyone about the existence of my wife, don't
take any chances, don't let her find freedom outside of this marriage.*

It isn't logical, but logic isn't the point. He should have told
her months ago, when he realized who Sydnee was sleeping
with instead of her. He should have been *her* friend. Athena
can't help but think of it as taking Sydnee's side. He kept this
vital piece of information from her. He left her in the dark,
and let her talk on and on about it. How many hours had
they spent dissecting how the two of them met? Deacon had
indulged her. That was not love. That was self-preservation.

She cracks her knuckles, fuming. Her father always said
that anger was alright, as long as you worked it through then
made way for grace. Mollie was more practical. Anger's like

drinking: it feels good going down, but overindulge, and the hangover will punish you the next day.

Athena couldn't even pretend to be surprised. Alex was everywhere, at all times. In the year leading up to their separation, Sydnee was always bringing up Alex when she talked about work, inviting her out to drinks with them, coming home late after happy hours extended into long dinners on weeknights.

Athena didn't read anything into it. She should have. But she didn't. That was the year of the rejections. The pain of them sent a streak of worthlessness through her. Lethargy took over. No one wanted her ideas, her thoughts didn't matter, her observations were best left kept to herself. The self-pity was, perhaps, self-indulgent, but she couldn't pull herself out of it. Going out wasn't an option. Having fun did not appeal to her anymore. She didn't want to hold Sydnee back, so she told her to go on without her. So much time spent without Athena must have made her realize how tethered she'd become to someone who couldn't keep up with her anymore. Next to Athena, Alex must have seemed wild and free and easy.

*There's something I haven't told you...*

A Saturday outside in March, in Montrose, at Menil Park. A picnic blanket, a cheese board, a plastic cup full of Sancerre. Sydnee's bright yellow T-shirt with a small smiley face in the middle, tucked into her ripped, whitewashed jeans. Ponytail, no makeup, beautiful. Sydnee never said her name. She didn't have to. Who else was there, besides Alex?

"It's not a relationship," Sydnee explained. "But it's not a one-time thing, either."

Exclusive, not exclusive, dating other people. It didn't matter. It all meant the end for Athena. She waited for the next wave of depression to come, this one more intense and all-encompassing. But it stayed the same. No better, no worse.

Another rejection, another heartbreak. She was more than numb. Ambivalence reigned supreme. She felt nothing. She was armed. No one could hurt her anymore.

But Deacon did. That he had introduced Alex to Sydnee was a disappointment. That he had kept it from her felt like a breach of trust. Was she so fragile, so delicate? It's an injustice, and her cheeks grow hot with the fury it brings. That he didn't believe in her, that he didn't think she was strong enough to handle the truth. Hadn't she survived the truth over and over again? The truth that mortality comes for all of us, even when love binds you together. The truth that some relationships are too broken to be bothered with mending. How dare he try to protect her. She was strong enough to handle anything. She didn't need anyone's help.

Deacon stands across the room, next to Daisy, laughing with her, his back turned to Athena, so he does not see her glower in his direction. She clenches her fist and sips her tequila, her mind reeling and raging.

She still has to give a speech. About love. About gratitude. The thought of both makes her nauseous. Betrayal. Liars. She has more than a few things to say about such subjects, though she doubts this is the venue for them.

She thinks of platitudes about love. Love at first sight, absence makes the heart grow fonder, love conquers all, opposites attract, love is patient, love is kind, love will set you free, *Unable are the Loved to die For Love is Immortality*—

For a moment, Athena pretends that love is enough.

If it were, Athena could drop the past from her shoulders, shrug off that great albatross, and forgive Sydnee. They could have an honest conversation, with kindness and respect. Flush out all the bitterness of the end. Athena could communicate. She could heal.

If love were enough, Athena would be able to corral Mollie

and Leo into the living room, share a meal at the table they've had for decades, and revel in their memories of Jason so that she doesn't feel so alone in her longing for him. She'd institute a language of grief, which is to say, she'd usher in the memories everyone kept to themselves. She'd make them share, like Jason used to. She'd find a way to embody his magic touch, which always summoned the tender, vulnerable and joyful parts of every person in every room.

If love were enough, then words of Dickinson, chicken scratched on the back of an envelope, could come alive and fill Athena up with the meaning she's forever seeking in the ghost of a woman she'll never know. Athena would no longer have to depend on her unreliable mind to dissect the lines that haunted her, the meaning of which shifted depending on the year and her mood. They were acrobats, contortionists, a circus of words that drew her into herself and her imagination. Athena wants to know her, to study her enough, to love her enough, that she's summoned into existence. Athena can almost picture her. But it's translucent, not fully formed. She was a woman, redheaded, like Mollie, trapped and privileged and full of rage and passion. She was in love with her sister-in-law. Athena had read enough letters to be certain of it. A hedge away, but a world apart. How quiet were the halls of her house? What echoes haunted her mind? Thousands, it must have been, with the ferocity and consistency of her writing, which, the more Athena studies it, seemed to be an exorcism more than a quaint pastime. She'll never know for sure, though. It is a study without an end, there will never come a conclusion to her excavation. You cannot, on your own, piece together a soul, and love is not enough to bring back the dead. Love is hardly enough to build a bridge over her anger so she can walk toward forgiveness.

No, love is not a subject she can breach. A wedding is rarely the best day of anyone's life. It's a beginning, an ending, the middle of the road. The past drags behind everyone, a train of memories and regrets, stitched together with lace, delicate and ornate, years spent threading it together. The future shines on, the ever-present sun, closer every day. The present, the here and now, it surrounds. Athena runs through more clichés in her mind. No time like the present, it's now or never, no time to lose, today is a gift, don't dwell in the past, don't ruin today, *I felt a Funeral, in my Brain*—

There are only ghosts and clichés in the air tonight. Give up the ghost, white as a ghost, it's a ghost town, a goose walked over my grave, there are skeletons in the closet, over my dead body, *The only Ghost I ever saw Was dressed in Mechlin*—

She shakes her head, trying to shift her mind. A wedding is no time for haunting. She squeezes extra lime in her drink before draining it.

Dinner wraps up too quickly. Her stage time approaches. Athena's stomach's in knots. She can't eat. But she can drink. She grabs another tequila soda and drains it, trying to find courage in the bottom of her glass. She wants to punish Deacon for telling her the truth. For placing Alex directly in Sydnee's path. She wants to punish Sydnee, too, for so readily straying from their marriage. Daisy, for inviting Alex. Katie, for making her speak. All the people she cares for, seem deserving of only her wrath. If they're going to give her the mic, she might as well use it to say whatever she wants. She'll bring the house down before it even gets built up.

The band stops playing. The speeches begin. The singer hands the mic to a groomsman, who tells a story about Daniel's time as a pledge in their fraternity, how he got lost on Highway 6 trying to take them to Austin without a map, convinced he knew the way, which landed them smack-dab in the middle of nowhere. "While Daniel has many strengths, you should probably be the one to navigate, on road trips and otherwise." Everyone roars with laughter. He continues on with the funny, humiliating stories about Daniel, before transitioning into all the ways that Daisy is perfect for him. He ends on a heartfelt note of congratulations. It's a perfect speech.

He hands the mic to Athena as she assumes the stage. Up there alone, she takes a deep breath. She's ready to rip everyone to shreds. But she can't quite get herself to start.

People cough and shift in their seats. Athena still doesn't speak. She remembers the malachite. Transformation. Healing. Moving forward. As her eyes scan the space, she sees Sydnee looking up at her, her head cocked to the side as she holds a bottle of Shiner. She stands alone. Her hair is down and natural, the tight, dark curls cropped short, just above her shoulders, where the spaghetti strap of her red dress slides down her arm. She pulls it up, never taking her eyes off Athena.

Deacon sits with Daisy and Daniel at the center table, closest to the stage. The three of them stare, almost hypnotized by her silent presence onstage. Daniel gives her a smile and starts to clap and cheer, encouraging others to do the same, as if this moment was all part of Athena's plan. Athena's touched by the gesture. The small act of kindness. The sight of Daniel and Daisy and Deacon gazing up at her, their faces a mix of curiosity and fear and tension, Athena sees herself as they must see her now: unpredictable and yet never changing, clinging to a pain so desperately that nothing else can come from her. It's jarring to understand who you've become and humbling to know there are those who stick with you despite all you put them through.

"If you know me," Athena starts, her anger slipping off her back and puddling at her feet. "You know I love Emily Dickinson. Some would say a little too much." The crowd laughs. Athena raises her glass to Sydnee, who winks and does the same in return. "There's this line of hers that I love. *Forever—is composed of Nows.* I'm not great at prayers or blessings or anything like that. But that's my hope for y'all. Marriage is a gift. It will change you and challenge you." Athena pauses. Looks at her feet. "And make you better, if you let it. Never stop letting it make you better." Athena lets that land, for the room and for herself. "More than anything, I hope you always, forever, keep every moment close to you. Today, tonight, I see now composing forever—a picture of love and devotion. Of a marriage built to last. So, cheers, I guess, to this new adventure."

The guests raise their glasses with Athena and toast to Daisy and Daniel, cheering all the while. Athena exhales, relieved and surprised with herself. It feels strange, the earnestness. But it's good, too, an out-of-practice muscle finally getting some use. She didn't know that what was lost can come back again with time.

Athena and Sydnee lock eyes. Sydnee smiles and taps two fingers to her lips, their old signal for when they heard something they liked. They invented it in Austin, when their world was insular and full of house parties packed with people they hardly knew. In a crowd, with the music blasting, they'd never hear each other, but they used it when something funny happened or, more likely, when a straight man interrupted the conversation to add in his two cents about a case he was working on (Sydnee's world) or make the case for David Foster Wallace's genius (Athena's world). They'd remember the moment and talk about it later on their way home, laughing so hard their sides split and their eyes watered, marveling at the courage some men had to talk with such authority about something they clearly knew so little about.

*The world's greatest privilege,* Sydnee would say. *Getting to make a complete ass of yourself and never realize you're doing it.*

Onstage, Athena taps her lips back at Sydnee. As she does, she makes a decision. To let her back in.

Then, suddenly, out of the corner of her eye, a blond man approaches. He heads straight for the microphone, a blur of motion and noise. There's no time to react. Her shock makes her submissive. She hands over the microphone.

"Excuse me," he says, shouldering his way in front of Athena. "I have something to say to the bride."

# DAISY

The day wasn't perfect. The text from the Youth Pastor, Athena's haircut, Leo's presence bringing back the memories of before, the uncontrolled imaginings of the life she could have had if she'd waited for him like she knew he'd wanted her to do.

But once she sat down to get her hair done and her makeup, too, she closed her eyes and steadied herself in the moment. The day she'd dreamed of since Daniel slipped the diamond ring on her left finger had finally arrived. She thought of him, and a calm came to her that she could not explain. His presence had that effect on her. Their thighs touching when they sat close together on the couch. Their hands brushing underneath tables at dinners out with friends. The moments alone, gazing down at him, his eyes crinkled at the corners and barely visible for how wide he smiled when he saw her. It was love, it was comfort. The wedding was her dream come true, but her hope was laid away in the life she would build with him, the promise that his comfort would never leave her, no matter what.

The calm stayed with her through the pictures she took with her bridesmaids, and now, through the waiting before the wedding begins, as she stands with her father.

"My dear Daisy," her father says, holding her shoulders. He wears his army blues, the gold buttons down his jacket shining in the sun. Daisy adjusts his service ribbons, which have gone askew. "You look beautiful."

"Not too shabby yourself, Pops." She flattens his lapels and brushes a piece of lint off of his broad shoulder, the same one she'd rested her head on so many times after long days at school, the sheer width of him enough to cover her and all of her worries, a protected place where she could rest.

"You sure you don't want to do it like Daniel's family?" her dad asks. "With your mother, too?"

"This one tradition I wanted to keep." She puts her arm into his. "Just you and me down that aisle."

He clears his throat as he nods, making a show of it, doing his best to hold his tears at bay. He tightens his tie and straightens his back. A military man through and through.

Standing with her father, wearing her perfect dress, only a few feet from seeing the love of her life at the end of the aisle, no negative thought can touch her. Not thoughts of Leo or the past, not the text from the Youth Pastor. Nothing. All else falls away. Only this moment exists, and she roots herself in it, in the present, next to her father, in the dress of her dreams, about to marry the most wonderful man she's ever known.

The string quartet switches to an instrumental arrangement of her favorite by Maggie Rogers. She goes on her tiptoes and kisses her father's cheek.

"Ready?" she asks.

"No." He blinks away a rogue tear, shrugs and smiles. "But yes. Of course."

They walk toward the aisle. The sun sparkles on the water behind the chuppah, the white canopy billowing in the wind, held up by four wooden poles staked into the sand, each wrapped in jasmine. Daniel's mother and grandmother designed it. Daisy sees Daniel's grandmother in the front row, wiping tears from the corners of her eyes. His mother waits at the end of the aisle, beside Daniel under the chuppah. She puts a hand to her chest when she meets Daisy's gaze, and Daisy understands it as an invitation into her family, which is to say, her heart.

Daisy's mother rises from her seat at the front and takes her place under the chuppah, her expression dignified and put together as ever, her head held high. As Daisy gets closer, though, she sees her chin shaking, her eyes wet with tears, the corners of her trembling lips pulled up in a smile. Down the line of Daniel's groomsmen, Deacon, hands clasped in front of him, nods at Daisy as he clenches his jaw, containing his emotions. Daniel's rabbi waits patiently at the center, beaming. And, to her left, Daniel in his black tux, his face split open into the biggest smile Daisy has ever seen.

Daisy takes him in. Tailored tux, curls contained with mousse, cream-colored yarmulke on the crown of his head. He signs *I love you*, and then wipes his eyes. The beach is white as snow. The waves drown out the cellist, nature's music laying claim over its dominion. The sun sets behind the chuppah, lighting Daniel and everything else in silhouette. She walks toward the sun and shadows, clutching the arm of her father, which holds her steady, as it has for every other major moment of her life.

Life and love have not always been kind to Daisy. But in that moment, walking toward the person with whom she will spend the rest of her life, Daisy knows nothing except the faint hum of peace that thrums through her body. A frequency of faith: that she will love this man and be loved by him for all of her days and all of her nights, as long as they both shall live. A vow that binds her in this moment, a preservation of a promise. Here, now, forever, this day will be perfect.

And, as it so often goes, it was perfect until it was not.

She and Daniel had a moment together, alone, to eat and take in the moment, without the cameras or people coming up to them, offering their congratulations.

"We'll be good hosts soon," Daniel said, raising a glass of champagne and clinking it against hers. "But for now, here's to us."

Their moment together was just that, gone as quickly as it began. They were ushered into the reception, the tent packed with people and lights and flowers. The band played their first dance song as their MC introduced them. They swept onto the floor and danced together, their song upbeat and full of joy. Daisy danced with her father, and, after, Daniel with his mother. Then, the speeches, and with Athena still onstage, it happened.

The only thought running through Daisy's mind when she sees the Youth Pastor onstage.

He's too old to be so blond. It's not natural. It's platinum, like boy bands in the '90s, a bad Barbie and Ken highlight job. His hair used to be dark brown, just starting to salt and pepper, the color of the beard he has now. He rips the microphone from Athena's hands and presses it too close to his mouth, so close that his panting echoes in the speakers.

His dark jeans are straight legged and cuffed at the ankles, he wears a black, polka-dot button-down. There is nothing remarkable about him. He could be any white man in his forties.

But he is, undeniably, the Youth Pastor. Onstage, he glances back at Athena for the briefest moment. Daisy can tell his eyes are bloodshot and wild. They twitch every few seconds, and dark circles shadow underneath. He reaches into his back pocket, and a few people in front of the stage duck down.

"I don't have a gun," the Youth Pastor says. He lifts up his phone as proof. "I'm not a violent man, I'm in the ministry. I'm a man of faith, all y'all are safe. I just—I'm going to start recording now."

He presses something on his phone, holding it out in front of him. He glares back at Athena again, annoyed that she's still there. He gestures toward the stairs that lead down to the dance floor, as if she's disrupting him.

Preparing for the band to start playing, Daisy and Daniel had already walked out onto the floor after Athena's speech. They stand there now, frozen. Daisy clutches Daniel's shoulder. Out of the corner of her eye, she sees Daniel adjust his yarmulke, his eyes narrowed and his head tilted to the side, as if trying to place the man onstage. Daisy spots her father at the bar. He clutches his scotch, his mouth agape, the shock, like Daniel, seeming to render him incapable of action or speech.

"Everything's alright," the Youth Pastor says again. He's trying to calm the room like they're his congregation, obligated to follow his lead. "There's no need to panic!"

The rumbling continues. A few people call out at him to get off the stage. The band tries to take their places, the lead singer walking toward the Youth Pastor.

"Just give me one second," the Youth Pastor shouts, holding the microphone out of arm's reach. "I'm not leaving. No. I need to talk with my wife. She's right there!"

The Youth Pastor points down to Daisy, her bridal gown bustled and ready for dancing. In the spotlight, she imagines her white dress glows bright, like a moon made out of lace and silk. She closes her eyes. His appearance, while shocking, is not altogether surprising. The text had been an omen, Daisy knew it. There were no coincidences when it came to the Youth Pastor and his people. There was always a reason. There was always a plan.

In the Youth Pastor's particular sect of Christianity, men were not complete until they found their women. They were created for marriage and heterosexuality. Especially pastors. There was a lack, it seemed, when a pastor didn't have a wife. It was like presidents: when there wasn't a spouse, people started to ask questions.

Those questions stopped after he met Daisy, and the opportunities he'd been waiting for finally rolled in. The church leaders hinted that they were eyeing him to take on a lead pastor role at a new church plant downtown. He would have his own congregation. He would get to shape hundreds of minds every Sunday.

Daisy leaving destroyed what the Youth Pastor had so carefully built: the illusion that his life was perfect, that God was blessing his every step, that he had what it took to handle a church, to reign people in and force them to focus on the Gospel, despite all the delectable distractions of the secular world. It made him seem weak. There was no worse fate for a man in his position.

The evangelicals Daisy had known might not believe in revenge, but they did believe in retribution. If God and his people were slighted, there would be consequences. Men like the Youth Pastor made sure of it.

The Youth Pastor was a shadow. Wherever the light in her life shined brightest, there he would be, close behind, never letting her go. She'd forged ahead, made a new life for herself. But in the back of her mind, there was a dense darkness swirling with shame: that she had loved the Youth Pastor, that she had thought like the Youth Pastor, that she had almost given up all of her agency in the name of the Youth Pastor, though of course, he would have said it was in the name of God.

As the Youth Pastor rips the microphone out of Athena's hands, waving his phone in front of him, declaring that he's recording everything that happens from there on out. Daisy squeezes Daniel's hand and kisses him on the cheek. She clenches her fist, preparing to face her fear, to take on her shame and plunge headfirst into the fire.

The crowd is silent, unsure if this act is part of the reception. Is it a bit? A sketch? Everything has the potential for entertainment. So, they sit back and watch it play out.

"I prepared for you," the Youth Pastor says, swaying to the side. In the lights, Daisy sees flecks of spit fly out of his mouth. A bead of sweat slides down his face. He wipes his brow with the back of his sleeve. "Ever since you were in youth group. We prayed. You remember, Daisy? The Lord spoke with you. You said so. You promised, remember, Daisy?"

Daisy joined the youth group her junior year, when two girls from her class invited her and Athena to come along. Leo refused to join, it would cut into his rehearsal time. Deacon had nothing better to do, so Daisy dragged him along with them. The first meeting was a youth group dodgeball tournament, and, after a sweaty half an hour of pelting rubber balls at one another, they all gathered in the center of the gym for their midtourney sermon.

The Youth Pastor was twenty-two. Just starting Seminary School, he felt wired with the word of God. He wore a navy blue polo and dark, pressed jeans, his hair clean and well-kept. He was tall, but not too tall, with broad shoulders and narrow hips. He was an imposing presence, athletic-looking with kind eyes. He made jokes. He talked about the Good Samaritan. Daisy listened with reverence and wonder, never once taking her eyes off this man, who she thought was one of the most beautiful she'd ever seen.

It is difficult, when you're in high school, to differentiate the voice of God from the developing echo of your ego and subconscious. So, when Daisy looked at the Youth Pastor, in his well-fitting polo and skinny jeans, with a full head of dark hair and sideswept bangs, she thought, that's the one. She attributed the little voice to God, and told her friends that, if she had a choice, he was the man she was going to marry.

In the back of her mind, she compared all other men to him. All fell short. They were boys. He was a man. No one else her age ever stood a chance.

Daisy told the Youth Pastor this on their first date, and he asked to hear the story repeated almost every time they saw each other in that first month. It gave him great pleasure to be seen as ordained, chosen, holy enough to draw the voice of God.

"It reminds me that I've chosen the right field," the Youth Pastor said. "That God put me in this place for a reason."

And now, it seems, God has placed him in Watercolor, Florida, for one simple reason: retribution.

"We were fine," the Youth Pastor says into the microphone, twirling the chord on his finger, pacing back and forth on the stage, just like he did when he delivered a sermon. The move is effective, almost hypnotizing. Even Daisy finds it hard to peel her eyes off him. "And then you left."

"Hey, Dais," Daniel's dad comes up from behind. "Who's this guy? We good?"

"He's my—"

"As witnessed by Christ and His Body," the Youth Pastor answers, as if he heard the question, "I am her husband."

"That's me," Daniel shouts back, finally mobilized out of his shock into anger and action.

"But you don't know Jesus," the Youth Pastor says, turning his phone on Daniel. "Christ is not at the center of your marriage. He wouldn't recognize it. The rituals you performed. They're not right. Unlike ours."

"Sit down," one of Daniel's uncles cries out.

"Of course he'd recognize it. Jesus was a Jew, you idiot!" Daisy's cousin screams.

The crowd, now understanding the threat, joins in on the heckling. It comes from the groom's and bride's sides. It's mostly men. Deacon is in the back corner, watching Daisy carefully. She shakes her head. No. This is not his fight. She wants him nowhere near the Youth Pastor, who's never hid his animosity for Daisy's brother. Deacon steps up anyway. She's worried he's going to go up to the stage, confront this man, this plague from her past. Instead, he jogs up to Daniel. At the exact moment her husband starts to charge the stage, her brother holds him back.

The other men at the reception gather on the dance floor, moving toward the stage. Slightly drunk, revved up, Daisy can sense the energy shifting for the worse. The men push past her, trying to get at the stage, trying to get at the Youth Pastor. And as satisfying as it might be to see him take a punch across the jaw, she knows it will only embolden him further, only martyr him more. And there was no thought more nauseating than that.

She sees Leo loosen his tie and make his way to the front of the stage. The Youth Pastor uses his phone as a shield, shoving it in Leo's face, letting him know that he's recording everything that happens. Leo looks into the camera and takes a swipe at it, but the Youth Pastor is too quick for him. Leo charges forward, then, thinking better of it, backs off, as if remembering that every action will be caught on camera.

The second he retreats, Daisy's father comes barreling over from the bar, his face red, the veins popping out of it, as he screams up at the Youth Pastor, shaking his fists, giving no regard to the camera or the threat of recording. Before he can clamber up the steps, Leo braces him in his arms, holding him back, stronger than he's ever been, which is necessary to hold back a military man on a mission. Her father thrashes, trying to get away from Leo's grasp, but he makes no headway. Leo has him locked tight.

Athena, still lurking behind the Youth Pastor onstage, gazes out into the crowd, lost and shocked. She makes eye contact with Daisy, who gestures for her to come down.

"Sir," a woman says, elbowing her way through the crowd. Daisy's surprised to see Sydnee striding to the front lines. "You do realize you're putting yourself in a position to be charged."

"I'm not touching anyone." The Youth Pastor raises his hands. "We're all having a good time, right? He's the one you should worry about." He motions toward Daniel, who Deacon holds back with great restraint. He won't last much longer. Daisy knows she must do something.

"You're trespassing." Sydnee gestures to the tent. "This is a private event. That—" Sydnee points to the phone in his hand "—suggests an intent to trespass, and, in doing so, cause harm to the guests."

"You're just making up stuff. Just 'cause you say it all gruff and tough doesn't mean anything. Daisy, she one of those angry lesbians you like to hang around with now?"

"Sure am," Sydnee says. "Getting angrier by the minute looking at you. Bar certified, by the way, willing and able to take your ass all the way to—"

"Put down the phone, John." Daisy keeps her focus on the Youth Pastor, ignoring everyone else. It's the only way.

"Why shouldn't I try and do what you do? Your internet proselytizing of secular values. At least I'm spreading the Gospel. You're just spreading more evil, vapid and pointless, making people think girls can get happy by being independent and wearing the right eye cream."

"Put down the phone, John," Daisy repeats. "And I'll talk to you. Outside. Alone."

"Like hell you—" Daniel interjects.

"Fine." The Youth Pastor makes a show of stopping his recording and putting the phone in his jacket pocket. "Alone. Outside. Now."

He says it with that same tone he used so often when they were together, as if she were a soldier hardwired to take his orders. To obey. Only tonight, only this last time, will she do so.

He drops the microphone on the stage. A horrible screech echoes through the speakers. The lead singer quickly runs toward the mic to place it back in its holder. The rest of the band files out behind him. They seem unsure of what to do next.

"Play, please," Daisy says. "Loudly."

And they do, starting with Springsteen, the sax player using every inch of space in his lungs to play like the Big Man did back in his day.

The song recedes as Daisy leads the way out of the tent. She holds up her hand to her parents, who want to intercede. This is her fight. This is her shadow to slay.

Once they're outside, the Youth Pastor tries to hug her. Daisy shoves him away.

"You won't touch me again," Daisy says. A warning.

"You gonna slap me?"

"Worse," Daisy says, balling up her fists. She's never thrown a punch, but if ever there is a moment to try something new, it is now, here, in front of this man she loathes.

"Geez, Daisy." The Youth Pastor runs his hands through his platinum blond hair. His eyebrows are still his natural dark brown. "How'd we get here?"

"We split up five years ago." Daisy's voice shakes. She clears her throat, hoping to steady it. Her body trembles. Her legs are numb, but they hold her up anyway. She straightens her back, like her father taught her to. She will not shrink in front of this man. "Why come here? You don't love me. You never did. You were cruel. You wanted me to choose between—"

"We miss you at the church," the Youth Pastor says, cutting her off with a frown. She's not supposed to talk out of turn. That was the expectation of women. "Folks don't like your posts. The secular world. It's eating you alive."

"Why? Because I've finally found—"

"When I say eating you alive," he says, holding up a hand to stop her, as if she's still a child in youth group, in his presence to learn and be corrected. "I mean in a spiritual sense. You understand that?"

"It was implied." Daisy clenches her fist. The fury, though, is nothing compared to her confusion. "We divorced five years ago. Why are you here? Why do you care?"

"Because you are my wife, and you are not living out your purpose. You were created for something greater than what you've become."

"I'm still becoming," Daisy says.

"The Lord spoke to me this week," the Youth Pastor says, still looking down at his shoes. Scuffed white tennis shoes that never stay clean. "In a dream. He told me to come here. To intervene. With his blessing and his power. To bring you back. To Him."

"To you, you mean."

"I speak on God's authority." He snaps his head up to finally meet her eyes. "You've soiled yourself. With the ways of the world. You've soiled me."

"Your shoes are dirty, that much I'll admit."

"Divorce," the Youth Pastor says with disgust. "What woman will want me now?"

"Just check your youth group roster and wait a few years."

"Bitch," the Youth Pastor says before he can stop himself. He's said nothing that she hasn't heard a thousand times.

It hurts him more than it hurts her. "I didn't mean to—I shouldn't have—"

"Go, John," Daisy says. Her voice no longer shakes. How was she ever afraid of him? He is no shadow. Just a man standing outside of the light. "It's time for you to leave. You've had your say. Tell your God you did good. You tried. But leave here, now."

He opens his mouth to speak once more, but nothing comes out, as if he doesn't trust himself. As if he's lost the script. He hangs his head. He leaves. Anticlimactic and unfulfilled. An apt end for a man like him. Daisy doesn't watch him go.

"Hey," a voice says from the tent's entrance.

It's Daniel. He peeks through and finds Daisy alone. Her heart bursts at the sight of him: his curls, his beard, his short arms and long torso. She walks to him, burying herself in his chest. She breathes him in. Sweat and his cologne, light citrus and cedarwood and tobacco. The violation of her previous encounter melts away. She remembers who she is. Who she wants to be.

"Am I good enough for you?" Daisy asks, pulling herself away to look at him. The moment the question leaves her anxious mind and hits the air, she realizes how ridiculous it sounds. "Wait, don't answer that."

"That guy is a pill, huh?" Daniel says as he rubs her back. "That was pretty fucking weird. Not on my wedding day bingo card."

"He texted me earlier. Deacon and I thought it would resolve on its own. Or, we were hoping it would."

"Did it work?"

"Manifesting is not as powerful as Katie makes it seem," Daisy says.

His eyes are big and bright and full of love.

"The moon as my witness," he says, pointing up to it. "I'll love you forever, through whatever."

"You promise?"

"As long as you fork over that dowry," he says. "My folks are counting on it."

Daisy shakes her head and succumbs to the laughter that bubbles up inside of her, a burst of joy that cures all the doubt of before. She hiccups through her tears and holds Daniel close. He kisses the top of her head. They take a moment for themselves.

"Want to go back in?" Daniel asks. "Hear they've put on a great party for us."

"In a second," Daisy says, knowing she'll have to fix her makeup and practice her smile in the mirror a few times before she'll be ready for the cameras. But right now, she doesn't want any witness but the moon and the man at her side.

She squeezes his waist and feels the shadow of the Youth Pastor, the shame of her past, recede into the air, away from her. Not all at once, and not every ounce. But enough to lighten her heart. She is healing. She is loved. That's as close enough to perfect as she ever needs to be.

# MOLLIE

After Daisy leaves with the Youth Pastor, the guests break their silence, all launching into conversation at the same time, so that the tent sounds like an angry swarm of bees. Mollie stands next to Eli by the bar at the back of the tent, farthest from the stage, processing what she's just seen, shocked that such a man could have ever wormed his way into Daisy's heart.

"So, who was the gate-crasher exactly?" Eli asks, his wide eyes darting around the room, assessing reactions. "Can't believe that just happened."

"I don't think his arrival was on the itinerary." Mollie sees one of Daisy's aunts break out into hysterical sobs. Aunt Rita, she remembers, a Juilliard-trained actress who never made it big, so now she, as Shakespeare compelled her to, treats all the world as her stage. "He was Daisy's first husband. I don't know his name."

"Prick."

"Who was also her youth pastor?"

"Sicko." Eli lets out a whistle. "Surprised Daisy's dad didn't lay him out flat."

"Scott would have if Leo hadn't stopped him," Mollie says. "Probably better for us all."

"Ex-military man going off? Yeah. This is a family affair. Don't need that kind of violence."

"Well, now you're sure to never forget this wedding."

"Think this one was already going to stick before that man even showed up." He winks at her. "Gonna go for a smoke." Eli pulls out his carton of Marlboros from inside his jacket. "Meet me outside?"

"Just give me a minute." Mollie looks around to make sure her children aren't watching. "Gonna grab another beer."

"Snag me a Love Street?"

"You got it."

Mollie walks over to the bar, reaching into the ice bucket for their two drinks, doing a quick cost analysis in her head. She didn't know Eli smoked. Leo will call her a hypocrite if she dates a man who does after she drove away his first girlfriend out of college because she came into the house smelling like an ashtray. It seemed important at the time. She can't remember why, now. It doesn't bother her anymore. Such a small thing to get hung up on at the end of the day. Life is too short for that kind of thinking, Mollie knows that now. And, anyway, it isn't like Eli's hiding it from her. Pretending to be someone he's not, trying to reel her in with false information.

Every person has a secret life. Something they aren't willing to share. Even Jason had one. Over the years, Mollie would often hear him talking to himself in other rooms. She couldn't understand him. He was speaking Greek.

When they were younger, Mollie told her children that he was praying. She didn't want them to be afraid or to realize how angry it made her. For years, she suspected that he was talking on the phone with his mother or uncle or sisters, some part of the family from which he had been banished. She let her anger simmer below the surface, never letting it release, because what was there really to be angry about? It was his family. Just because they rejected her, didn't mean he needed to reject them, too, though he'd promised Mollie that if they couldn't accept her, he wouldn't accept them. It felt like a breach of trust, but it also felt like an intrusion to ask too many questions. Every marriage has its secrets, though hers and Jason's were few and far between.

One day, ten years before Jason died, Mollie walked by the room where he sat alone, speaking Greek. There was no phone in sight. No computer. He was sitting on the chair with his eyes closed. Speaking to no one.

Mollie suspected dementia. She kept her eyes peeled for the signs: forgotten phone numbers, lost keys, something said out of turn. But nothing came up. His mind was sharp as ever. She was not afraid of her husband, but something about his near meditative state, eyes closed, brow furrowed in concentration as he softly spoke words she would never understand, felt private, almost sacred.

It took her years to ask him about it. His answer was simple, and he was not ashamed to tell her about it. Jason was afraid of losing his first language. He'd tried—and failed—to teach his children Greek when they were young. His parents had taught him their language before they taught him English. Knowing Greek was crucial to communicating with his grandparents and great-aunts and uncles. There was a closeness, an intimacy, that came from learning their language and communicating with it on a regular basis, a rich reward. He dreamed in Greek as a child. As a man, the dreams were less frequent, but they still came. He felt like it was a sign whenever it happened, a whisper from the past, as if it was planting seeds in his mind, hoping it would take and flourish into something real.

It was different for his children. Everyone in their life spoke English. Plus, their attention spans were short, and his patience was thin. At the end of the day, they all wanted to go outside and play soccer more than stay in and learn a new alphabet. As the years went on, Jason felt a loneliness he could not articulate to his family. He loved them with his whole heart, but they would never know a specific part of him, the quadrant that loved his family, his heritage, his language.

So much had been lost in his family, taken without their consent, ripped away with the violence of genocide and the pursuit of empire. Even Jason's own choice to make a new kind of life, with a new kind of woman, was a cataclysmic loss and betrayal to his family, just one more pile of ashes to add to the already stacked collection. Jason never felt guilty about choosing Mollie, but he did feel the absence of the world he'd known before. Greek was the one tie left. He was determined not to lose it. There used to be an older couple from Crete at the specialty store down the road who spoke it, and Jason would go in after work every Friday to pick up yogurt and feta and pita. The woman would give him a free piece of baklava and a cup of coffee while the man talked about Arsenal and the Astros, always wearing a jersey for one of the teams. It was a weekly ritual he'd kept up for more than two decades. One Friday, though, Jason went in, and both of them were gone. A stranger rang him up. When Jason asked where the couple had gone, the young man frowned and said, "Retired, I think. Or died. I can't remember. I just started yesterday."

Since he had no one left to speak with, Jason simply spoke to himself. It was more satisfying than merely thinking in the language. He liked the way the consonants felt on his tongue, the way they contorted his mouth to take different shapes as he used the pronunciation his grandfather had taught him. *Strong, like Sparta and the sea*, he would say when Jason stumbled over a word during their lessons. It was hard work, but it was worth it.

He worried when Athena stopped practicing Spanish. The effort mattered. Jason knew it did.

"Sydnee doesn't care, Dad," Athena said, flipping through the channels for the Astros game.

But Jason knew better. He put in the time and effort and learned Spanish instead. The conversations with Sydnee were elementary at first, but as the years went on and he spoke to more people in the language, their conversations became more intimate. Jason never knew how seen it made Sydnee feel, but he understood it was important to her. He wanted to get Athena on board. They'd been talking about it right before he went to make them drinks.

After he died, everyone got quiet. There was no room for any language. A home became a house, empty and too big.

With time, though, that can all change. A home will be built again. Surely they have a regenerative life. Mollie hopes so.

A few minutes after Eli goes outside, Mollie sees Athena leave with Sydnee. She doesn't know what that means, but it can only be good news. Athena had avoided her for months. Now, at least, she seems willing to confront all she has lost. Mollie knows, more than most, that is the first step to healing.

Eli is not the first man she's considered dating since Jason. Athena is scared of them, but the dating apps weren't so bad for Mollie. She hasn't had any luck with love so far, but she's had some fun. Once she figured out how not to get catfished— Athena helped diffuse a mild situation with a man who's profile pictures were just photoshopped red carpet portraits of Paul Rudd—she'd met up with a few salt-and-pepper men from various walks of life. They took her to restaurants and bars and parks that she never knew existed in Houston. It was wonderful—not the men, but the food. She found her favorite pho in the city, the best frozen margarita, excellent Ethiopian (*yebeg tibs* with extra injera on the side to sop up the sauce), and brisket so tender and so lean she almost asked her date to leave the table so she could have a moment alone with it. Houston, Mollie discovered after four decades of residence, was the great provider of global flavor. Give me your saffron, your garam masala, your star anise, and you'll find an open door by the Bayou.

Food was the healer of her heart. It had always been a source of comfort, an escape from the world. Growing up, Mollie's mother had never cooked with spices, usually going for the "heart healthy" boiled, skinless chicken breast with boiled Brussels sprouts and peeled, boiled potatoes. It was hearty and flavorless and kept everyone's cholesterol in check. A meal was just a place to fuel. Little enjoyment came out of it. Sit, fill up, be on your way. Food was unremarkable for the beginning of Mollie's life.

Then she met Jason and everything changed. He introduced the flavors of the Mediterranean. She made dinner most weeknights for the family, incorporating the recipes Jason taught her: *paidakia*, moussaka, dolmas, lemon potatoes, rice pudding, baklava. It unlocked a love that Mollie had never known. The joy of oregano, the beauty of olive oil, the necessity of cumin and citrus and cayenne. Sautéed garlic and onion gave her a sneak peek into heaven, the aroma filling her house with a sort of magic, the promise that something wonderful was soon to come.

Even though they've only known each other for a day, meeting Eli is full of a similar promise. A new world unlocking, shedding light on a corner of her heart that she hadn't even realized was shrouded in shadow. She thinks of Jason, and all the light he brought into the world and her life. How could it ever honor his memory, forever hiding her heart in darkness?

With Athena out of sight and the rest of the reception roaring drunk, Mollie takes her chance. She ducks out of the tent and finds Eli leaning against a fence post, lighting up. In the moonlight, with his well-tailored velvet, burgundy suit, he looks like a movie star. Audacious and stylish with the shoulders and the confidence to pull it off.

"So," Eli says, handing Mollie his cigarette. "You in Houston?"

"Why?" Mollie says, taking a drag, then immediately succumbing to a coughing fit. She hasn't smoked since high school, and even then, she only did it to impress the boy she had a crush on. How little changes with time. After she collects herself, she asks, "You want to take me out or something?"

"That's the idea," he says. He inhales and exhales rings of smoke.

"Now you're just showing off."

"Trying to impress you," he says, grinning, the dimples on his cheeks becoming unplumbed indentations, two apostrophes of joy. Mollie wants to kiss them both and trace them with the tips of her fingers. "Is it working?"

Mollie tries to play it cool. "Think I could get a better gauge if you'd ask me to dance, like a gentleman."

"A gentleman?" He tosses the cigarette to the ground, stomping it out with his heel.

"That's right."

"Well, m'lady," Eli says, holding out his hand. "I don't have a carriage or anything. But may I escort you to the dance floor?"

A Sinatra song starts as they walk into the tent. The floor is packed with couples cheering as the first lines are sung. The lead singer does a passable impression of Sinatra. If Mollie closes her eyes, it could be Ol' Blue Eyes on the mic.

There's little room for them on the dance floor, but they find a stretch of unoccupied lawn near the back of the tent. Mollie kicks off her heels. They dance together in the grass, the blades tickling the bottoms of her feet. She puts her hand in Eli's. They're smaller for a man of his height, calloused but still soft and warm and inviting. It feels right. They sway back and forth, his hand on her hips, hers on his shoulder, keeping up with the beat. It's the first time Mollie forgets to compare a man to Jason. She's too focused on maintaining her balance, on not stepping on Eli's toes. He laughs when he realizes how focused she is on the ground.

"Let me lead," he leans down to whisper, pulling up her chin with his thumb, meeting her eyes with a smile. "You're gorgeous."

"Oh," Mollie says, her cheeks heating up. She knows she's blushing hard, which makes her go even more red. "That's kind of you."

"This is where you say I look handsome." Eli twirls her as the brass section picks up. He tugs her back into his chest, falling back into step with the rhythm. Every movement is smooth and confident. She feels safer here in his arms than she has in years.

"You're beautiful," Mollie says in a rush. Grief had, at least, given her this great gift: she says what she means, when she means it, and she never apologizes when it is true.

"Then we're quite a pair," Eli says.

They continue dancing. Even as the song changes to an upbeat, modern pop song, they sway back and forth, getting closer with each new tune until they're holding each other, gazing into each other's eyes, feeling the heat of the moment

become magnetic and irresistible. They kiss. Soft, subtle, taking the first steps into the unknown.

Perhaps, here, under the twinkling party lights, in a too
small tent with too loud music, Mollie can finally find her
footing, barefoot in the grass, and begin again.

# SYDNEE

"That was unreal." Athena still stares at the stage, as if waiting for the Youth Pastor to come back for one more round. But the band sets up. They tune their instruments. Then, they start to play. The show will go on. Hopefully, soon, Daisy will return, alone, and everyone can move on as if nothing out of the ordinary occurred.

"What a dick." Sydnee steps closer to Athena, shocked into their old patterns of conversation by the bizarre appearance of that man. Sydnee leans in close to her. She can smell Athena's perfume, sandalwood and sea salt. It's heavy, Athena always sprayed too much, but Sydnee welcomes it. Her mind becomes dizzy with memories she didn't know were lost: falling asleep in her arms, Sydnee's face pressed into Athena's neck; pinkies held on morning walks to breakfast in Montrose; Friday evenings in the kitchen, experimenting with too strong cocktails and lazy mornings the next day on the couch with heavy limbs and foggy minds, drinking black coffee and reheating frozen bagels from their favorite shop in town, refusing to move an inch until the late afternoon sun streamed through their living room window, beckoning them to revive and walk to the closest icehouse for a beer and street taco. An entire life preserved and safely held, encased by salt water and sandalwood.

"You came in so hot," Athena says, stepping nearer, resting her forehead on Sydnee's shoulder in fake exasperation. "Like you were in *Law & Order* or whatever that show is that you love."

"My Benson moment, okay, I had to take it."

"You wore it well."

"Can't believe he used to be y'alls actual youth pastor." Sydnee tucks her hair behind her ear. "Catechism's a bitch, but at least our youth leaders knew what they were talking about."

"I always thought he was full of shit." Athena clenches her jaw and shakes her head. "Only went for the free pizza, you know."

"Little Athena," Sydnee says, imagining it. Her tight ponytail, serious face, no-nonsense attitude. The Youth Pastor would have a tough job convincing her of anything. "A David Bowie, 'Rebel Rebel' type. Who knew."

"Don't know if I was flashy enough for that." Athena's lips tug up at the corners, the first sign that she'll let Sydnee in if she tries to get there.

They stand together in a corner, leaning against one another. Sydnee presses her shoulder into Athena's, and Athena wraps her hand around Sydnee's waist, pulling her in close. Sydnee loves the feel of those hands, the ones she's known for so long. A comfort floods between the two of them, thawing all the ice that had separated them for the past year and more—it had been hard, in the years after Jason died. They never found their rhythm, the pace with which they could both comfortably walk, side by side. She welcomes it like an invitation. Sydnee may have imagined it, or wanted it so desperately to be true that she wills it into reality, but she senses that some kind of truce has been established between them without either of them saying a word. *For one night, just one night, let's be free.*

"Want to get out of here?" Athena asks, interlacing her fingers with Sydnee's.

She nods and Athena leads her out of the reception and down the boardwalk toward the beach. Athena grabs two towels from an abandoned bucket at the edge of the board- walk and hands one to Sydnee. It can't be sanitary, but she takes it nonetheless, not wanting to break whatever spell the two have found themselves under. They remove their shoes and head into the sand, walking in silence down the beach, away from the noise and prying eyes. They settle on a spot away from the inn and the houses, all packed close together. Athena sets down both towels, sits on one and pats the other to her right. Sydnee plops down next to her.

Behind them, the sand dunes are covered in seagrass and weeds and bushes that sway gently in the breeze. In front of them, the Gulf. The waves are calm, the tide pushing the water in and out in a smooth, hypnotic motion. Sydnee and Athena stare out at it for a while. The moon has risen high and bright, the light reflecting on the water, making the movable darkness sparkle and shine. It feels almost unreal, like they've entered a space outside of time and humanity. It is just them, the moon, the waves and the wind.

"So," Athena says without looking over at Sydnee. "How's Alex?"

"Wow." Sydnee laughs. "Cutting straight to the big stuff. No small talk?"

"Technically, that is small talk," Athena says. She still stares straight ahead, but her eyes crinkle at the corners as she smiles. Sydnee knows that means Athena is a little tipsy. "Just asking about your partner. Pleasantries, you know. The only thing that makes it unpleasant is that this particular partner happened to bulldoze our marriage."

"She's not…" Sydnee says quickly. "We're casual, I guess."

"You hate casual," Athena says.

"I do," Sydnee agrees.

Her admission hangs heavy in the air between them. Sydnee glances over at Athena. Her new haircut gives her an androgynous silhouette in the darkness, a curvature of broad shoulders and a pointed nose in profile. She can't see her face, but she can sense the tension in her body, pooling up at her shoulders, creating knots at the base of her neck. Sydnee has to stop herself from reaching over and squeezing it away like she used to after Athena came home from adjuncting all over town—two community colleges and the University of Houston, at both the downtown and main campuses. Only after she met Athena did she understand the importance of *tenure*. A few months before Jason died, Athena finally landed a tenure-track assistant professorship at the University of Houston. Sydnee had put in a good word with the dean there. One of the partners had invited him to a work function, and Sydnee made sure she stayed near him all night. They talked, and she schmoozed, and he flirted and stared at her chest, and she didn't object because that's the sort of thing you have to do for love. Athena didn't know any of this. Why should she? She was qualified. She'd make a great addition to the staff. Another lesson from law school: it paid off to be in proximity to power.

"How's work?" Sydnee asks, breaking the silence.

"Really? That's what you're asking?" Athena's voice is monotonous but not displeased.

"Believe it or not, no one talks to me about Dickinson anymore," Sydnee says, resting her head on Athena's shoulder. "Give me a line."

Athena takes her time. They sit in silence as she does. The waves crash gently on the shore. The band plays Bob Dylan. Sydnee wonders how anyone can dance to such a sad song.

*"The Moon was but a Chin of Gold A Night or two ago,"* Athena says, staring up at the sky as if reading the words in the stars. *"And now she turns Her perfect Face, Upon the World below."*

"I like when they rhyme." Sydnee studies the moon in the sky, trying to view it like Dickinson. It's full and glowing, casting eerie light onto the sea, a moving mass of darkness, like a spotlight on a film set.

"Why'd you do it?" Athena finally asks. No accusation in her voice. No defensiveness. It's the curiosity she'd had when she was younger, when Sydnee first met her. The eagerness to know, to learn, to expand.

"Oh, I don't know." She'd known this question was coming and had long since prepared an answer for Athena, an airtight argument that couldn't be questioned.

She lets that fall away, now, her own defensiveness washing by the wayside like the waves crashing upon the shore in front of her feet. "I never got to live, you know," Sydnee says, staring up at the stars, digging her hand in the sand, letting it fall through her fingers. "We were so young when we met. And you had this great family…"

"You were part of it," Athena says, gazing at Sydnee, as if drinking in everything about her. She'd do the same thing whenever Sydnee got home from a weeklong business trip, as if seeing her were some sustaining force she'd had to live without for five days.

"And I just…" Sydnee tries to explain herself, though there is no real excuse, no real reasoning to justify the way she left. "I'd been white-knuckling everything for so long. It was nice. To breathe. To be taken care of by someone else."

"We loved you, that's why we took care of you."

"Everything got set so fast. I finished law school. Got my job. We got married…"

"That was a good day."

"Yeah," Sydnee faces Athena. She smiles and strokes her cheek. It's soft and cold. "That was a great day."

"But not enough for you."

"It's not that," Sydnee says, sighing. She lies down on her back. Sand clings to the side of her arm. Athena brushes it off. "I needed to find myself outside of you. Outside of your family. Your friends. When your dad died…"

Athena inhales sharply, as if hit with a stabbing pain. Sydnee remembers that the reminder always takes her breath away.

"I know," Sydnee says, her voice soft and strong. She grabs Athena's hand. "I miss him, too."

"I miss you," Athena whispers, as if they are the only words she can think to say. Sydnee knows that they are true.

Her face softens with her heart, her eyes wide, her lips downturned and open as she quietly exhales, like Athena's words have knocked the wind out of her. In a way, they have. It's like something splits inside of Sydnee. She remembers the Dickinson line she loves: *Split the Lark—and you'll find the Music.*

They'd always been able to find the music between them, a score written in their bodies or their souls or their minds, always connected, on the same wavelength, humming the same tune.

When they come together, it is a practiced instinct, a comfort and a conflict.

They kiss, and there is nothing else in the world.

They trace their fingers down each other's bodies. Everything is covered in sand. They reach out to the ocean, the tide coming in close to their feet, and let the Gulf wash their hands clean.

They embrace the heat in each other's bodies as the cold wind blows around them, every touch unlocking a memory, shooting pleasure through them with a frantic, feverish energy. Noses buried into necks, breasts, in between thighs, the inhalation of all that has been and could become. The soft music of gasps and exhales, names whispered and barely heard above the wind. It is a homecoming of the senses. It is a pleasure reborn.

When it's over, they both stay on their backs, taking in the stars. Sydnee grabs Athena's hand, and they stay like that for a long time, fingers intertwined, the waves filling the silence between them.

Athena squeezes her hand. It's a comfort, the pressure of someone else. Athena repeats the gesture, continuing to rub the edge of Sydnee's palm, right below her thumb, where Athena knows Sydnee holds tension from typing all day. Will a person ever know her as completely as the woman beside her now?

"With the stars," Sydnee says, staring up at them. "Do you ever wonder what it would be like...?" Her voice trails off, not sure how to articulate her question.

"What they would be like," Athena says, picking up where Sydnee left off. "Without the light? Without the moon and the city. Yeah. That's why I always tried to get you to go to Big Bend."

"I don't like nature."

"But that's where you can see the stars."

"There's always a sacrifice to get what you want."

"That's life." Athena rests her head on Sydnee's chest, burying her face in her neck. Goose bumps shoot down Sydnee's arm. She holds Athena closer. She shuts her eyes.

An emptiness fills her. A calm. A void. Little memories trickle in, the ones she'd kept in the back of her mind, shadowed and silent. Athena's face at the park when she told her about Alex. When she told her that she wanted to end the marriage. When she told her that there was nothing to be said or done. The decision had already been made. She never gave Athena the chance to make a counterargument, to give them something to fight for. Sydnee had shut down the road to healing before it could even emerge. Why had she done it like that? Acting as if the love of her life were a case she could file away as finished and move on to the next one. When had she become so callous? Trading her instincts for impulse, acting on them without a second thought, and never apologizing for them when they hurt other people.

What is it that she fears? Home. She's run from it all her life, she's run toward it all her life. A contradiction in constant motion. She has always wanted it, and she has always had it, here with Athena.

Sydnee studies Athena. Upturned, pointed nose, heart-shaped face, her sharp chin coming into clearer focus with her sheared hair, her full cheeks, soft and ruddy from the wind, dimpled as she smiles. A face full of contradictions, a face that Sydnee knows well and loves instinctively.

*I want this*, Sydnee thinks. An observation as casual as noting the freckle on Athena's left cheek. She holds on to the thought for a few moments before she realizes that it's true. *I have always wanted this.* It's the only thought in Sydnee's mind now. She forgets about Alex and all the other details that might inconvenience this sudden rush of realization. She wants what she had before. With this version of Athena, a grown-up version of that woman she fell in love with nearly a decade ago. How could she have forgotten this? The way she felt next to Athena, who always finished her sentences, who made Sydnee so comfortable she felt she could melt into herself, truly relaxed and unselfconscious, the greatest privilege born of trust and love. How could she have let all of that go so quickly? Her callousness and frustration and need to break free had blinded her to what she'd had all along. But she can get it back. She must get it back.

The last year cannot be erased. Sydnee knows that. What she did. How she hurt Athena. The years before could not, either. The coldness of Athena, the distance that had become so habitual, and the unkindness that had become a practiced instinct. All that had driven Sydnee into the arms of someone else. (She cannot reflect on the steps that she took, her own agency in the betrayal. That will take years and many miles. Weddings are powerful, but not powerful enough to change the chemistry of someone's reaction. Another story, for another time.)

None of that matters. Not really. Athena is here, with her new hair and her same smile, and her head is on Sydnee's chest, and Athena's exhales tickle Sydnee's collarbone, and it feels like nothing has changed, and Sydnee can almost allow herself to believe that nothing *has* changed, that they are still those twenty-four-year-olds in the coat closet, kissing until the crowd outside picks up on what's going on and starts banging on the door, laughing and catcalling and forcing them apart for another twenty-four hours, before they can be alone, before their life can begin.

The air is heavy with salt. She can taste it on her tongue. She inhales deeply. Her exhale blows back the baby hairs near Athena's temple, ungelled and untamed, flying free. She smooths them back with her index finger. She kisses the temple, an act of devotion.

Sydnee has always been great at persuasion. She can convince herself of anything. Trick her mind to go toward the light instead of into those dark spaces that hide a mirror in which she'd be forced to look at herself and understand how afraid she is of being alone.

She shakes away the thought. That's not what matters. What matters is that Athena's hand in hers feels like destiny by design, that their very fates have been etched into their palms, a hint at where their stories were always supposed to end. Side by side, clasped together.

No consequences cross her mind. She only thinks of what she wants. Whether instinct or impulse, she cannot be sure. She has never been sure.

Because she still has much to learn, Sydnee cannot imagine a world where realizing what she wants might come too late.

# ATHENA

This is where it ends.

They sit there on the beach, together, alone, legs wrapped around legs, arms twisted together, hearts beating fast. It feels natural, which gives it the illusion of feeling right.

"This just feels right," Sydnee says, as if she can read Athena's mind. She runs her hand down Athena's arm and kisses her shoulder. "Who are we kidding? Not being together."

"Nobody's joking about us."

"It's so silly." Sydnee props herself up on her elbow so that she can evaluate Athena's reaction to her carefully chosen words, waiting for an invitation to proceed, to open up. Athena's face is still, not wanting to give away an inch, forcing Sydnee to take a chance, to open up when she doesn't know how she will be received. "Let's just forget last year. You know? We could try again. Can't we try again?"

Athena rolls onto her back and studies the sky. The full moon is bright, its light dimming the surrounding stars. She finds the belt of Orion and the handle of the Big Dipper. All else is obscured by the moon.

She doesn't want it to end. But how could it not? Healing for them seemed a valley too impossible to cross. The month after Sydnee left, Athena couldn't eat. Perpetually nauseous, her stomach tied up in knots, she subsisted on smoothies and saltines. Her colleagues at the university congratulated her on how great she looked, as if the skeletal were a cause for celebration. If she'd had the energy, it would have enraged her. But every feeling died inside of her before it could grow, like a match lit in a room without oxygen. Her body was a room without oxygen. Shallow breaths, stitches in sides, tension clenching every muscle, her jaw sore and too tired to chew. She was a husk. Sydnee had left her hollow. It had taken her months to find herself again, to fill that emptiness inside her. There is still so much left in her. She has not yet grown solid again.

A life with Sydnee after that seemed unfeasible. But if she tries to imagine it...

How would it go?

Athena would start small. Couples therapy. They'd tried that before, after Jason died, six months or so into the grief, where it strangled them both so badly they could no longer communicate. It helped Sydnee more than it helped Athena. Sydnee kept seeing the therapist long after their joint sessions were through. This time, though, Athena would make an effort. She would open up. She would share. She would learn to trust again.

Athena would go on a date with Sydnee. Just one. Start small, start slow. A dinner at a restaurant they've never been to before. They would have to begin fresh. No places from before. They would not be haunted by their past. They cannot be, if they have any hope of making it.

How long would it take? A month? Six? For Athena to move back home. Their home. That alone would be enough to break her. They'd spent so many years in their little corner bungalow, with the begonias in the garden and the lemon tree in the backyard that Athena would pick in the winter and squeeze to make lemonade for their Arnold Palmers. Sydnee's grandfather's guitar in the corner of the living room that she would pick up on rainy days and mindlessly strum, creating melodies from her mind that would become the soundtrack to Athena's life. The kitchen—Athena loves that kitchen— with its gas range and oven just big enough to fit the roasted chicken she'd make on Sunday nights. The house would come alive once more with the sound of skin crackling in the oven and the smell of sautéed garlic and onions and cumin on the stove top. Sydnee does not cook if she can help it, Athena knows. The house might have gone stale without Athena there. When she returned, it would remember itself. The full expansion of who it could be.

They would expand. Learn how to express their feelings, even the deepest, darkest ones, and communicate better. Athena would no longer lash out at Sydnee, Sydnee would no longer...

But Athena keeps seeing it. A flash of red hair. A flash of Alex. A flash of kissing. It accumulates. Visions of Alex interrupting their dinners out. Alex talking to Sydnee at work. Alex taking Sydnee out for happy hour drinks...

*Many Things—are fruitless. 'Tis a Baffling Earth.*

Beneath the history, beneath the shared memory bank, beneath the patterns of behavior that tied them together like fate, the trust had cracked and left their foundation broken beyond repair.

Eight months ago, when she had found out about Sydnee and Alex, all Athena wanted was for Sydnee to fight for them. To stick around and dig through the hard feelings and find a new place to grow from there.

But Sydnee left.

Everyone thought it had been Athena who ended it. She let them. Some days, she even tricked herself into thinking it had been true. But no matter how much you want to believe in something, you can't change the past to fit the more palatable narrative. It is impassive and unmoving. An old Texas live oak sustaining through the years. Rooted. Stuck.

At the end of it all, Sydnee was done. Their marriage, she said, had ended a long time ago. They were just waiting for someone to call time of death.

She hadn't just given up on their marriage. She had declared it incapable of revival. Without hope. Nothing left to be done.

Nights were spent listening to the saddest song Athena could find as she wept, imagining Sydnee's new life without her, imagining all that they had lost. Her body ached with the pain. Her legs and lungs were exhausted and numb, as if she'd run on a too fast treadmill of grief, the shock and heartbreak coursing through her, taking all her energy, sinking itself into her muscles. She can still feel it, her entire body clenching as she imagines Alex assuming her place in Sydnee's life, sleeping on her side of the bed, using Sydnee's rusted cast-iron skillet, the only pan in the kitchen that had not been Athena's, trimming her trees and picking her fruit and not caring that someone else had been there before, planting all the seeds.

She'd been cast aside so carelessly after so many years of tenderness and love, as if marriage were a switch you can flip on and off. At this moment, Sydnee wants it on again. But what would happen in a month, or two, when their communication broke down and they got into their first fight and the past kept popping up because neither one of them has really forgiven the other? You cannot set flame to the past, let it burn while you walk away. Scorched earth leaves no stories, no lessons, no memories. Athena will not move forward like this.

She hadn't noticed it happening. Perhaps it hadn't happened until this moment, when Sydnee watches her with such hopeful eyes, her warm, green eyes, barely perceptible in the darkness, glowing orbs reflecting the light of the full moon. But something has shifted for her during the course of the wedding weekend. Maybe it was the way Daniel looked at Daisy when she walked down the aisle, or it was Deacon telling her the truth, or it was seeing Leo again with Mollie, or it was the shock of feeling when Katie touched her hand. But she suddenly feels more grounded in the present than she has in years, since before Jason died. And in the present, she finds, for the first time, a vision for the future. A future she can navigate alone, without Sydnee. A prospect that had seemed unfathomable in months past, now feels inevitable.

"It's a nice idea," Athena says as she sits back up. She scans the ocean, wishing her father were there, helping her, holding her, giving her strength to do the impossible.

"So you agree?" Sydnee asks. Her hand reaches down for Athena's, gripping it tightly, transferring all the hope in her heart into Athena's hand. "You think we should try again?"

Athena says it gently, but her tone is firm. "No." There is no way to soften that word when it is meant. Her conviction gives the decision no loopholes for Sydnee to find.

"Oh." Sydnee sucks in her breath like she's taken a gut punch. "Okay."

They sit in silence, Sydnee's labored breathing lost among the sound of waves crashing to the shore. Athena glances at her. Hunched shoulders, clenched fists, eyes closed. A small fragment of her heart shatters at the sight. Athena blinks away the tears.

If only she could find a way to stay. Create a tool to crack open the claustrophobic existence she'd created with the great love of her life, to crash continents inside herself and make mountains, a vast terrain for them to explore, wander, learn and grow. If they could come together, allow themselves to expand so that they could contain a country, become an ocean, large enough to live a new life without needing to heal from the past.

But there is, for now, too much damage done. They contain multitudes, yes, but not continents. It is not enough. Athena must find the space she needs to move on, without Sydnee.

Sydnee stands and gives Athena's hand another squeeze before pulling away. After a moment spent fixated on the ocean, she turns to Athena.

"I love you," Sydnee says. Her eyes are full of that fierce fearlessness that Athena fell in love with.

Athena says it back. No words that have ever left her lips have ever been more true. They hold each other's gaze. Neither of them wants to break first. Athena knows that she must, but she holds on for a second longer, savoring this last moment of connection. Despite everything that has transpired between them, they are, for the last time, still intimately connected by all that tethered them together: wives, lovers, confidantes, family.

Sydnee blinks. She grabs her bag and walks down the beach, away from the reception, toward her hotel. She is stronger than Orpheus. When she leaves, she does not look back.

So it ends here. In the sand, by the ocean, with the only woman she's ever loved. Athena watches Sydnee walk away. A silhouette in the night. A ghost leaving its haunting for another world.

Athena closes her eyes. The last time they were together, she didn't know it would be the end, so she savors the final moment of their collective life.

She wants to remember every detail. The crook of Sydnee's neck, covered in sand and her perfume, a heavy lavender-honey mixture that takes Athena back to their mornings spent cramped in the tiny bathroom they shared in Houston, both getting ready for work, both needing more room than the other was willing to give, knocking knees and elbows, the air thick with steam from the hot shower, crowded with all their scents: the eucalyptus bodywash, the gardenia hand lotion, the perfumes and hair sprays and face creams all applied in a frenzied flourish as they rushed out the door.

Sydnee's fingertips, familiar and foreign, so much distance between their last moment of contact, yet each graze transported Athena to another time, when touch was not a scarcity and love was never something to question. Sydnee's hair, shorter now, tickled her forehead as she made her way down Athena's body, which felt every movement with a heightened sense of awareness. It had been so long since she'd been touched. It opened up the crag of loneliness and despair she'd kept at bay, and it released a euphoric, wild wanting—for more. An impossible desire, of course. More does not exist here.

It would be easier if it felt different. If Athena could feel the finality in their bodies. If memory wasn't wrapped around every finger, if tongues couldn't trace the past. When they are together, it is like nothing has changed. Context slips away. It is just them and the air, and they are all free, and the past doesn't matter, nor does the future, and the only truths they have to hold are the sand and the stars and the resurrection of who they were before.

Then, it's over. Athena comes back to herself. She feels the distance that never left them. There is no closeness and, worse, no conclusion. She is still in love. They are still divorced. There is no saving what is already lost. It's for the best, but it still hurts.

Athena continues to stare down the beach, toward the bustling reception. She can't see Sydnee anymore, or anything else from the party. The band plays an upbeat pop song Athena doesn't recognize, but she taps out the bass line with her thumb anyway, creating a minicrater in the sand.

A figure walks out from the tent and comes down toward her. Athena thinks it's Sydnee at first and her heart rate spikes, always hoping where it's already lost, a habit she prays will break with time. It's not her. It will never be her.

It is Deacon. He stumbles slightly in the sand, swaying a little back and forth. Everyone's had too much to drink, trying to drown the pressure of the day in a euphoric toast, an indulgence in numbness that will punish them in the morning. He plops down next to her, where Sydnee had sat just moments ago.

"You're gonna fuck up your tux." Athena brushes sand off the lapel of his jacket.

"Gotta dry-clean it anyway, been sweating like nobody's business all day," Deacon says. "The reception did not help. Unexpected stress."

"Didn't you feel like he was gonna pull out a gun?" Athena asks.

"Thankfully, he's a pacifist," Deacon says. "What a relief."

"Unarmed, yet still dangerous. What a concept."

Deacon mimics the motion of the Youth Pastor, swiftly opening up his jacket, reaching his hand inside. When he pulls it out, he has two beer cans. He gives one to Athena.

"To chaos." Deacon raises his can in the air. "May it never die down."

"Speak for yourself," Athena says as she knocks her can against his. "I could live without the stuff for the rest of my life."

"Drink up," Deacon says. "You might change your mind."

Athena takes a swig and sets the can down in the sand. Her head buzzes with booze, tipsy but not drunk. Fully cognizant

and wistful. She leans back on her hands, tilting her head up to
the sky. It's cloudless and pocked with scattered stars. There's
a full moon, a great glowing orb. The breeze has a bite to it.
Athena shivers and remembers the heat of her hand between
Sydnee's thighs. She tries to feel guilt or shame or regret. It
does not come. She feels everything else, though. Past and
present. Right and wrong. Coolness and warmth. *Forever—
is composed of Nows*. But Dickinson got it wrong. Forever is
composed of contradictions.

"You missed the hora." Deacon unties his shoes and slips
them off, putting them at his side. He flexes his feet, his socks
covered with a thousand hearts and cropped pictures of Daisy's
head, a masterpiece he made himself.

"Did Daisy fall?"

"Total pro."

"Good for her. She was worried about that."

"Saw Sydnee walk out here with you," Deacon says. He
doesn't look at Athena. There's no hostility in the question.

"Just saying goodbye." Before, Athena had needed to express every detail of her thoughts, the depths of her exasperation and pain and isolation. Now, though, she wants to keep
it close and save it for later, so she can feel the memory flood
her chest. "Leo got that part."

"No shit?" Deacon says.

Athena knows he wants to hear what happened on the
beach. Thankfully, he doesn't say anything more. They sit in
silence and sip their canned light beers, the lack of flavor a sacrifice for calories, coating Athena's tongue in half-hearted af-
tertaste that sours, leaving her mouth drier than it was before.

"I meant what I said earlier," Athena says, clearing her
throat like a conscience. "I want to meet Mel."

"Well," Deacon says as he digs a hole in the sand with the

heel of his shoe. "How about tomorrow night? After we get back in."

"Tomorrow?"

"Sure," Deacon says. "Why waste time, you know?"

"Feels like we won't make it to tomorrow. Like this day will never end."

"But it will."

"It will," Athena agrees.

"I'm not good at, you know," Deacon says, his blond hair gelled back and unmoving as he turns toward Athena, not quite able to meet her eyes. "Apologizing. You know. It's just…"

"It happened." Athena shrugs. All the fire from before dissolved, the anger quelled. There is no ground left for her to stand on.

"You're my best friend," Deacon says, finally able to meet her eyes.

In the darkness, it's hard to make out any detail. But she can see the silhouette of him, that face she knows so well. High cheekbones, large forehead, long, dark lashes on his small, beautiful, blue eyes. Without thinking about it, she reaches out to touch his cheek, cupping it into her hand. He leans into it. She feels his eyelids flutter closed. Her thumb strokes the arch of his eyebrow.

No words mean more than this, so they sit in silence, listening to the waves crash on the shore, then recede back into the sea. The wind is cold. The air is full of salt. Athena feels a tear run down Deacon's cheek, pooling in the curvature between her thumb and index finger. She removes her hand, gently, and wipes it on her gown. He reaches out and squeezes her shoulder before wiping his eyes and standing up. He holds out his hand to help her.

"You go ahead," Athena says. "I just need a few more minutes."

Deacon nods and walks back to the wedding. The band plays on. Daisy paid them extra to stay past midnight. There are still hours of music left in the air.

She watches Deacon's shadow move toward the party. Once he ducks his head back into the tent, she stands up and walks down the beach, the blaring bass of the band slowly fades as she makes her way through the cool sand, her toes digging into the ground as she tries to anchor herself to something. The wind swells, November's fingerprints all over the cool gust, the saltwater air still thick and unrelenting.

*Find the sea, Athena, you're built from the sea.* Her father's voice is as present in her mind as his absence is in the world.

The ocean crashes at her feet, the tide undeterred by anyone's anguish. It moves in and out. It stops for no one, it answers to nothing.

Seeing Sydnee, touching her, feeling her, hearing her laugh again, it didn't heal Athena in the way she thought it would. Was there no cure for heartbreak? Was love never enough? She has no answers. The only certainty is the sand between her toes.

Athena walks closer to the shore, pulls up the hem of her dress and lets the tide knock into her legs as she stares into the abyss, the vast darkness of ocean and sky merging as one. She bends down and lets the water pool in her hands, watches it trickle out.

What comes next? The ache in her heart still throbs through her, extending into her lungs. For months it had remained like this. Perpetual pain. She wants to move forward, but she worries she's become too hard, too calloused by the past. Could she be tender? Or would she need to be pulverized first, like a meat mallet coming down hard on a butcher's table? The love of her life left her at the first sign of turbulence. How would any of her next loves abandon her? Is it too early for her to wonder what would happen if they stayed?

When the next tide comes, she cups the water once more, then splashes it on her face. The cold is a shock. It snaps her senses to attention. She licks the salt from her lips, and lets it sting her eyes. She blinks her vision clear. She gives herself a minute more in the silence, then walks back to the reception. There's nothing out here for her anymore.

She focuses on the present. The air in her lungs. Her fingertips tickled by her freshly sheared hair. Sand-coated bare feet on the grass, the blades creating a cushion of comfort for her to stand on. The beat of a good song moves through her, forcing her forward.

She's inside the tent. The reception roars on. Leo and Deacon dance together. They jump up and down, out of sync with one another, their seesaw rhythm propelling their motion as they scream the lyrics in each other's faces. The loss of inhibition is so pure and so spontaneous it feels to Athena like a true picture of heaven, or, at least, the only kind of heaven she'd like to be a part of. Behind them, Mollie, in the back of the room, dances with a man Athena does not recognize. It's comforting to see her mother lost in someone new. There's hope in that. She holds on to it.

Athena goes toward the scrum of bodies in the middle of the dance floor, all jumping up and down together, clapping off the beat, their heads banging back and forth. It's chaotic. It's wonderful. There's Katie, on the outskirts of it all. Her hair is down and wild. She rocks her head. The song is familiar, pop punk and upbeat, with lyrics that devastate. Katie is devastating. Hips swaying in rhythm with the bass line, her eyes closed as she belts out the words, the veins in her neck visible. She looks possessed. She looks free. Without thinking, Athena walks toward her, drawn in, like she's a siren, like she's a sign. Katie opens her eyes. She sees Athena. She smiles. She reaches out her hand.

★ ★ ★ ★ ★

# ACKNOWLEDGMENTS

The rumors are true: the second book is harder to write than the first. That this book ended up in your hands is a result of these amazing people, who I now have the great pleasure of thanking for their support and kindness.

To my editor, Melanie Fried, for the incisive editing and insightful notes throughout this process. Drafting is difficult for me, but her keen eye and excellent notes helped me see this through. At every turn, when I couldn't see the way forward, she shed light in the right places so that I could continue on the path. All my gratitude for every edit and suggestion, which has made this book so much better. And once more, I'm delighted to thank the wonderful team at Graydon House Books, for all of their hard work in helping to bring this book into the world.

To my agent, Amy Elizabeth Bishop, who champions, celebrates, and delights in the work of her clients, of which I am so proud to call myself one. When I didn't think I could write another book, all it took was a quick, "So, what's next?" from Amy to get my pen to the page again. She truly is the best in the biz.

To Martha Nell Smith, Ellen Louise Hart, Marta L. Werner, Jen Bervin, Jerome Charyn, and Alena Smith for their scholarship on and imaginings of Emily Dickinson's life and poetry, which made the poet from Amherst come alive for me when

I needed her most. And to the poet herself, who has proved a faithful companion during periods of isolation and despondency. Misery loves company, and there is no company better in dark times than Dickinson.

To all the people I've stood beside on their wedding day: I love you! This book is not about you! I promise!

To Reghan Gillman, who has been the best social media assistant ever, in addition to being my best friend of twenty years. And to Tiffany Navarro, for the excellent content consultations and strategy when it comes to social media and marketing. I'm a reluctant curmudgeon with such things, but this team makes every step fun.

To my parents, David and Diantha, for always supporting me and loving me and taking me out to dinner on Sunday nights.

To Anastasia, for the enthusiasm and encouragement, even when I respond to both with, "Yeah, thanks. So, anyway…"

To Hayden and Payton, for their friendship and fun, and, to Sunny, for being such sweetness and light.

Finally, to Miranda, ever patient and kind and curious, for seeing me through this process with laughter and understanding. I imagined love in many ways, and you surpass them all.

# *TODAY TONIGHT FOREVER* PLAYLIST

1. "All My Friends"-LCD Soundsystem

2. "The 1975"-The 1975

3. "Overdrive"-Maggie Rogers

4. "Ode to a Conversation Stuck in Your Throat"-Del Water Gap

5. "DIRTY WHITE VANS//"-KennyHoopla

6. "AMHERST"-Kevin Hacket, Aaron Marcus

7. "The Heart Is a Muscle"-Gang of Youths

8. "Age of Consent"-New Order

9. "May I Have This Dance"-Francis and the Lights

10. "Televangelism"-Ethel Cain

11. "Not Strong Enough"-boygenius

12. "Loose Garment"-MUNA

13. "Dawns"-Zach Bryan, Maggie Rogers

14. "Sugar"-Amythyst Kiah

15. "F2F"-SZA

16. "Mastermind"-Taylor Swift

17. "life you lead"-niceboy ed

18. "GOODBYE"-BROCKHAMPTON

19. "Strangers"-Mt. Joy

20. "Changes"-Joy Oladokun

Find it on Spotify: *bit.ly/TTFMKS*